cut to
the chase

Joan Boswell

RendezVous
Crime

Toronto, Ontario, Canada

Cover design by Emma Dolan

Le Conseil des Arts du Canada | The Canada Council for the Arts

We acknowledge the support of the Canada Council for the Arts for our publishing program. We acknowledge the financial support of the Government of Canada through the Book Publishing Industry Development Program (BPIDP) for our publishing activities.

RendezVous Crime
an imprint of Napoleon & Company
Toronto, Ontario, Canada
www.napoleonandcompany.com

Printed in Canada

FSC **Mixed Sources**
Product group from well-managed forests, and other controlled sources
www.fsc.org Cert no. SW-COC-002358
© 1996 Forest Stewardship Council

13 12 11 10 09   5 4 3 2 1

Library and Archives Canada Cataloguing in Publication

Boswell, Joan
Cut to the chase / Joan Boswell.

ISBN 978-1-894917-89-6

I. Title.

PS8603.O88C8827 2009   C813'.6   C2009-904779-9

For Nick, Katie, Francis,
Trevor, Christy and Brendan

Prologue

The old-fashioned word "besotted" exactly described Danson Lafleur's feelings for Angie Napier, his fiancée. He'd fallen for her in high school and never lost his amazement and gratitude that she loved him. Now, university behind them, they planned to marry. They'd be together forever—the thought filled him with joy.

Rays of late afternoon sunshine filtered through the trees encircling the patio behind a popular Danforth watering hole and bathed Angie in light, setting her apart like a beautiful painting. Danson wanted to hold the moment forever. He wished they were sitting in their own garden instead of a crowded, noisy restaurant.

Angie, laugh lines crinkling, brown eyes flashing and shining brown hair swinging, pushed her hair behind a delicate ear as she leaned towards him. "It's time for us to make a decision. Should we elope? Do you have a long ladder?" she asked and laughed.

Danson grinned and grasped her slender hands. "No, I expect you to let down your long brown hair and let me creep up into the tower." Her engagement ring sparkled as her hands moved.

"Seriously, should we have a wedding wedding—brides-maids, ushers, fancy dinner, speeches or..." she lowered her voice and whispered, "should we recruit two witnesses, your sister and my brother maybe, and hurry off to City Hall?"

Danson would do anything that made her happy. He

loved her with an intensity he'd never believed possible. "Whatever you want," he said.

"We could have a party afterwards. That way we'd be relaxed, and we'd have fun. Maybe a strawberry social or a fancy dress ball or—" she stopped, as a loud bang startled the diners. Then she looked surprised, let go of Danson's hand and clutched her chest.

Danson watched an obscene red stain flower and spread over her pale yellow dress before she pitched forward face down on the table. He was vaguely aware that others were screaming and fleeing from the restaurant.

He could only focus on Angie's stillness as her head rested on the table. It had to be a bizarre joke. How could this be happening? He sat frozen for seconds while his mind processed what he was seeing.

Jumping to his feet, he leaped to Angie's side. "Call 911. Help us," he shouted.

Not that anyone could. She was dead.

Danson felt as if a huge earth-moving machine had torn out his heart.

*   *   *

Eventually, Danson learned that a gang member who'd briefly served time before being deported had returned to Canada and taken up his old life. Angie had died in the gun fight between rival gangs.

Anger at the system that had allowed this to happen consumed Danson, and he vowed he would track down returning criminals and have them deported. He owed it to Angie to see that no one else died as she had, and to himself that no one else should suffer grief as he had.

No longer interested in his promising career as a tech consultant, he took a job that would put him on the fringes of the crime world and give him access to the information he needed.

2

One

Brush in hand, red-framed glasses perched on her nose, Hollis Grant studied the large canvas positioned on the easel set under the north-facing skylight. Earlier she'd cranked the window open to allow Toronto's unseasonably warm late October air to flow into the room. The third floor attic apartment remained hot, but she ignored the heat, focused on her work and tried for the moment to ignore her concern for her landlady and friend, Candace Lafleur.

She intended to create a golden puzzle, a painting that would draw the viewer in and make them search for meaning. There would be tones and textures of gold with half-revealed hidden messages. Except for the reference to gold, this description could refer to Candace. For the past week, Candace had been a women obsessed with a problem but unwilling to share the details.

The painting wasn't working. Damn.

She plunged the brush into the water on the tambour beside the easel. She felt like pulling out her hair. She momentarily envisaged herself bald as an egg and the floor littered with curly blonde hair.

What if she couldn't fix the painting? Couldn't paint what she visualized? Couldn't succeed as an artist? These depressing thoughts sidling into her mind frightened her.

Not again. She'd suffered bouts of depression in the past, and they'd immobilized her. Bad enough to have painter's block—she couldn't allow depression to overwhelm her.

Exercise—that would help, she decided.

Several years earlier, her soon-to-be ex-husband had challenged her to take up running to lose weight and improve her fitness. Surprisingly, once she'd accomplished these goals, she hadn't given up running; the process and the joy it produced had hooked her. Another plus had been its slimming effect on her slightly corpulent golden retriever, MacTee. They'd become committed runners, although sometimes, when she found herself plowing along in snow or rain, she wondered if "committed" wasn't exactly the right word.

Today, probably one of the last warm autumn days, instead of running, she'd sit in the garden, enjoy the sun and read the Saturday paper. Maybe she'd solve the cryptic puzzle; that always boosted her ego. Entertaining diversions also helped to chase away the black dogs of depression.

She opened the fire escape door which overlooked the garden, noting that the latch needed to be repaired. Paper tucked under her arm and a thermos of coffee clutched in her hand, she enjoyed the view over the neighbourhood before she cautiously descended. As always, the rusty railing alarmed her. She chose not to touch it but to edge her way down, allowing her free hand to touch the wall. MacTee, nervous about the see-through stairs, hesitated for a long moment before he reluctantly followed.

On terra firma, she breathed deeply and stared up at the intense blue autumn sky. They'd had a cold snap and a few flakes of snow earlier in the week. Today the temperature hovered at twenty, and the radio weather reporter had promised this warm weather would last through Hallowe'en, the following Tuesday. Great for the kids who wouldn't have to wear parkas and snow pants under their costumes.

She dropped the newspaper on the round cedar picnic table, retrieved a sling-back canvas deck chair from the garage, unfolded it and prepared to relax for an hour and think of anything but painting or Candace. As she sorted through the sections, deciding which to read first, MacTee,

4

after rolling ecstatically on the leaf-covered grass, flopped down, groaned with pleasure and stretched out in the sparse shade of a maple almost devoid of leaves.

The ground floor door banged open.

Hollis, halfway through reading editorial speculations about an unidentified mutilated murdered man and his possible connection to the murders of male drug users in the downtown core, lifted her head. Candace emerged, leading two-year-old Elizabeth and carrying newspaper and coffee mug.

"Good morning. Hope you don't mind company," she said, releasing the toddler's hand. She spoke in a flat tone.

Whatever had been bothering Candace was still affecting her. She'd been tense and nervous each time Hollis had spoken to her during the week. She wasn't likely to be very good company, and certainly she looked anything but peaceful. What could Hollis say? The yard belonged to Candace who allowed Hollis and MacTee to use it.

Elizabeth, wispy blonde curls escaping from her pink baseball cap, chortled when she spied the dog. Clad in overalls and a pink windbreaker, she toddled toward him shouting, "Tee, Tee, Tee."

MacTee adored children and tolerated their unintended abuse. He always allowed Elizabeth to catch him, grab great handfuls of hair and hug him. When she opened her mouth and bore down on his nose, he shrugged her off and moved away. She'd follow and repeatedly throw herself on him as they continued the game they both enjoyed.

Eyes bleak, mouth set in a straight line, shoulders slumped, Candace radiated distress.

Maybe Hollis would finally root out the cause of her friend's unhappiness.

"Always glad to see you and Elizabeth. Aren't we lucky with this weather?" she chirped.

"We are," Candace said without conviction. "I'll get a chair." After she'd hauled one from the garage, she folded herself into it and said, "I'm being selfish. I should have stayed inside. I'll drive you crazy. I'm so jittery, I can't concentrate on anything."

Hollis examined Candace. Early in their friendship, Candace had identified herself as a fellow Virgo and a woman who prided herself on being an organized positive pragmatist. Dressed in tailored clothes, accessorized with conservative but high-quality accessories and shod in highly polished, "sensible" pumps she was a quintessential polished professional executive assistant. Today, baggy jeans, a stained and faded T-shirt, and a misshapen navy cardigan not only drew attention to her short, stocky body but emphasized her state of mind. Her square-cut chin-length brown bob, wide-set brown eyes and regular features devoid of makeup normally underscored her no-nonsense approach to life. Today the tension in her face telegraphed that she was anything but "in charge".

Candace reached into her sweater pocket and yanked out a cell phone. She pressed buttons, listened, snapped it shut and stuffed it back in her pocket.

"My god, where is he?"

Her anxiety hung in the air.

"Who?"

"My brother."

Hollis had met Candace's brother, Danson, several times and knew that the muscular and athletic young man supported himself as a nightclub bouncer but spent time promoting and playing box lacrosse, the indoor winter version of the summer game.

"What's the problem?"

"I've been calling him for days. Days and days. I've phoned his friends and his boss. He worked last Saturday. That's the last anyone has seen or heard of him. His tenant, the guy who rents the second bedroom in his apartment, isn't there either."

"Is that unusual?"

Candace shrugged. "Search me. I haven't met him. His first name is Gregory, and I haven't a clue what his last name is." She shrugged. "Apparently Gregory's a sales rep who hates motels and wants his own place when he comes to Toronto."

"So no one is there to answer the phone."

"Not the apartment phone and not Danson's cell phone. Last time I talked to him, he scared me, because he implied he was on the trail of something important. I'm frightened that something terrible has happened to him."

"What and why?"

Candace shook her head. "It's a long story, and it's taken me a few days to get really worried. At first I was furious, especially when Jack showed up on Wednesday."

"Jack?"

"Remember two weeks ago, when you and Danson came for Saturday lunch?"

When she'd met Danson in July or August, he'd struck Hollis as intense and obsessive. Her first impression had been confirmed at that mid-October lunch. It had been warm, and they'd eaten out here in the garden. She recalled lobbing an innocuous question. "Candace says you play lacrosse and…"

Danson hadn't waited for her to finish. "Play, recruit, organize—lacrosse is officially our national sport. I bet you didn't know that. Hardly anyone does." He didn't require a response.

"It's a totally demanding game. You have to be totally fit, totally committed. I wish the government would pass legislation to make it compulsory in our schools. Forget football or even soccer. Lacrosse is the sport all young people should play."

Candace intervened. "Hollis, it *is* a great spectator sport. You and I should go to a game after Christmas."

Danson reached across the red and white checked tablecloth and laid his hand over his sister's. "Candace, I have a favour to ask—a big one."

7

Hollis sensed that whatever the request, the answer would be 'yes'."

"Remember when I went to Montreal a few weeks ago?"

Candace sipped her wine and nodded.

"I recruited a great player, totally great, and he needs somewhere to stay until he gets a day job and place to live."

Candace toyed with the stem of her wine glass and waited with a half-smile on her lips as if she anticipated what was coming.

"Since you don't have a tenant in the basement studio apartment, it occurred to me that he might camp out there for a few weeks. It wouldn't be for long, and he'd pay rent," Danson said.

Candace had looked as if she wanted to refuse but found it hard to deny her baby brother anything.

"It was a lovely lunch," Hollis said now. "Danson wanted a lacrosse player to crash in your basement apartment. I recall that you said yes, but your expression said no."

"Absolutely right. It's hard for me to say no to Danson. He has a generous heart, and he's always taking care of others. Sometimes it's us, sometimes it's friends, this time it was a lacrosse player. It's a wonderful quality, but last week a woman at work told me her daughter would like to rent the basement apartment for a year. I didn't want to turn down a year's guaranteed rent. When I called Danson with the news, he understood and promised to tell Jack."

Candace ran the fingers of both hands through her hair, interlaced her fingers behind her neck and pressed her head back as if trying to squeeze her tension away. She released her hands and crossed her arms over her chest. "Jack Michaels phoned Tuesday evening. He sounded so pleased that he had a place to stay that I couldn't say no. He moved in on Wednesday."

Elizabeth howled. MacTee had accidentally upended her, and she'd banged her head on the edge of the sandbox.

Candace jerked to her feet and rushed to comfort the little girl. "You're fine, Elizabeth," she said as she picked her up.

Almost simultaneously, the basement door opened, and a young man who had to be Jack Michaels emerged. His face resembled an inverted white-enamel pie plate on which a kindergarten child had drawn round eyes, curved eyebrows, and a bow of a mouth. After that, the child would have smacked on a playdough blob for his nose and declared the face finished.

He took in the scene but said nothing.

Since Candace literally had her hands full, Hollis spoke up. "Hi. You must be Jack," she said. "I'm Hollis, the upstairs tenant. What can we do for you?"

Jack stared at Elizabeth, who continued to scream. "I have to do laundry. Can I use the machine in the basement?"

Candace, who'd quieted Elizabeth, nodded. "You may."

"I'd like to make sure I do it right."

Candace put Elizabeth down and held up her hand to indicate she'd address Jack's concerns in a minute. She spoke to Elizabeth. "Why don't we give MacTee a break? I'll uncover the sand box? Would you like that?"

Elizabeth stopped sniffling as abruptly as if she'd thrown a "do not cry" switch. "Water?" she said hopefully.

"Good thing I didn't get around to turning it off for the winter," Candace said to Hollis and Jack with a poor attempt at a smile. "I'll fill your watering can," she told Elizabeth. She unrolled the hose, partially filled a child-size, green plastic watering can and handed it to the toddler.

Elizabeth parked it on the sandbox's seat, clambered in and plunked down amid a bright plastic toy collection. She grabbed a yellow shovel and scooped sand into a plastic pail. After adding two more shovels of sand, she poured water into the pail, stirred, looked thoughtfully at Candace and dumped the contents on her head.

Candace, squatting beside the sandbox, wasn't quick enough to stop her.

Water and sand splashed over Elizabeth's baseball cap and dribbled down her face and neck. She scrubbed at the mess, balled her hands into fists, jammed them in her eyes and wept.

"Anything to get attention," Candace said and folded her arms around Elizabeth. "Time for a quick spray in the bathtub."

Her gaze swung between Jack and Hollis. "Hollis, would you show Jack how the machine works?"

Hollis would have preferred hearing why Danson's failure to phone had terrified Candace, but this wasn't the time to pursue the topic. "Sure," she said, called to MacTee and followed Jack to the basement laundry room.

Before Hollis left, Candace lowered her voice and said, "When Elizabeth's cleaned up and had her morning nap, would you join us for lunch? There's more to Danson's story."

Hollis agreed almost before the invitation left Candace's lips.

Jack had parked a large blue duffle bag on the basement floor in front of the washer.

"It's a basic machine," Hollis said. She showed him which dials to turn. "Do you start practices right away?" she asked.

"No. They told us to come early to find a job and a place to live. We're semipro, and we don't make enough to live on. Too bad, or we'd be better players. That's the way it is. I have interviews this afternoon," he said.

"What do you do?"

Jack stopped sorting his laundry. "Anything. I don't have specialized training, but I've worked in fast food restaurants, and I can probably get something that will mesh with the training schedule."

"Good luck. I'm an artist, and my studio is here. If you need to know anything about the house or the neighbourhood, feel free to come up and ask me."

"You're here every day. I forget that people work at home," Jack said.

10

"I do. Candace's mother is here off and on during the daytime too." She pointed to the ceiling, "She's above you on the first floor. You may wake up at three in the morning and hear her. She's a dancer and practices at all hours."

"It's already happened. I figured college kids lived upstairs, although the music was kind of strange. I figured they were Latin Americans." Jack's eyes widened, and his mouth made a perfect "o" before he said, "Candace's mother is a dancer?"

Leaving him to digest his surprise, Hollis and MacTee headed back outside. Hollis didn't know what had been causing Candace such distress, but it hadn't just been her obsession with her brother's whereabouts. Danson seemed like a normal, caring if somewhat fanatical guy. Hollis wondered why his sister was so concerned. What revelations was she about to hear?

TWO

Back in the garden, reading the *Globe*'s pontificating columnists, learning what was happening in the city and immersing herself in the details of others' lives no longer attracted Hollis. She had a real-life issue to deal with.

Why had Danson disappeared?

Maybe he'd run away from life's responsibilities or done a flit with a gorgeous girl? Maybe the explanation was simply that he'd forgotten the charger for his cell phone. Men frequently took off. Modern life was hard on them. Whatever the last conversation had been about, it had to have been something serious, or Candace wouldn't be panic-stricken. Since no answers danced before her eyes, she'd work.

Upstairs, Hollis studied the large canvas. The day before, she'd saturated sheets of tissue paper with a transparent water colour. Now she tore the paper into smaller pieces and coated each fragment with the acrylic medium she used as an adhesive before layering it on the canvas. Laying the paper pieces over the gold paint allowed the gold to partially shine through. She wanted the viewer to wonder what lay beneath. She stood back and shook her head. What a mess. Tempted to grab a wide, commercial paint brush, slather white gesso over the entire surface and begin again, she resisted the urge and took her brushes to the sink in her tiny minimalist kitchen. Better to forget the painting for the time being and work on it later. Maybe inspiration would filter into her subconscious while she did something else.

Something that made money. Dollars and cents mattered now that she'd relinquished a regular paycheque from the Ottawa community college where she'd taught history.

She moved carefully to her work space, a long trestle table set up on one side of the room. Being almost six feet tall, she had stopped bumping her head on the sloping roof only after several weeks of living in the small apartment.

At the trestle table, she created life-size papier-mâché animals. Mostly cats and dogs, but there was a waiting list for parrots and other birds. Although she loved malevolent crows, brightly coloured macaws appealed to a wider audience. The craft store on Yorkville Avenue sold them as fast as she produced them and charged astronomical sums. These beings weren't "art", but they engaged her energy, and she enjoyed the creative process. Each animal acquired a personality as she worked. When she finished but before she sent the creatures into the world, she attached appropriate name tags.

Chickens, a flock of five, sat partially assembled on the oilcloth-covered table. She finished wrapping and stapling chicken wire around their wooden frames and reached into the container of thin plastic gloves. These not only protected her hands, they also allowed her to dip paper strips into paste without feeling the paste's slimy consistency. She applied a first coat of paper strips.

Not her day.

The last chicken, supposed to have its head down and tail up as if pecking in the dirt, was lopsided. She ripped off the paper and pried the wooden frame apart. Before she forgot, she scribbled "Buy eyes" on her shopping list. The chickens would look great with beady black eyes. Buttons would do, but eyes would be better. The doll hospital sold a good variety. The question was, would buyers like chickens with blue or green or even violet eyes? Hollis felt her mood lighten when she considered making them with a variety of colours. Maybe she'd name the group—chicks flick eye

13

tricks. Different rhymes, some scatological, raced through her mind, and she laughed aloud. Oops, this was scary. She definitely needed to get out more if this was the kind of conversation she was having with herself.

While she cleaned up, she listened to the noon news on the radio.

Lunch time. She headed downstairs. MacTee bounded ahead of her.

When she knocked on the shiny black door, she noted a patina of small handprints on the lower half. Maintaining a pristine house and a happy toddler were mutually exclusive goals. She smiled. Invited to enter, she stepped into the kitchen, which was immediately to the left of the front hall. The entryway's cream-painted wainscotting continued in the kitchen. The glass-fronted cupboards with old-fashioned brass knobs, green slate floor and green granite countertops gave the room a warm country kitchen appeal. Elizabeth, bibbed and waiting, sat in the high chair beside an antique pine table.

"Hi Howis, hi Tee." Elizabeth accompanied her greeting with a barrage of spoon-banging on her high chair tray.

"Sorry if I'm late. Sometimes time escapes me when I paint."

"Elizabeth napped longer than usual. We haven't started yet," Candace said.

Clean chinos and a pressed blue button-down had replaced the baggy jeans and stained T-shirt. Candace had made an effort to return to her "take charge" persona, but the tight lines around her mouth and raised shoulders told another tale.

Impatience gripped Hollis. She knew that Candace would feel better once she told what she thought had happened to her brother. Unspoken fears stripped away your confidence and your equanimity like piranhas moving in for a kill. If only they could bypass all the domesticity and get on with the story.

14

"Grilled cheese sandwiches, carrot sticks, applesauc and tea okay?" Candace asked. She cut bread into strips and handed them to the child, who abandoned her spoon to scoop them up with pudgy fingers. "I've pretty much given up gourmet delights for the duration. I did try her with smoked salmon and capers, both of which she adored, and sushi, which she didn't. Probably just as well. If the experts suggest pregnant women give up sushi, I'm sure children should avoid it too." She was babbling.

"Anything I don't prepare for myself is wonderful." Hollis munched a carrot stick and watched Elizabeth mash the bread on the tray before she dropped it to MacTee, who snatched it in midair.

"That should keep her entertained if not well-nourished," Candace said. Candace's cell phone shrilled as she motioned for Hollis to sit at the table.

After she flipped it open and said hello, a range of emotions that Hollis identified as relief, anticipation and anger sped across Candace's face. "No, this is not a good time to call. I don't give to charities that phone." She clicked the phone shut. "Damn. I hoped it would be Danson."

"I thought about Danson. I remember his intensity when he talked about lacrosse. You said he had other passions— what's he doing that worries you so much?"

Candace gave Elizabeth a bowl with raisins and chopped apricots along with more cutup bread before she spoke. "You're right. Danson reacts with passion when he loves or hates something. Even as a little boy, he fixated on issues, particularly injustices, and always wanted to take corrective actions." She grimaced. "You may think it's weird that he's an adult, and we're so close. But there's a reason—I feel responsible for him."

Responsible—an odd word to use to describe a relationship with a functioning adult man. "Why is that?"

"I'm more like his mother than his sister. Poppy isn't maternal. I'm glad she had us, but given her personality,

15

it surprises me that she did. I'd say she's never visualized herself in a traditional mother role. One small example— from the get-go, she insisted we call her Poppy. She's never married, never lived with a man."

Speaking of men, there were no signs of one in Candace's apartment, nor had Hollis ever heard Candace mention Elizabeth's father. Maybe single parenting was genetic, or maybe, if that's what your mother did, it was what you did. Interesting idea. Not that she could ask. That sort of information had to be volunteered.

"Poppy always provided for us, by hook or by crook." Candace frowned. "I'm not sure she always draws the line between the two and, however politely I inquire, she won't discuss her financial affairs. Anyway, that's beside the point. The day she and Danson came home from the hospital, she passed him to me." She paused, widened her eyes and raised her eyebrows. "I was seven."

"You cared for him by yourself?" Where had the social service agencies been?

"Not exactly. To give you the background, Poppy was fifteen when I was born. My grandparents opposed her decision to keep me. When she insisted, they decided they didn't want her living with them or even staying in the same community. Unwed mothers weren't part of their world." Her lips drew down. "I never got to meet them. They died when I was five, and unfortunately Poppy hadn't reconciled with them. To give them their due, they weren't prepared to allow Poppy and me to suffer real hardship. They paid Adele, a housekeeper who'd worked for the family, to step into the breach and care for me while Poppy finished school."

"Times were different then," Hollis said. How would her mother have dealt with a similar situation? She felt sure her mother would have chosen abortion. It said something for Poppy that she'd made a decision that was long-term, life altering and took strength, particularly if you weren't a maternal sort of person.

"To continue my story, seven years later, when Poppy became pregnant again, she persuaded Adele to return. By then, the woman was over eighty and couldn't lift or bend. I did those jobs."

"You must have been a responsible kid."

Candace pursed her lips. "I would have preferred to have been just a kid, but I didn't have a choice. Anyway, now you know why I think of Danson as my baby. As for his personality—from day one he was a crusader. Always on the side of the underdog. In the Middle Ages, he would have galloped off to battle the Infidels."

"We need those passionate people, or society would never change."

"I wish Danson wasn't one of them." Candace's lips tightened. "Oh, God, if only Danson was an ordinary guy."

"Danson coming?" Elizabeth said. She smiled at Hollis and repeated, "Danson coming," hopefully.

"No sweetie, not now." Candace teared and gulped. "Maybe soon. Eat your raisins."

Elizabeth's smile disappeared, but she obediently bent to her time-consuming task, picking up raisins one by one.

"Tell me about his passions, the ones you think are dangerous."

"Give me a minute," Candace said, struggling to maintain her composure. Once she'd taken several deep breaths, she continued. "Let me set the scene. One Saturday evening three years ago when Danson and Angie Napier, the love of his life, were sitting in an outdoor café on the Danforth planning their wedding, Angie was killed when she was caught in the crossfire between two gangs. Later, Danson discovered Angie's killer had been convicted of another crime, deported, returned and, within months, killed Angie."

"How could that happen?"

"We deport criminals to their home countries after they serve minimum time in our prisons. They reenter Canada

17

with phony passports. They're mostly men, and frequently they commit more crimes. Our immigration officers don't do a great job."

"How does that connect to Danson?"

"Since that terrible Saturday, he's waged his own crusade. He track downs the men or women who've been convicted, deported and slithered back into Canada."

"Are there many?"

"The numbers would horrify you."

"How does he locate them?"

Candace toyed with the knife with which she'd cut up the bread. "I haven't asked many questions. The more I know, the more I worry, and I do enough of that. I gather it's mostly through the street grapevine. That's why he works as a bouncer; he gets to know people and hears things."

"You said passions. That's plural. What else?"

"I think it's because of Angie that he worries about us and does his best to keep us safe. He goes to great lengths to make sure we aren't connected to his tracking activities."

"All done, all done," Elizabeth squawked. "Down, get down."

Candace sighed. "Conversations with kids around are fragmentary at best. Sometimes I think it's a recipe for early Alzheimer's." She tapped the toes of Elizabeth's sneakers. "I have to buy shoes for her today. Her daycare sent a note home last week saying she needed bigger ones, but I haven't had time." She attempted a smile. "I don't want them to set the shoe police on me." She unlatched the high chair's tray with one hand, clutched Elizabeth and eased her to the floor.

"I understand. When you have a full-time job, you do your shopping when you can."

The stress lines around Candace's mouth relaxed slightly, and she smiled fondly at Elizabeth. "Elizabeth has extra-wide feet. Finding the right ones will be difficult."

Elizabeth studied her feet and lifted one for Hollis to inspect. "New shoes. Lizabet get new shoes."

Despite the tension in the room, it enchanted Hollis to hear the toddler refer to herself in the third person.

Candace brushed the crumbs from Elizabeth's jeans before raising her gaze. "With every passing moment, I'm more fearful. You can't imagine the physical effect it's having on me."

"I don't understand what it is that you fear," Hollis said.

"I'm afraid something terrible has happened to him. I'm scared to death." While Candace talked, she repeatedly snapped the cell phone open and shut.

"I don't get it. Exactly what do you think might have happened to him?"

Candace closed her eyes for a moment as though trying to block out something she didn't want to face. "I don't even want to admit I'm thinking this," she said, then stopped and took a deep breath. Finally her gaze met Hollis's. "It's the unidentified murdered man they're talking about in the news. I keep thinking, 'what if it's Danson?'"

Three

Hollis recalled the article she'd been reading when Candace had come outside. It had speculated that a mutilated and unidentified man's murder might have been connected to the five male drug addicts who'd been killed in the last months. She shivered. It was a terrible idea, but she understood why Candace thought Danson's obsession with tracking could have drawn him to the attention of the wrong people. He could be the unidentified man.

Time to deal with practicalities. "Exactly when did you last talk to him?"

"Sunday night, October 15. Almost two weeks ago. The day after the four of us had lunch in the garden. He doesn't work Sundays, and he always calls, even if he's talked to me the day before."

"What did he tell you?"

"Said he was onto something—that he was closing in. Lot of excitement in his voice." Candace shook her head. "That's what's frightening me."

"Closing in on what?"

"I don't know." Candace took a deep breath. "What I'm about to ask is really off the wall. It's a huge imposition. I apologize, but I don't know where else to turn." Hollis suspected she knew what was coming. "Would you help me track him down?"

Candace hurried on before Hollis could respond. "You can say no, and I'll understand, and we'll still be friends.

20

But you do have experience. You have helped solve two murders." She placed her hands palm to palm in the classic prayer pose. "I'm praying that you won't refuse."

Hollis, who was holding her sandwich halfway to her mouth, lowered it to the plate. Finding missing persons— that's what private investigators did. Not amateurs. On the other hand, Candace was right. If she wrote a comprehensive resume, it would say, "amateur sleuth who assisted in solving two murders". Most women didn't possess that skill set.

Candace needed her. Thinking selfishly, focusing on Danson's disappearance would allow her subconscious to work out her painting block. Moreover, concentrating on someone else's problem might stave off the black dogs.

"Where do we start?" Hollis said.

Candace clapped her hands. "Thank you, thank you." Relief filled her eyes.

Hollis had felt like that when a plane she'd been on had managed to land safely after its landing gear failed to lock into place. Feelings of absolute relief and profound gratitude along with a determination never to take life for granted.

"What does Danson do when he fingers these criminals?" Hollis said.

"Thank god he's smart enough not to play superhero. He reports them to the appropriate authorities. Twice, when nothing happened, he contacted the *Star*, and it did an exposé."

"Are many people aware that he does this?"

"I hope there isn't a single person, but I suspect many people know. That's one reason I'm worried." Candace hesitated and, glanced at Elizabeth as if seeking confirmation that what she was about to say was important. "Since he left, I've had calls asking for him. When I say he doesn't live here, the callers—there are different ones—hang up without identifying themselves. It's frightening me."

"Do you ask who they are?"

"Yes, they won't say." She shuddered. "Then there are the

calls where someone breathes heavily—I've had those too. I'm convinced they aren't random, that someone wants to scare me, to stop me from searching for my brother." Again her gaze focused on the toddler. "I'm afraid for Elizabeth. Her daycare is secure, but I've warned them to be extra careful, not to allow her to leave with anyone but me."

If there had been more calls, and they did relate to Danson's disappearance, it was another reason to worry and to take the problem seriously. "Is it happening more often than usual?"

"Maybe I'm exaggerating the number, but it has been happening. The breathers upset me the most."

"Creepy. Have you reported them to the police or thought about getting an unlisted number?"

"I have, but what about Danson? What if he needs help, and when he calls the number, is no longer in service? No, I couldn't do that."

"Would your mother know where he is or what he's doing?"

"Poppy!" Candace's eyebrows rose. "As I said, Poppy lacks the maternal gene and the 'worry' gene. She figures things will work out, and for her they usually do. Right now it's even more unlikely that she knows anything or has talked to Danson about anything serious."

"Why is that?"

"Something's preoccupying her or maybe them. Alberto, an Argentinean, is Poppy's business partner. I'm sure he'd like to be more than that, but Poppy has had a long-term relationship with someone. We've never met him, and she's been careful not to mention his name. Recently I've had the sense that something has happened to him or to their relationship, because she's seemed sad. From a lifetime of experience, I can tell you Poppy doesn't spill the beans until she's good and ready. Worrying about Danson isn't on her agenda at the moment. When I tried to talk to her about him, she fluttered her hands dismissively and said, 'Danson will be fine.'" She paused. "Families. Always something."

"I only have my mother, who's an accountant determined to save the environment. She's in Halifax. Although we talk once a week, if she isn't off on an ecological tour, it's a tenuous connection. She's obsessive about her causes and isn't interested in my life. I'd give anything to have a close family. I envy you."

Candace's eyes widened. "You're right. Because I'm always worrying about Poppy, Danson or Elizabeth, I sometimes forget how much I love them. Poppy and Alberto are coming to dinner tonight. Join us and see what information you can winkle out of them."

"Tell me about Alberto."

"I don't know much. Spanish is his first language, and he isn't that fluent in English." She grinned. "Poppy talks for both of them. She and Alberto own and run a dance studio on Queen Street west and compete professionally in ballroom dancing. They specialize in Latin American dances, particularly the tango. That's another reason she isn't worrying about Danson. She and Alberto are flying to Vancouver this coming week for a major dance competition.

"They're business partners. They don't live together because Poppy adores Siamese cats. Certainly the current two, Bubbles and Smokey, run the show. Alberto's allergic to cats. He can't spend five minutes in Poppy's apartment without grabbing for his inhaler. Poppy would not give them up. She once said her cats provided continuity and kept her anchored to reality."

When she heard the cats' names, Elizabeth shouted, "Bubbles, go see Bubbles?" When no one responded, her voice rose and became more insistent.

Candace stopped talking, bent down to Elizabeth's eye level and smiled at her. "No sweetie, not today. Poppy's coming up for dinner, but she's not bringing them. You have MacTee—you don't need the cats." She looked up at Hollis. "Use your detecting skills and find out what the hell is going on with Poppy. She loves an audience. Not surprising, considering what she did for years."

People and the details of their lives fascinated Hollis. She supposed that was why she'd taught social history, the story of ordinary people. In intimate conversations, she'd found that there was a confessional pattern. Individuals wound their way into a tale, always aware if the listener lost interest or found intimate details shocking. She found that revelations grew increasingly significant if she didn't comment but listened attentively. Some Americans surprised her, because they readily revealed the most private details on the shortest of acquaintances.

"What did Poppy do before?" Hollis asked.

"Right now she not only dances in competitions herself but also designs and sews costumes for other ballroom dancers." A faint smile twitched at the corners of Candace's lips. "Not for those with whom she competes. There's a strict code the dresses must conform to, or the wearer is disqualified." She twirled a strand of Elizabeth's fine hair around her finger. "But these are second careers." Her eyes danced.

A big revelation was coming.

"What was the first?"

"Exotic dancer," Candace said with raised eyebrows. "Bet you weren't expecting to hear that." She grimaced. "Thirty years ago, I don't think it was quite so awful— more like old-fashioned burlesque." Her eyebrows rose, "At least that's what I choose to believe. I do know lap-dancing wasn't allowed."

Hollis stretched her mind around the idea. You seldom thought about parents' younger lives.

"Poppy also creates outfits for people for special occasions—Mardi Gras, Hallowe'en, fancy dress balls. She's talented. If the arrival and departure of UPS trucks is any indication, she does a steady business."

"Is the dance studio profitable?"

"Something must be. She lives well. Three or four years ago she made a great fuss about buying an expensive fireproof safe. Said she needed to protect her valuables. When I asked what that meant, she winked and said it was better for me not to know." Candace shrugged. "Maybe she's right. Maybe it's something I don't want to hear."

Hollis revised her view of Candace's mother. Who thinks that a friend's middle-aged mother has been an exotic dancer, let alone has secret sources of money? Given this information, she wondered to whom the house belonged. She paid her rent to Candace, but if Candace owned the house, wouldn't she live on the first floor?

"Is this her house?"

"Because I live on the second floor?"

Hollis nodded.

"It's mine," Candace paused. "Well, to be precise, the mortgage company and I own it. I live upstairs because no one wants to have a dancer over her head and certainly not a night hawk who may have a tango inspiration at three a.m. As it is, I sleep with ear plugs. Poppy claims volume allows the music to penetrate 'the essence of her being.'"

Elizabeth climbed onto Candace's knee and snuggled against her. Candace pulled her close. "Hollis, tell me quickly what else you need to know about Danson?" She buried her nose in the toddler's hair. "You will never know how wonderful it is to have an ally, a friend who knows the ropes."

"I'm flattered, but don't get your hopes up. I'll do my best, but I've never searched for a missing person."

Hollis had been making mental lists, an embryonic attack plan. Their first priority was to decide if Danson had left of his own free will.

"If it's not an invasion of Danson's privacy, we should examine his apartment and possessions. You said the man who rents the room isn't there. What's his schedule for coming to Toronto?"

"Haven't a clue. Gregory was here briefly a couple of

weeks ago. Danson said he'd like me to meet him the next time he came to Toronto." She paused. "I can be more precise. He was there two weeks ago when you were here for lunch. If you remember, Danson said Gregory would leave in the morning, and he didn't know when he'd be back, but we'd meet him when he did make another appearance."

Sometimes roommates were not as they presented themselves. It was a theme Hollywood had explored in a number of movies where a seemingly innocuous roommate emerged as a psychopathic killer.

"Where did Danson connect with Gregory?"

"It was the other way around. Gregory found Danson. Apparently he hung out with Danson's crowd at Concordia University in Montreal. Anyway, it's a perfect setup. Danson needs the money to carry the apartment's costs, and Gregory won't often be there."

"A visit to the apartment is first on our list."

The tension around Candace's mouth and eyes had lessened marginally. She ventured a smile. "It will be such a relief to do something. I'm wearing out my phone flipping it open, hoping there's a message. You may think I'm extremely paranoid, but I'm wondering if I should file a missing persons report with the police?"

"Good question. Why don't you wait until we've seen his apartment?"

"I guess a few more hours won't hurt," Candace said slowly and reluctantly. She shook her head. "For him not to have phoned...he knows how I feel. It's not like him. My sixth sense tells me he's in terrible trouble."

Four

Hollis itched to get going, to visit Danson's apartment and search for signs that he hadn't intended to be away for an extended period. Despite Candace's anxiety, Elizabeth's shoes came first.

"You and Elizabeth are going shopping, aren't you?" Hollis asked.

Elizabeth, sitting on Candace's knee, straightened her legs and shook her feet. "New shoes, new shoes," she chanted as she kicked.

"She has her afternoon nap first. Then we go." Candace placed a restraining hand on Elizabeth's legs. "Now that you've agreed to help, I hate to waste a minute, but Elizabeth will be a bear if she doesn't sleep. After that, I don't have a choice—we must buy shoes." She lowered Elizabeth to the floor and steered her toward the door. "No matter how often I repeat it, you'll never realize the extent of my gratitude. You can't know how relieved I am that we're doing something." She stopped halfway to the hall. "I have a set of Danson's keys, including those for the front door, mail box, apartment door and garage. To speed things up, why don't I hand them over and let you begin?"

Action at last. "Terrific. The garage. What does Danson drive?"

"He leases a sporty car. I don't know the make. It's silver and not expensive. I'm an idiot when it comes to cars, but it's pretty spiffy." She corralled Elizabeth. "We'll shop quickly and join you. Since you'll have Danson's keys, buzz us in when we arrive."

"Before I go, I'll grab some things—printer paper, notebook, camera, and maybe the thin plastic gloves I use when I construct papier mâché sculptures."

Candace held the toddler's shoulder as if she wanted to steady herself, as if Elizabeth's warm body provided stability and anchored her to reality. She shivered. "They say you do that when someone walks over your grave. It scares me to realize you're taking gloves so that we won't contaminate anything in case this becomes serious."

"Probably silly, but I've watched too many episodes of *Law and Order* and *CSI* not to think it's important." Hollis changed the subject. No point in upsetting Candace any more than necessary. "Write down the instructions for driving to Danson's. I'm hopeless with verbal directions, and I'm not that familiar with Toronto."

A few minutes later, after she'd walked MacTee, Hollis parked her truck across from a rambling three-storey brick house on Bernard Street. A relatively new three-car garage filled most of what had been a large garden beside the house. She sorted the keys, clutched what she thought might be the right one for the garage and, not wanting to alert or alarm anyone peering out of the window, walked confidently to the small door and inserted the key. It worked, and she entered the gloomy, musty space, where she flicked the light switch next to the door. A sedate dark-green Nissan sedan occupied one parking spot.

One question answered. Danson's car was gone.

In the building's vestibule, she confronted a closed door, three mailboxes and buzzers. Danson did not have his name anywhere. This surprised her. Advice columns warned single women not to advertise their state; to use an initial or simply a surname to indicate where they lived. She wouldn't have thought the advice applied to men. But given Danson's tracking obsession, maybe this was a wise precaution. Fortunately, the other tenants' bells were marked. She'd chat with them if the situation was serious.

She felt silly when she slipped on clear plastic gloves but ignored the feeling. She had a job to do.

No newspaper on the shelf under the mailboxes. That proved nothing. Danson probably picked up the *Sun, Metro* or *Star* on his travels.

After she inserted the key, the door flipped open, and mail tumbled out. She scooped it from the floor and bundled it into her large purse before she unlocked the door to the stairs leading up to apartment two. Inside the stairwell, it smelled stale, as if nothing had disturbed the air for days.

Upstairs, she unlocked Danson's front door, stepped inside a miniscule hall and took in what she saw. It fit the category—student transitting to young adult. Because of Danson's age and occupation, she'd expected college dorm or family castoffs. Clearly he'd shopped at Zellers or IKEA—she recognized the white assemble-it-yourself furniture. The black leather sofa and club chairs in the living room shrieked newness. Probably bought to replace a worn-out couch or a futon.

She flipped through the bills, flyers and letters she'd carried upstairs. No mail for Gregory—he remained the mystery man without a surname. Nothing useful, nothing she thought might relate to Danson's disappearance. She dropped the mail on the narrow white hall table. It too was a particleboard DIY creation, no doubt emitting toxic formaldehyde fumes.

Her first priority was to determine if Danson had intended to be away for an extended period. The bathroom would give her a clue. Inside the white room, she opened the vanity's door. A brown leather shaving kit, stacks of toilet paper and clean white towels occupied the space.

An electric toothbrush and toothpaste sat beside the sink in a mug commemorating a lacrosse tournament.

The medicine cabinet held two bottles of painkillers, a tiny bottle of wart remover, nonprescription allergy medication and a canister of Noxzema shaving cream. She opened a drawer in the vanity and found an extra tube of toothpaste, a package of unused razors and a hairbrush.

A clean-shaven young man did not leave without his shaving kit and toiletries. He had not intended to be away overnight. Now the question was—where had he gone and why?

She left the bathroom and moved methodically through the apartment. First, on her right, the kitchen. Four items graced the scarred Formica countertop—toaster, coffee maker, bean grinder half-full of beans and a telephone. She lifted the receiver and heard the buzz of a line. No beeps to indicate messages. Since she knew Candace had left messages, this meant Danson owned an answering machine. Because she would have required a PIN combination to access messages recorded by the phone company, she welcomed this knowledge.

Now for a gander in the refrigerator. She found the usual array of condiments, soft drinks and beer along with some small containers of yogurt, two light caesar salad bags and greenish uncooked chicken encased in plastic wrap on a styrofoam tray. Time-dated food long past the best-before date. More confirmation that Danson had not planned to be away for long.

In the master bedroom, two framed posters—lacrosse players in action—provided colour. The utilitarian navy-blue duvet and pillow cases, white chest of drawers, white bedside table, gooseneck lamp and clock radio were minimalist. The bed was made and the closet doors shut. Although she wasn't familiar with Danson's wardrobe, she peered in the cupboard and found nothing but clothes and shoes.

On top of the bureau, Danson's cell phone was plugged into a charger. More evidence to support her growing conviction that he had not planned a trip.

Perhaps that explained why he hadn't called?

There were many locations without cell phone accessibility but few without telephone service. The high Arctic, the northern tundra—not places Danson was likely to visit.

Would learning that Danson didn't have his cell phone make Candace feel better, even explain why he hadn't phoned? No way. It would give her even more reason to worry—few young men travelled far without a cell phone.

She plucked her notebook from her shoulder bag, copied his cell phone address book and wrote down the names of those whom he'd contacted and those who had called him. Unfortunately, it wasn't a photo phone. She knew how useful they could be. Recently she'd read that many companies had outlawed cell phones, since they provided such an easy way for staff or visitors to steal confidential information.

The second bedroom, impersonal as a motel room, epitomized austerity. If Gregory intended to establish a homey base in Toronto, he hadn't accomplished his goal.

She'd deal with establishing Gregory's identity later. Danson was her priority.

Back to the combination living room/dining room. A wall of Venetian blinds, no curtains, off-white walls. A collection of tall, healthy palms and ficus in large black self-watering pots clustered near the windows. The pristine leather furniture grouped around a small TV set on a worn chest of drawers flanked by three bookcases.

Books revealed facets of a reader's character. Danson had kept his college texts, along with books on kinesiology, brain patterning, psychological treatises on abnormal behaviour, books on treason, on the organization of the courts, on criminal law and more prosaic volumes on lacrosse. An interesting collection.

A sound system, CDs, jazz and more jazz, along with black cardboard file boxes, and large photo albums filled the remaining shelves. A peek inside the boxes confirmed that Danson seldom threw anything away, as he'd saved

31

memorabilia from his life along with outdated files and receipts. The photo albums, arranged chronologically, revealed his devotion to his family and to Angie, his murdered fiancée.

Opposite the recreational side of the room, yet another lacrosse poster presided over the mechanics of twenty-first century living. An unpainted door resting on two beige metal file cabinets served as a desk. A laptop, printer, phone and answering machine lined up like soldiers awaiting their marching orders. The answering machine's message light flashed.

Hollis pressed play.

"Your mortgage has been approved blah blah blah..." Pointless to save, but to erase would be tampering with evidence in the event there had been a crime. She pressed save and moved to the second one. "This is Boris," a heavy Eastern European accent, one she thought that she recognized. Boris must have done a blitz on every phone number in the book. "Do not move unless you talk to Boris..."

She stopped listening. Boris might vary his spiel, but many times before she'd received his annoying calls selling his moving company's services.

Number three. "It's Monday. Where the hell are you? You've got a job, in case you've forgotten. Actually, you fucking well haven't—you're fired."

Not good news. If he'd intended to be away for an extended period, Danson would have talked to his boss.

She moved on to the next message. "It's Cally. Let me know if your gorgeous mother still sews her wonderful costumes. I'd like her to design one for me with no other like it in the whole wide world. Oh, and tell her we're not in the same competitions. Call me." Cally sounded like she drew hearts as punctuation in anything she wrote and cultivated wide-eyed innocence. Probably her stock in trade in the competitive dance world.

Next call was a hang-up.

Several long messages related to lacrosse and recruiting for the team. The callers, and there were three different voices, became increasingly irate when they repeated their messages and demanded that Danson return their calls. Whoever they were, they'd phoned before Candace talked to them, or they'd be aware of Danson's absence.

And then it was Boris again.

No messages offered any immediately recognizable clues as to Danson's whereabouts.

The filing cabinet came next. The top drawer confirmed her impression that Danson was a tidy man. Financial records—paid bills, taxes, insurance, Visa and bank statements—filled the first drawer. Lacrosse schedules, contacts, equipment etc, memberships in lacrosse and alumni associations, newspaper clippings relating to lacrosse, to criminals, to the justice system, to trials—these files crowded the second drawer. Danson seemed to have recorded and saved every detail of his life.

If a crime had been committed, the apartment would be sealed, and she wouldn't get a second chance to burrow through his records. Hollis hoped she wouldn't need any of this information but pulled the paper from her bag and used Danson's printer to copy every potentially helpful file, including a chart detailing the organization of Toronto's Russian Mafia.

The Toronto police would do a thorough job. She'd had firsthand experience and knew how effective they were. Sometimes an unprofessional mind thought differently, approached problems in a different way. That would be her role.

Copy, copy, copy—it took forever; almost all her paper, and the printer alerted her that the ink cartridge must be replaced. Once done she carefully replaced the files and opened the laptop. If she needed a password, she would be out of luck. No one in her circle of friends used passwords for their personal computers, but given his campaign to round up criminals, Danson might. She flicked it on.

The intercom sounded. Candace and Elizabeth had arrived.

Hollis buzzed them through the downstairs door and stepped out in the hall to wait for them to climb the stairs.

"Touchdown. Mission accomplished. We have shoes," Candace called.

"Hi, Howis," Elizabeth said.

Inside the apartment's living room, Candace donned the gloves Hollis offered. Elizabeth watched and held up her hands.

"No gloves for you. They're too big. They're for Hollis and me," Candace said.

Elizabeth's lower lip quivered.

"You can watch TV," Candace said to the little girl, who immediately plunked herself down in front of the television.

Elizabeth held up her foot for Hollis's inspection. "See," she said displaying a pink running shoe with Velcro fasteners. "New."

"They're gorgeous. What a lucky girl you are," Hollis said.

Elizabeth ripped the Velcro tab to undo the shoe. She gripped the heel, yanked the shoe off and held it up to Hollis, who accepted the gift, admired it, and handed it back.

Elizabeth struggled to push it on, so Hollis bent down to help her. "Was it hard to track them down?" she said to Candace peering over the little girl's shoulder.

Candace smiled ruefully and ran both her hands through her neat bob. Hollis admired the way the hair dropped into place, the mark of great hair and a terrific cut.

"Hard enough. Three stores, two temper tantrums— then success. Coping with toddlers is not for the faint-hearted." She picked up the remote and flicked on the TV.

Elizabeth ignored it. Instead she peered up at Candace. "Danson?" she said. Her nose wrinkled, and her tiny, almost invisible eyebrows drew together in a frown.

"Not here, sweetie," Candace said.

Elizabeth glowered. "Lizabet want Danson," she said.

"I know you do. But not now. Elizabeth, this is one of your favourite shows—it's Curious George."

Diverted, the little girl settled to watch the monkey's cartoon antics.

Candace moved closer to Hollis. "Well, what did you find?"

"Danson's car, wallet and keys are gone, but he left his cell phone, toothbrush, and shaving stuff. He must have expected to return quickly from wherever he went." Hollis didn't want to look at Candace, to witness the devastation as the ramifications of this information hit home.

"He doesn't go anywhere without his cell." A long silence grew heavier by the minute. "This is bad news, isn't it?" Candace said.

No use denying it. "I think you should contact Missing Persons," Hollis said gently. "If you like, I can phone Rhona Simpson, a homicide detective I know, and ask her advice."

Candace shuddered. "Please. Do it immediately. I have to know that Danson isn't the unidentified man in the morgue."

Five

Late that October Saturday afternoon, Rhona Simpson hunkered down at her desk. She, along with an ever-growing pool of detectives, had been assigned to unearth the killer or killers preying on men in the downtown area. The killings had begun six weeks earlier. The police weren't any closer to solving the crimes than they had been on day one.

Six murdered men, five identified thus far, all stabbed with a long, thin blade. One unidentified—his face pulverized and his fingertips chopped off. No one had reporting a missing loved one, at least not a man with physical characteristics that corresponded to the mystery man's. A gangland execution—but which gang and why?

Rhona repositioned the elastic scrunchy anchoring her dark hair away from her face and covertly studied the partner assigned to her.

Ian Galbraith, the newest detective in homicide, zealously applied a yellow highlighter to the document in front of him. There wouldn't be much unmarked when he finished. Single-mindedness characterized his attitude. Like most new boys, he was determined to prove himself.

Physically, blazingly blue eyes, fair skin and black hair falling in his eyes marked him as a man with a Gaelic heritage matching his name. Tall, thin and intense, he'd launched himself into the investigation as if his position depended on it, and maybe it did.

"What are you staring at?" Ian said.

"Sorry, I do that when I'm thinking," Rhona said.

"I'm relieved. I thought I must have left half my lunch on my face," Ian said with a small smile that revealed perfect teeth and a dimple. He returned to scrutinizing the document.

They'd spent the morning on the street, interviewing women and men on the stroll and searching for fresh clues to identify the killer. Hours later, they were cross-indexing information from the murdered men's files, seeking a revealing, overlooked detail. For the last few minutes, they'd been reviewing information, searching for similarities in lifestyle, hangouts, diet, habits, medical conditions—factoids that linked the victims to each other and to their killer or killers.

Rhona leaned back in her swivel chair and shifted her weight to keep from resting on her left hip. She'd enrolled in a Pilates class several weeks before, and the previous day her ego had prompted her to do a leg-lifting exercise that the instructor had cautioned was for the "more advanced" in the group. Rhona had figured that as she was only in her late thirties, she was as fit as anyone, but watching the lithe twenty-year-olds, she should have known better.

She stretched her legs and contemplated the black tooled-leather cowboy boots chosen to coordinate with her washable black pantsuit. Aware of her foibles, she knew she wore boots almost daily not only because they were comfortable but because they gave her the added inches she craved. In the man's world of policing, being a short First Nation woman left her triply disadvantaged, and there wasn't anything she could do about it except wear higher heels. Enough self-examination. They had work to do.

"Six weeks since the first murder—it's too long," Rhona said.

"It is." Ian evened the edges of the paper piled on his desk and frowned. "Do you get a sense the killer doesn't care about his victims?"

Rhona felt her eyebrows rise.

"No, that didn't come out right. What if the killer hates what his victims do but isn't attacking them as individuals. That's what I mean?"

"Like the anti-abortionists who have nothing against particular doctors but kill them because of what they do?"

"An analogous comparison. A fervent crusader maybe?"

Analogous? Fervent? Not words commonly heard from her fellow detectives. She'd have to learn more about this new guy. "Maybe. They were all addicts." Rhona riffled through her papers. "No victim was sexually assaulted or fought back. No skin under fingernails, no semen, nobody who's come forward to say he saw anything—we'll have to catch the perp in the act." She rocked forward on her chair and winced.

"What's wrong?" Ian asked.

"Pulled a muscle doing Pilates," Rhona said. She cautiously leaned her body forward again. "These men were expendable. That doesn't explain why they were killed."

"It's the general opinion that they were involved in the drug trade?"

Rhona shook her head. "Too obvious. These guys were peripheral—small fry." She moved herself a fraction of an inch to the right. "They weren't operators—maybe mules, but I doubt it. I think the killer hates drugs and those who use them. Finding the person who hates drugs enough to kill men because they were addicted—that's who we're searching for. Whoever that someone is, he doesn't frighten those he kills. That's our perp."

"That might explain those crimes, but I don't see how it ties into the killing of the other man." Ian steepled his fingers, tilted his head to one side and waited for her response.

"In my opinion it doesn't. The perp beat the shit out of this guy before he died. His face smashed with something heavy—a crowbar, baseball bat—who knows. His fingers chopped off. No fingerprints. Whoever killed him didn't want him identified. We have to wonder why."

"No blood in the dumpster where we found him. Moved from somewhere—who knows—it's a big city," Ian said.

"The killer made sure the victim would be hard, if not impossible to identify. Why hasn't someone missed him?"

"Obvious answers. Either he isn't from Toronto, or those close to him don't dare call us." Ian swept up the pile of paper, held it aloft and shook it. "The answer is here. It would be good for our careers if we could identify the missing link."

Rhona's phone rang. She listened for a moment, pushed the button to activate the speaker phone and motioned for Ian to listen. "Repeat that, please," she said.

"My friend's brother is missing. She's afraid something terrible has happened to him," Hollis said.

Men disappeared every day; it was the nature of the beast. However, at this particular moment, Homicide had an unidentified male murder victim.

"I'm sorry to hear that. Give me his particulars," Rhona said.

"I'll put his sister, Candace Lafleur, on the line. She'll provide the details."

"Detective Rhona Simpson speaking. Sorry to hear about your brother. Give me his vital statistics—name, age, height, weight, eye and hair colour, marital status, occupation, address, everything relevant. After that, tell me why you're worried."

"Danson Lafleur. He's twenty-four, single, six-foot-two, about one hundred and sixty-five pounds, blue eyes and brown hair. Danson's a bouncer at the Starshine club, and he plays semi-professional lacrosse. He lives in an apartment on Bernard Street in the Annex."

"Tattoos or scars?"

"No. He hated…" Candace paused.

Rhona knew, as surely as if she'd been in the room with her, that Candace's eyes had widened; she'd spoken as if her brother was dead. "My god, that was past tense. That shows how frightened I am. Anyway, he's hated needles since he was a baby. I can't remember any scars. He suffered the usual number of childhood falls and accidents, but none left scars."

Too bad. A snake twining on his bicep or a heart on his shoulder would help identify him. Today being tattooed seemed to be a rite of passage. Rhona had contemplated getting one relating to her Cree background but had rejected the idea of voluntarily suffering pain.

Rhona said nothing about the man's body lying unidentified in the morgue. He didn't have identifying marks either, but comparing DNA or dental records would tell if Danson Lafleur and the man in the morgue were one and the same.

"Why are you afraid?"

"We always talk on Sunday nights. Always. It's never mattered where he was or what he was doing, he always, always phoned me on Sundays. I had lunch with him two Saturdays ago, and he hasn't contacted me since." She paused. She probably thought that this sounded a bit odd and required an explanation. It did. Most grown men did not phone their sisters once a week.

"I'm older than Danson and more or less brought him up. Kind of a surrogate mother. He's never missed a Sunday night. Never. He would have phoned or e-mailed me if he could."

Definitely didn't sound good, although a man might change his habits without it meaning anything more serious than a desire to alter routines.

"Have you checked his home to see if he took clothes, suitcases, cancelled the paper or anything else to tell you he left intentionally?"

"We're in his apartment right now. His car, wallet and keys are gone, but his cell phone isn't, and he didn't take shaving stuff or toiletries."

"Sounds as if it's time to report him to missing persons. Go to your nearest station and file a report. Take a recent photo. Let me speak to Hollis again."

"Hollis speaking."

"I don't want to alarm your friend, but if Ms Lafleur has access to his apartment, ask her to pick up and bag his hairbrush or something else that will have DNA and drop it off at the desk downstairs. Also get the name of the young man's dentist."

"May I ask why?"

"Pursuant to another inquiry," Rhona said. "We'll get back to you."

"How soon?"

"When the lab work is done."

Ian raised an eyebrow after Rhona had placed the phone in its cradle.

"Hollis Grant. I've dealt with her twice before," Rhona explained.

"In what capacity?"

"When I worked in Ottawa, her husband was murdered and here, in Toronto, the stepson of one of her friends was murdered."

Ian exhaled a puff of breath and shook his head. "I'd say you need hazard pay to associate with her."

Rhona nodded. "You could be right. She seems to be murder-prone. You heard what her friend said. Her brother is the right height, weight and has the same colour hair as the man in the morgue. For his family's sake, I hope it isn't him. But it would speed up our investigation and give us leads if we knew the victim's identity."

*   *   *

As Danson's TV blared and Elizabeth sat entranced, Hollis and Candace stared at one another.

"What did the detective say?"

41

Hollis gave herself a minute to think while she readjusted and resettled her red-framed glasses. She hated passing on the message, but Candace had every right to be told. "She wants something with Danson's DNA and asked for his dentist's name."

"Oh my god! Do you suppose his statistics match those of the unidentified man? Is that why they want…" Candace's voice petered out, as if she couldn't bear to say the words aloud.

"I'm sure she would have asked anyone reporting a missing man the approximate age of the victim to supply those things." Hollis made her voice sound offhand. "I expect it's totally routine—an elimination process. Probably doesn't mean anything."

Candace looked doubtful.

"Do you know his dentist's name?"

"Sure, I go to him too."

"You have his address and number?"

"At home."

"Why don't you go back to the house and write everything down. I'll pick up a couple of items here. Then you or I or both of us can take everything to the police station."

"Dental records. My god, this is awful. Waiting will be unbearable. Doing lab tests and matching dental records—it will seem like forever before they have the answer." Candace's voice rose. "I don't know if I can make it," she said.

Elizabeth, not completely absorbed in Curious George's antics, raised her head. "You cross?" she said conversationally.

Candace made a visible effort to pull herself together. She inhaled and exhaled slowly before she answered, "No, sweetie. But it's time to turn off the TV and go home."

Elizabeth frowned. "Curious George?" she said.

"Maybe later," Hollis said. "Right now, Hollis will follow us soon. Then we'll go for a ride." She pointed to the new shoes. "Let's see how well you and your new shoes go down the stairs?"

After they'd left, Hollis pulled a plastic baggie from her purse. Maybe it was a good thing Danson hadn't taken his toiletries. She collected the hair brush from the bathroom drawer and sealed it in the bag.

Back in the living room, she turned her attention to Danson's computer. She hated leaving before she saw his files. She temporized—maybe half an hour. No, she wouldn't do that. This wasn't the time to keep Candace waiting. Candace would feel better after they delivered Danson's things to Rhona. Before she left the apartment, she verified that she'd replaced every item where it had been originally.

At Candace's house, her Volvo station wagon idled in front of the building. Hollis parked and walked over.

Candace cracked the window open and waved a post-it note. "Here's the name and address. Stick it in with whatever you have. I'll drive you downtown. I don't want to slow down the DNA testing for a single solitary moment."

Hollis piled into the front passenger seat. Before she could slam the door, Candace squealed away from the curb. Hands gripping the steering wheel, she took her eyes off the road long enough to glance at Hollis. "Are you a praying woman?"

"I used to be married to a minister, so I should be. I'm not though."

"I'm not either, but I'm praying there will be DNA on the brush…" She took one hand off the wheel and tapped the baggie on Hollis's knee, "…and it won't belong to a murdered man."

Candace's driving frightened Hollis. She erratically sped up and slowed to a crawl, causing following drivers to honk and wave fingers at her as they passed. Twenty long minutes later, she deposited Hollis at the police building on College Street. At the front desk, Hollis dropped off the bag with directions to send it up to Rhona.

Returning to the car, she glanced at Candace, whose face was not as white and strained as it had been.

"Hi, Howis," Elizabeth said in a tone that suggested they'd been parted for at least a year.

Hollis swivelled cautiously and grinned at the girl strapped into her car seat in the centre of the back seat. "Hi, Elizabeth. Nice shoes."

Elizabeth held up her foot. "Nice," she said approvingly.

"Given what we've found, perhaps I should go back to Danson's apartment and keep working. I can come to dinner another time," Hollis said.

"Go back after dinner. Since we think Danson didn't intend to be away, you have to talk to Poppy and see if she can provide some insights into where he might have gone. They're close—Danson tries to take care of Poppy." A small smile crept across Candace's face. "Once you've met her, you'll know what a challenge that is."

"How much do you plan to share with your mother?"

"Nothing more than what she already knows—he's missing. But Danson calls her often and pops in to see her at least once a week, and he may have told her something. As I said, he's family oriented and always wants to look after us."

"Poppy, Poppy, Poppy," Elizabeth chanted.

"You'll see her soon. She's coming for dinner," Candace said.

"Getti?"

"No, lasagna, but you like that."

Hollis smiled. Candace had been right when she claimed that having a sustained conversation when a toddler was around presented challenges.

"Candace, you arrived at the apartment before I had examined Gregory's room or gone through Danson's files or opened his computer. We need to discover Gregory's surname and contact him. I hate to waste a moment."

Candace banged her fist on the steering wheel. "If *you* talk to Poppy, you'll find out more than I will."

"Why is that?"

"Because when she chooses, she manages to say nothing charmingly, and I'm not good at persuading her to talk about subjects she doesn't want to discuss."

Clearly dinner would be a command performance.

In the hour before dinner, Hollis walked MacTee and settled him in her apartment before she went downstairs. Candace, with Elizabeth behind her, answered her knock.

"Tee?" Elizabeth said and peered behind Hollis.

"I left him upstairs."

"Would you get him?" Candace said. "He's like Nana the St. Bernard in *Peter Pan*—he acts like a babysitter. If we're to have a good conversation, we need him."

When Hollis returned with MacTee, Elizabeth threw up her hands and shouted, "Tee, Tee, Tee." The buzzer signalled the arrival of Poppy and Alberto. The door to the front hall opened, and Poppy Lafleur, in a cloud of musky scent, made her entrance, trailed by the slim, elegant Alberto.

What presence Poppy had. Tall, auburn-haired, and beautifully made-up, her clingy black jersey dress revealed a spectacular figure. Patent-leather stilettos, a chunky jade-and-silver necklace and two armloads of silver bracelets that jingled when she moved completed the elegant presentation. A subtle cloud of aromatic scent floated in with her.

Her figure was evidence that dancing burned masses of calories—probably as many as running. Hollis asked herself if she should replace running with dancing, but even as she posed the question, she knew nothing would ever make her figure like Poppy's. Hollis's big-boned frame would remain her inheritance from peasant ancestors.

"We've met in passing," Poppy said and extended beautifully-manicured hands loaded with large, eye-catching rings. "But you haven't met my partner. This is Alberto."

Alberto grasped then kissed Hollis's hand.

Latin men did that in movies, but it seemed a little over the top in a Toronto living room.

"Charmed," he said with a heavy Spanish accent and a smile that revealed teeth so white, they had to be capped.

He made Hollis think of matadors or gigolos—handsome and fully aware of their effect on women.

"Darling," Poppy said in a low, throaty voice, bending down and opening her arms to Elizabeth.

"Poppy," Elizabeth trilled. No Grandma or Nana for this exotic creature.

After a big exchange of hugs and kisses, the two moved to the slip-covered cream cotton sofas. The couches sat at right angles to one another with a long, rectangular black leather bench in front of them. Elizabeth hoisted herself onto Poppy's knee and snuggled ever closer as she moved the bracelets up and down on Poppy's arm.

Conversation swirled from the unseasonable weather to the possibility of an election before Candace pulled an ottoman over to face her mother.

"Poppy," she said, "I'm worried about Danson. Do you have any idea where he is?"

"Darling, you worry too much. Danson is a grown man. If he goes off for a few days, it isn't anything to fuss about. There is something I want to ask you."

Candace shifted on the ottoman and waited.

"Were you in my apartment recently?"

"No. Why?"

"I saved a section of Saturday's *Globe* from two weeks ago, and I've misplaced it."

Hollis would have pegged Poppy as a *Sun* or a *Star* reader. The Saturday entertainment section must be the attraction.

Poppy toyed with a dangling earring. "I'm sometimes forgetful, but I'm sure I didn't throw it out. I thought you might have picked it up."

"I didn't. Danson's in your apartment all the time. He cares for your plants. Perhaps he took it or tidied up before he went wherever he's gone," Candace said coldly.

Poppy, ignoring Candace's comment, directed her next remark to Hollis. "Darling Danson. I owned masses of gorgeous, expensive artificial flowers and plants and my darling son objected. He said silk plants were totally déclassé." She tossed her head, and the swinging red hair caught the light. It's glory reminded Hollis of the shampoo commercials in which hair was impossibly shiny and beautiful.

"As if I cared," Poppy continued. "Anyway, I refused to replace them with real ones, because I knew, absolutely knew, that they'd die. Darling Danson said he'd help me buy real ones and look after them. He's been as good as his word." She frowned. "My poor plants—without Danson around to attend to them."

She focused on Candace. "But why would you suggest that Danson would take it? Do you have a copy of the *Globe*?"

Candace shook her head. "The recycling pickup was Wednesday. Sorry."

"Darling, it isn't that important, but I am worried about my plants."

Looking at Candace's fists and white knuckles, Hollis feared her friend would launch an attack on her mother. Instead, Candace slumped back and sighed. "Poppy, the plants are in self-watering containers. They'll be fine, but if it will make you happy, I'll come and tend them."

Poppy clearly expected those close to her to bail her out of difficulties. Candace had performed the role since she was seven and continued to do so.

"Thank you, darling."

Given the exchange and Danson's disappearance shortly after his visit to Poppy's apartment chances were good the paper was significant, Hollis thought. Did she have Saturday's paper? Not likely. She'd dragged out a clear green plastic bag for recycling and was sure the paper was gone. Even if they found a copy, how would they know what they were searching for unless Poppy 'fessed up, and that seemed unlikely.

Poppy shrugged, slanted forward and peered down. "Elizabeth, darling, are those new shoes?"

Elizabeth stuck a foot out to allow Poppy to admire her shoe.

"It's time to eat before Elizabeth has a major meltdown," Candace said.

In the dining room, Candace fastened a large plastic bib around Elizabeth's neck and anchored her in her high chair. MacTee settled underneath, ready to catch any morsels dropped or thrown his way.

The adults helped themselves. After Candace assured herself that everyone had what he or she needed, she said, "Poppy, what section of the paper did you save?"

Hollis smiled. Exactly what they needed to know.

Poppy waved a finger in front of her lips to indicate her mouth was full. Finally, she said, "The financial pages. Something triggered an idea for a contact for costumes. I can't remember what it was." Poppy spoke rapidly without meeting her daughter's eyes.

Hollis glanced at Candace and assumed her friend's lifted eyebrows expressed doubt.

"Poppy, if it was important enough to ask us if we had copies, you must be able to be more specific. It has to be related to Danson."

With another forkful halfway to her mouth, Poppy paused. "You can be so dramatic. Did I tell you we'll be away at the Vancouver dance competition next week? Candace, darling, if you could see to the cats, I'd appreciate it."

Candace laid her fork on her plate. She stared at her mother as if confronting a rare and unfamiliar species. "I'll do it," she said frostily.

Alberto pleaded the onset of a migraine and left soon after dinner. Elizabeth insisted Poppy supervise her bath and read her bedtime stories.

Candace and Hollis listened to gales of laughter while they cleared the table and loaded the dishwasher.

48

"She's terrific with Elizabeth—never worries about getting messy. Elizabeth loves her," Candace said.

"Fascinating woman."

How did you say to a friend that you thought her mother was a liar? Hollis ventured what she hoped was a diplomatic question. "Did you think she told us everything about the newspaper article?"

Candace blew a noisy raspberry. "No. She only tells you what she chooses. She didn't want to enlighten us, and she didn't."

When Poppy rejoined them, she gathered her handbag and said, "Darling, I can't stay. Alberto and I have to rehearse for the competition. Tomorrow morning we've reserved our studio for ourselves, and we hired a cameraman to record our routine so we can study it." She smiled at Hollis. "Delighted to finally talk to you. As an artist you must come down and see my art collection."

"Love to," Hollis said. The opportunity to pump Poppy had evaporated. How could they uncover the information she seemed to be withholding?

Six

With her detecting supplies stashed in her bag, Hollis set off for Danson's. Lights shone from the apartments above and below his black windows. She hated entering unfamiliar unoccupied space at night. She'd once been trapped in a dark, deserted church with a murderer and knew this experience partially accounted for the phobia.

That was then, and this was now. She locked her truck, squared her shoulders and marched into the building. Inside, she unlocked Danson's downstairs door and climbed the broad, once-grand mahogany stairs as if she carried heavy iron bars that increased in weight with each step she took. When she faced his apartment door and slid the key into the lock, her stomach contracted, and her throat dried. She swallowed convulsively but without releasing any saliva. The taste of hard, metallic fear filled her throat.

How could she overcome this paralyzing dread? If she propped the door open, the other tenants would hear her scream. What if they didn't come? What if they thought it was on a neighbour's TV and cranked up the sound on their own set?

Scream—what was wrong with her? She'd searched the apartment hours earlier and seen nothing to frighten her and no evidence that anyone else had been there. Silly, silly, silly, she scolded and ordered herself to get a grip.

One deep, calming breath and she opened the door.

Then she retreated to the hall, removed a hefty pad of

printing paper from her bag and wedged the door open.

Briefly she contemplated ringing the other tenants' bells, asking if they knew where Danson was and telling them she would be in his apartment but decided against it. Later, if it became necessary, she'd interview them but not tonight.

Finally, after another steadying breath, she crept into the apartment and flicked on the three light switches just inside the door before she froze and listened. Silence. The bedroom and bathroom doors were closed. Had she shut them when she'd left?

If only she'd brought MacTee.

She really was being silly. Who had ever heard of a golden retriever protecting anyone?

She inched along the hall, flung the bathroom door open and hit the light switch. Earlier in the day she'd bunched the shower curtain back, and it remained just as she'd left it, an empty white room. No one lurked here.

The closed bedroom door came next. She tiptoed to the door, carefully rotated the knob and banged the door open. Nothing moved. The only sound was her breathing and her thudding heart. No one there. She flipped lights on as she progressed from room to room. Nothing. She was alone, totally alone.

Once her heart had resumed its normal rhythm, she started her search in Gregory's room, confident some item would have his surname, his employer's name and a contact number to confirm that he was who he said he was.

An old-fashioned maple bed, matching dresser and straight chair, inexpensive white particleboard desk and bedside table furnished the room. Yet another lacrosse poster adorned the walls. A laptop, boom-box and a stack of CDs sat on the desk, a shaving kit rested atop the bureau and several paperbacks, one splayed open, spine up, lay on the bedside table.

What did this tell her?

She'd been through this with Danson's belongings.

Guys didn't leave without their shaving kits. Furthermore, businessmen seldom parked their laptops at home, certainly not in a temporary pad like this. They might have a desktop at home, but laptops were for travel, for bringing work home from the office. Wherever he'd gone, Gregory hadn't intended to stay. No, not quite true. He could have a razor, shaving cream and toothbrush at a lover's or relative's place. It was peculiar that both he and Danson had left at approximately the same time.

She unzipped the cheap black pseudo-leather case. Not much inside the main compartment besides the essentials for keeping oneself clean and healthy: toothbrush, Colgate toothpaste, Noxzema shaving cream, nail clippers, comb, Advil and an unopened package of condoms. No medical prescription with his name on the label.

The side pocket's contents told a different story. She'd been building a picture of an innocuous young man, but the tin foil, spoon, matches, hypodermic needle and a baggie of white powder erased that image. Gregory used cocaine, maybe crack, maybe heroin—this equipment belonged to a heavy, not a recreational, drug user. An even more unsettling question—why hadn't he taken his paraphernalia with him?

Had Danson known? Was he too a drug user? How would Candace react if she found out that he was an addict? Like most family members confronted with unpleasant realities, Candace wouldn't want to believe it. Fortunately, no evidence supported this idea this far. Back to Gregory.

She dragged the wooden chair to the desk, sat down and found she needed a password to open the computer. Her disappointment was mixed with suspicion. Computers revealed so much about their owners, particularly e-mails and saved files. Few people employed passwords for personal computers. If you had something to hide or weren't who you claimed to be, of course you'd guard your information. Was this why Gregory's required a password?

The almost-empty top desk drawer held three Bic ballpoint pens, a yellow legal pad, envelopes, a few paper clips and a calculator. The other drawers were empty except for traces of ancient dust. No bills, no receipts, no address book—nothing to identify Gregory. Granted, he'd moved in recently, but putting herself in the same situation, she would have had address stickers in with the envelopes, extra chequebooks—personalized items you used frequently.

Perhaps his clothes would reveal more. Brand name dress shirts, golf shirts, a tweed sports jacket, grey flannels, chinos and jeans hung in the cupboard. On the floor, black oxfords, brown loafers and worn Nikes. Everything was standard issue, brand-name clothing. She rummaged through the pockets and came up with crumpled tissues, a half-empty package of Lifesavers, a match folder with a gas company logo.

Again—nothing useful. Gregory, the mystery man.

What methods would the police use to identify him? They wouldn't learn anything from his clothes, but they'd have the expertise to bypass his computer's password and log in. No doubt this was the motherlode, and they'd come up with a wealth of information. Gregory would remain a mystery to her unless she found information about him in Danson's computer files.

The big question—would Danson's computer require a password? She'd been about to open it the other day when Elizabeth and Candace had arrived. She should have followed up immediately—locating Danson was her priority.

In the living room she sat down in front of Danson's open computer. Disappointment engulfed her. Again she needed a password. Futility marked her evening's work. She snapped down the lid, unplugged the computer's cable and packed it in the case she found under the desk. Her last hope was that Candace, who knew many details of Danson's life, would have the password. She probably shouldn't remove it from the apartment, but since they only suspected Danson was in trouble, it wasn't a crime.

If Candace provided the magic word, Hollis would zip through the information in Danson's computer. If his electronic life was as well-organized as his paper files, she calculated that she could race through the data. She'd transfer whatever struck her as relevant to her own computer. She didn't allow herself to hope she'd uncover the reason for his disappearance, but it was a possibility. Either way, it would be a matter of hours before she returned it to his apartment.

Computer bag in hand, she felt the knot in her shoulders relax as the heavy front door clicked shut behind her. If she returned, she'd visit during the day. Back at her own building, Hollis parked and glanced upward. Lights glimmered in the second floor windows. Not too late to talk to Candace.

Before she had time to knock, Candace's door flew open. "Did you find anything?" Candace said. She was holding her breath and stiffening her body as if she expected a blow.

"Nothing earth-shattering," Hollis lied, but the hallway wasn't the place to deliver bad news.

Candace breathed again. She peered at Hollis and braced her hands on either side of the door frame. "I can tell by your expression that you did. What was it?"

"Let me in and I'll tell you," Hollis said.

They moved to the kitchen, where Candace, operating on automatic, plugged in the kettle ready to prepare the ever-soothing cuppa. "What was on Danson's computer? Did you get any leads? What about Gregory? What's his last name? Who does he work for?"

Hollis raised both hands, palms toward Candace, to fend off the barrage.

"Whoa. One question at a time. First, I brought Danson's computer with me. It needs a password, and I figured you might know it. If you do, I'll go through his files and e-mails tomorrow."

"I do, but should you have done that? What if he comes

home and thinks there's been a break-in? What if..." Candace stopped as Hollis again extended her arm, palm raised.

"Relax. I'll skim quickly and forward anything important to my computer. If all goes well, I'll have it back in twenty-four hours. Maybe I shouldn't have taken it, but as far as we know, Danson's absence is innocent. We'll work from that premise until we learn otherwise."

Candace stepped back. "I suppose you're right." As she poured the pale, pleasant smelling camomile tea into flowered blue china mugs, she spoke over her shoulder. "Did you discover any more about Gregory?"

Hollis waited until Candace swung around and handed her a cup. "Gregory is more and more of a mystery man. There was nothing, absolutely nothing with his surname on it, nothing to say where he worked or where to get a hold of him. Surprisingly, his laptop was there, but I couldn't open it without a password." How to phrase what she was going to say next? A statement, nonjudgmental and factual, would be best. "I did find out something important about him. Gregory's a drug user, the heavy stuff. He stored what I guess was cocaine, although it could have been heroin in his shaving kit. Given that drug-users generally keep their supply with them, the fact that it was in the apartment is bad news."

"My god." Candace clapped her hand over her mouth.

Hollis watched her friend absorb the information. First, she lowered her hand then she stared into space as if marshalling information.

"That changes things, doesn't it?" Candace said slowly. "Changes it a lot. Gregory's in the equation now. It's alarming that he didn't take his drugs or computer with him." She tapped her index finger against her lips.

No wonder she was hesitating. There was a basic and frightening question waiting to be asked.

Finally, Candace's gaze met Hollis's. "Did Danson have drug stuff?" Her voice betrayed her anxiety and her need to hear the right answer.

"No."

Candace sighed. "Thank god. Because Danson was so obsessed about physical fitness, I can't imagine him using drugs. Steroids maybe, if he thought they might improve his lacrosse stamina, but not street drugs."

"I saw nothing to indicate that he takes anything." Hollis unsuccessfully stifled a yawn. "Sorry. I've just realized how tired I am. That's what happens to early risers who try to stay up late. I still have to walk MacTee. Tell me Danson's password, and I'll talk to you tomorrow after I've searched his files."

"Before you go, there's one more thing to think about," Candace said.

"Related to his computer?"

"Yes, Danson's wallet is gone. That means his credit card and bank card are also missing. Let's see if he's used either one since the Saturday he disappeared."

"How could I have missed that?" Hollis said and answered her own question. "It may have crossed my mind, but I dismissed it because you need a password for internet banking."

Candace smiled. "You can't think of everything, and of course you assumed we couldn't get in. But I do know his password plus the answers to the questions they ask to ascertain if it's you."

"I'm impressed. How come?"

"Because Danson's girlfriend was murdered, he knows how fast and unexpectedly death can strike. In addition, he tracks 'bad guys', very bad guys, and that's risky."

"Too true."

"After Angie died, he put his bank accounts, his condo and his car into joint ownership with me. He also made a will. If anything happens to him, everything is transferred to me."

Hollis knew her face must show her surprise. "Did he expect something terrible to happen to him?" Given this information, it was no wonder Candace was worried.

"No, but he felt that since I'd been the mother-figure in his life, he wanted Elizabeth and me to inherit."

"That's why you have his information—to make life easier if he dies?"

"Right. I was going to give you the information and suggest that you go back to the apartment tomorrow. Now that you have his computer here, I won't be able to sleep until I've seen his accounts. I'll come up with you."

She shifted from one foot to the other and gestured towards Elizabeth's bedroom. "I don't know whether to bring the baby monitor and plug it in upstairs or to ask you to stay here with her."

"You can see her crib on the monitor. Why would I stay?"

"Because another call came tonight. It scared me."

"Why?"

"The person, I think it was a man's voice, whispered, 'Where's Danson', gave a sick sort of laugh and added, 'gone, gone, gone', and hung up."

"A sicko. It has to be someone who knows he's missing."

"Hardly anyone knows."

"Not true. You've contacted his friends and his lacrosse cronies. They've probably told their friends, which means it could be anyone. You should call the police."

"He didn't say anything threatening. They wouldn't take it seriously."

"Maybe not, but you should do it."

Candace shook her head.

"It explains why you're afraid to leave Elizabeth, but the outside door is locked, the door into your apartment from the vestibule is locked. How could anything happen to her while you're upstairs?"

Candace's lips twisted into a wry smile. "I guess you're right. I'm paranoid. I admire your lack of fear."

If Candace had seen her at Danson's apartment, she would have realized just how frightened Hollis could be.

This was not the time to reveal that. Hollis was tired. She'd anticipated taking MacTee out for a last walk before she pulled on comfy pyjamas along with sheepskin-lined slippers and flopped in front of the TV. She rationalized that a few moments delay until she indulged herself would make the pleasure sweeter.

Wearily, she trudged upstairs, followed by Candace, unpacked the computer and plugged it in. Candace jittered around the room, and even before the screen lit up, dropped down on the chair, tapping her fingers impatiently, waiting for the machine to boot up. Once it had, she clicked, located the banking site and entered the important information.

"I'm in," she said. "First I'll look at his chequing account."

Hollis waited.

"Bad news. No activity at ATMs since the Friday before."

"It could mean someone stole his card and didn't have the number combo to open it," Hollis said.

"And no activity in his Visa account," Candace said in a low voice.

"Again, if someone stole it or he lost it, that could be the explanation," Hollis countered.

Candace spun around to face her. "Don't be such a bloody Pollyanna," she said. "Admit it. You know this isn't good news."

"Okay, it isn't, but we have to be hopeful."

"You be hopeful. I'm going to bed, and I'm anything but hopeful," Candace said. She rose, scooped up the baby monitor, patted MacTee and left.

Was this investigation a pointless waste of time? Should she stop playing amateur sleuth and simply wait for the DNA results? If the DNA wasn't Danson's, they'd be no further ahead. No, they had to assume he was alive and keep going.

In the morning she'd plod through the computer files. Tedious work, but it would distract her from her painting problem. She stepped back to examine the large work on the easel. It stared back at her—a huge canvas shining with gold paint but lacking any character or message.

Maybe she could make a Rothko out of it? Fat chance. When you saw his colour field paintings in books or on slides, they underwhelmed. When you parked yourself in front of the real thing, they vibrated, the colours pulsed, moved and left a retinal afterimage. Her painting looked as if you'd stick it in Holt Renfrew's store window behind mannikins dressed in clothes accessorized with gold.

She removed the work and turned it to the wall. Tomorrow, after she finished with the computer files, she'd work on her chickens. Maybe she'd make a papier-mâché needs an accent dog for Elizabeth. Not too big. A bulldog would be perfect, with its short legs and squashed face. Whenever she took MacTee to the off-leash park, they met Winston, a French bulldog crossed with a Pekinese—a Bullnese, one of the new breeds beginning to gain acceptance by the Kennel Club. He was the friendliest and most charming dog she'd ever seen, and MacTee loved her. She'd wheel Elizabeth in her stroller. After the toddler fell in love with Winston, she'd present her with the papier mâché replica. Elizabeth would love it. She'd be able to carry it with her wherever she went.

*   *   *

Hollis awoke to hear the sparrows in the cedar hedge at the side of the property greeting each other and celebrating dawn's arrival. She lay in bed mulling over what she knew about Danson and his life. MacTee stood beside the bed, sighing and staring at her.

"I hear you. You know perfectly well you could wait another hour—it's your breakfast you want."

MacTee continued to fix her with an unblinking stare.

"Okay, I'm up," she grumbled and slid out of bed.

Outside, the clear sky and gentle wind promised another glorious Indian summer day. It would be lovely

59

on Centre Island. If she finished reading Danson's files and found nothing that required more work, she'd return the computer, postpone her chicken work and take MacTee to the Island on the subway and the ferry. They'd spend the afternoon walking and enjoying the glory of Lake Ontario. Today, those sailboats not stashed in dry dock for the winter would be skimming across the lake. She envisioned the white sails interspersed with multi-striped or vividly coloured spinnakers crisscrossing the waves.

MacTee padded after her as she headed for the bathroom.

"There's only one door. I'm coming out. I do not. I repeat, do not, need your help," Hollis said and shut the door in his face.

Outside, moving along the sidewalk, she picked up her pace. MacTee and she both needed a fast walk to pump up their heart rates and keep them healthy. Almost an hour later, she let herself into the apartment and portioned out MacTee's kibble, which he inhaled almost as soon as his dish touched the floor.

She should eat, but cereal and fruit had lost their appeal, and she lacked the energy to prepare anything else. Maybe a banana and a granola bar would do. The phone rang.

"I saw you come in. Checking out the computer will take up your morning, but Elizabeth and I want you to come down for an eleven thirty waffle lunch. Elizabeth loves waffles and insists she needs them this morning. I'm not up to waffle-making for breakfast and put her off until noon. It occurred to me you might enjoy them too. Since I'm making batter and hauling the waffle iron down from the cupboard, we should have a bang-up lunch—waffles, blueberries, raspberries—the works."

"Sounds great." What could she contribute from her nearly empty refrigerator? "I do have cottage cheese and vanilla yogurt. I'll bring both?"

Cheered by the prospect of a tasty lunch, she plunked down in front of the computer.

Now to Danson's files? She tapped his password and watched the screen as his e-mail messages downloaded. A deluge flooded in. Two hundred and forty-seven to be exact. Some from friends, mostly concerning lacrosse. She shuddered seeing the number of messages with attachments. A quick glance told her the majority involved the upcoming lacrosse season—practice and game schedules. She printed seven cryptic ones that might relate to criminal tracking.

Next she surveyed the sidebar of folders. Family, friends, criminals. Well, that was certainly straightforward.

She opened "criminals". He'd begun his crusade three years earlier, shortly after Angie's death. The first three cases involved Haitians. Not surprising, since immigrants to Montreal came from French-speaking parts of the world. She'd read that the largest Haitian population outside of Haiti lived in Quebec. Newspapers had published the information when the Queen had appointed a Canadian woman, born in Haiti, to be Governor-General.

The next correspondence involved two Jamaicans in Toronto. Then an Eastern European case and most recently an American. Interesting. Given the U.S. hysteria about border security, they'd allowed a deported criminal to return. She thought about airport security. Actually the U.S. agents' gimlet eyes assessed incoming and had nothing to do with outgoing. Presumably these criminals had passed Canadian immigration without any trouble. A worrisome thought.

Time for a plan. She plucked a sheet of newsprint from the pile beside her worktable. At the top she printed "Danson" then drew downward radiating lines to Gregory, recent phone calls, lacrosse, criminals, Poppy, bouncer and e-mail contacts. She left room on the right for more entries.

Gregory. Who was he? Where would Danson have recorded correspondence with Gregory? She ran her eye down the sidebar files. Concordia might provide an answer. When opened it revealed a vast correspondence with friends, including Gregory.

Don't know if you remember me? We took Soc 300 together. I was in George's section, and he tells me you might have a room to rent. I'm going to be on the road in the Toronto area next week. Would you be interested in giving me a Toronto base? Let me know soon. Cheers, Gregory.

She recalled her own university days. The classes always held dozens of people you nodded to but didn't know. Almost anyone could say they'd been a friend, and you wouldn't have a clue. If you were a nice person, you wouldn't want to write back and say that you didn't have the vaguest idea who the person was. What a great ploy to infiltrate someone's life. She double-clicked on Gregory's message to see if his surname came up. It didn't.

Gregory4000@xyzabc.com was the e-mail address. She connected to e-mail and dispatched a message to Gregory asking where he was and if he knew where to locate Danson.

She opened the "sent" folder to read Danson's correspondence with Gregory.

"Not sure I remember you but come and see me when you're in Toronto. I'm interested in renting the room." Then she searched for exchanges with George and found nothing. Maybe Danson had phoned to verify Gregory's bona fides.

Back to the Gregory and Danson's e-mails. They'd decided Gregory would drop in on September 10 to see the room and, if it suited him, arrange to move in. When had this been? Mid-September, almost a month ago. His most recent phone bill might have numbers.

When she'd returned from Danson's, she'd bundled the photocopies of Danson's documents and left the pile on her work table. Now she trundled over, sorted through the stack and extricated September's phone records. Area codes—what was Montreal's? Back to her desk, where she logged on to Canada 411. 514 was the code.

An examination of the phone records. Bingo. Four numbers in the 514 area. No time like the present—she'd call.

First one. "This number is no longer in service." There had been two other calls from that number. Presumably this one had belonged to Gregory, who'd cancelled the service.

The fourth call rang and rang. Finally someone answered. *"Âllo. C'est un téléphone publique. Personne est ici."*

French. How did she ask? High school French to the rescue. *"Où est le téléphone situé?"*

"Concordia University," the respondent said, switching into English when she heard Hollis's poor attempt at French.

The call from the university could have been anyone. No help from Montreal. Where did that leave her? For the moment she'd give up on Gregory. She moved to the next heading on her list—recent phone calls.

The land line wasn't going to help—she only had September's bill. Too far back. She needed October's. The most recent calls made from his cell phone would tell her something.

At Danson's apartment she'd copied the numbers along with his address book—it had taken forever, and she'd wondered if she was wasting her time. Now she'd get the answer.

Danson's phone, a Motorola, had saved the ten most recent messages.

On the Sunday before he disappeared, he'd called Poppy three times during the afternoon. Interesting that she hadn't mentioned it. Later that day there had been a call to a Toronto number. She dialed and allowed the phone to ring on, hoping there would be an answering machine. No such luck.

He hadn't called Candace that Sunday evening. It had been his regular time to call, but he hadn't done so. He'd been home Sunday afternoon, gone out and not returned.

She booted up her computer, typed Canada 411 and found that the number he had called was "unlisted". Another dead end.

On the Friday there had been a call to the nightclub where he worked and a second one that she dialed. A lilting woman's voice told her she'd reached the correct number, asked her to leave a message then wished her a happy day.

"My name is Hollis Grant. I'm trying to locate Danson Lafleur. Please call me."

The other three calls connected to answering machines. She left the same message on each one.

Discouraged didn't begin to describe how she felt.

Seven

"Hi Howis, waffles," Elizabeth said and launched herself at MacTee.

"Anything on his computer?" Candace asked.

"I went through his recent phone messages first and didn't get any leads. As for his computer, he saved many messages, which is a good thing, but none have provided clues about his whereabouts."

In the kitchen Candace placed the ingredients to build combinations to order on the counter. Elizabeth, given the opportunity to choose, surveyed the plates and bowls.

"Strawberries, bananas, finger puppets, yoghurt," she said.

"Finger puppets?" Hollis asked.

"That's her name for raspberries, because she can put them on her fingers," Candace explained. She spoke to Elizabeth. "You forgot the magic word."

"Please," Elizabeth said, and they smiled at one another.

Plates loaded, they ate in silence for a few minutes.

Hollis rose, plucked the coffee pot from the machine and refilled their coffee mugs. "I'm curious about Gregory, the invisible tenant without a surname. You haven't remembered what it is, have you?"

"No. Danson told me a Montreal friend gave his name to Gregory. That's not much help, is it?"

"I figured out that much from the e-mails. The friend's name was George Rostov. Does that mean anything?"

"I met George once or twice. He and Danson lived in the same student housing their first year at Concordia."

"I've downloaded his address book, and I'm contacting every name to see if anyone knows where he is. I'll also ask George about Gregory."

"Should I be doing this?"

"You could, but since I have the names and addresses, it's easier if I do."

Hollis, acknowledging the size of the task, had reluctantly relinquished her plan for a Centre Island visit. "When I return the computer late this afternoon, I plan to talk to the other tenants. Since it's Sunday, they may be home. I'll see if either one has any idea where he might have gone or can report anything unusual."

"There must be something I can do," Candace said as she collected the dishes and opened the dishwasher.

"Talk to Poppy again. I learned from his phone records that Danson spoke to her three times the Sunday before he disappeared. Going through the phone records for previous months, I saw that this was the one and only time this happened. See if you can jog her memory and get her to tell you what they talked about."

"I'll do that. Come down tonight, and we'll talk again."

Hollis finished lunch, walked MacTee, collected Danson's computer and set off to his apartment.

Inside the apartment she realized she hadn't finished with Gregory's room. Once she'd found the drugs and the locked computer, she'd raced to Danson's computer, become distracted and not returned to Gregory's room. It was a long shot, but his books might provide some insight into his personality. Or, if she was lucky, he might have written his name in his books. She initialed hardcovers but only those she lent and wanted back. Not that it helped. Particular friends were on her "do not lend to" list as they seldom returned books. If they did reappear, it would be years after they'd been borrowed.

Five books, all espionage novels. Interesting! Did he like vicarious excitement or use them as primers? Now she was being fanciful. The first two, James Pattersons, told her nothing. When she opened the third, a John LeCarré novel, a tightly-folded sheet of paper tumbled out. She unfolded and smoothed it out. Cyrillic writing almost filled the eight by ten sheet. Was it Russian, or did every Slavic eastern European nation employ this script? She tried to visualize a map and name the countries. Bulgaria, Romania, the Ukraine, other former republics of the USSR. She didn't know the answer, but it didn't really matter.

Someone had communicated with Gregory in Cyrillic characters, meaning he had understood. Or not. Maybe he'd known who the letter came from and was waiting for the opportunity to have it translated. She mustn't jump to conclusions. It was possible Gregory was a Russian. Maybe he'd been reading the espionage novels because he was a mole? Too far-fetched to be believed, but maybe he was with Danson because the Russian Mafia hadn't liked Danson identifying returning criminals and had wanted to know who he was after and how much he knew.

Should she take it with her, or was it "evidence" that should remain at the site?

She'd asked herself this question before—the answer remained the same. This was not a criminal investigation. As far as the police were concerned, they only knew that Danson was missing. Missing was not a crime.

This piece of paper might help her locate Danson. She'd stash it in her bag, make a copy and search for someone to translate what could be a grocery list, a letter from Gregory's mother—something entirely innocuous.

Where to have it deciphered? Back in the living room, she removed the phone book from the bookcase, flipped to the yellow pages and confronted many choices. Given the thousands of Russian immigrants in the Toronto area, having the paper translated should be easy.

Time to talk to the other tenants.

Downstairs she knocked on the door of the first floor's resident whose mailbox was labelled Bryson. She listened and heard someone moving around inside.

The door didn't open, but a voice she couldn't identify as male or female said, "Yes?"

"I'm a friend of Danson Lafleur's sister—the man who lives upstairs. His sister hasn't spoken to him since two weeks ago Saturday. We wondered if you know where he is or have heard anything out of the ordinary from upstairs?" It felt very stupid to talk to the tightly closed door.

"I said hello if I saw him in the foyer. I didn't know him, and I haven't heard anything, but I can tell you one thing," the voice said.

"What would that be?"

"Two weeks ago Monday, he was here. I know, because I nap in the afternoons, and he stomped around up there like he was auditioning for the infantry. This is an old building, and the floors squeak. It drove me crazy."

"Thanks," Hollis said. Had it been Gregory or Danson? If it had been Danson, why hadn't he called Candace? "I'll slip my card under the door. Please call me if anything else comes to mind."

She traipsed to the third floor and thumped hard to attract the attention of a resident who obviously loved opera played at full volume. After a barrage of forceful banging, she cradled her aching knuckles before continuing the attack.

The door cracked open. A diminutive, elfin-faced man did not undo the chain. He peered at her. A chorus from Verdi's *Masked Ball* threatened to drown out any exchange of words.

Hollis held out her card, introduced herself and explained her reason for being there.

"What?' the man shouted.

Hollis cranked her voice even louder and gave her spiel.

The man scrutinized her over narrow, gold-framed reading glasses. "I'll turn it down. Wait a minute," he shouted and shut the door in her face. Back again, he didn't release the chain but asked her to repeat what she'd said.

"Never talked to him. Don't know anything about him. He worked evenings and made a racket when he came home. Jazz—loud jazz. Meant to speak to him about that."

Opera played at full volume surely must have annoyed Danson as much as Danson's jazz had irritated this man.

"People like me who work nine to five don't appreciate noise after eleven. Nice car, though. I've always liked Camaros. No idea where he might be," he said with finality and closed the door.

Hollis sighed. She'd hoped one of the other tenants would be a garrulous retired person who tracked the other tenants' activities. No such luck, but she now knew Danson or Gregory had been home on the Monday.

If he'd been in his apartment on Monday, why hadn't he called Candace on Sunday or worked on Monday? Conceivably after he spoke to Poppy he'd travelled somewhere, stayed overnight, rushed back on Monday and left again.

Back in Danson's apartment, she contemplated the computer and hoped she'd downloaded everything she might need. If the worst came to the worst, she could come back, but it should stay in the apartment. It would provide evidence for the police if something terrible had happened to him. Given the leads she'd followed and the conversations she'd had with Candace, Danson remained an enigma. She glanced at her watch.

Still time to dispatch her e-mail query to the two hundred and seventy-five people in his e-mail contact list. She'd transmit it in small batches lest the ever-vigilant spam filters consign her message to junk mail limbo. Task done, she'd drop in on Candace and learn if she'd extricated any information from Poppy.

She sat at her table in her own apartment. Boring didn't

begin to describe the e-mailing process. Once they were flying through the ether or wherever e-mail flew, her conscience would be clear—no one could say she wasn't trying everything in her search for the missing man.

MacTee paced restlessly. He'd rise, come and stand beside her, sigh deeply and walk around before plunking down, only to rise again a minute or so later.

"Okay, okay, I know it's your dinner time, but you can wait a few minutes. Starvation isn't imminent," she said. A pang of remorse. Eating, even though he inhaled his kibble, was one of MacTee's great pleasures.

Leaving her computer, she scooped a cup and a half of Skin Support food into his red bowl. MacTee sprayed his surroundings with drool as he performed acrobatic jumps on all four feet while she carried his bowl to the plastic mat where she fed him. When given permission to eat, he homed in on his dinner and chowed down in record time. Each meal she asked herself if she should divide his daily portion into three or four rather than two meals? It would be wonderful to make him ecstatically happy several times a day. Fanciful thinking—trying to organize food at the same time twice a day was difficult enough.

Back at the computer, she moved through the list. Once the e-mails were gone, she felt a sense of satisfaction, along with a faint hope that they might bring in useful information.

After MacTee's walk, she knocked on Candace's door.

Elizabeth greeted the dog with squeals of delight and immediately initiated their catch-me-if-you-can game. Candace and Hollis chose chairs in the living room, where they could watch the child chase the retriever from living room to kitchen to hall and back to the living room. MacTee frequently allowed himself to be caught before he shrugged Elizabeth off, and the game resumed.

"Poppy claimed she only remembered that it had been about a fishing expedition. She joked about short-term memory loss and said she recalled that Danson wanted to phone someone and she'd vetoed the idea." Candace shook her head and pursed her lips in the universal expression of displeasure. "I didn't believe her. The mere fact that he called her three times in one afternoon just before he disappeared has to be significant. When I pointed this out, she said I could think what I liked, but she considered it a coincidence."

"What did she say when you told her again that he hadn't called you, and that he never missed his Sunday call?" Hollis said.

"Nothing, but she did say that although she couldn't remember exactly, she thought one of the calls might have been about Danson buying her new plants, because there was a late fall sale at Canadian Tire, and he thought their tropicals were good quality."

"That's an inventive evasion," Hollis said.

"It is. I'm sure it didn't take two calls to establish that information. But since I can't tie her on the rack and torture her, we'll have to wait until she accepts that this is serious, if it is, and share everything she knows."

"Obviously she doesn't believe something is wrong, or she'd tell us."

"Unless it's something so horrible or damaging that she can't bear to reveal it. Even with my vivid imagination, I can't think what that might be," Candace said.

"Too bad. We'll have to leave it for now. To bring you up-to-date, I've e-mailed everyone listed in his e-mail address book. I'll let you know if there are useful replies. I'm going for a walk. I need to clear my head."

Hollis and MacTee crunched through fallen leaves, and she allowed her mind to wander. How could a man vanish so completely? Was it unusual? What leads could she follow if none of the e-mails or phone calls brought in any information? Her thoughts spun and bounced like an Indian rubber ball run amok.

Maybe meditation would focus her mind. As an aspiring Buddhist, she'd created a calm oasis in her bedroom. A silvery drapery hung on the wall behind a low shelf, where she'd set a small statue of the Buddha and on the floor in front of it a square lavender silk floor cushion completed the setup. Initially, when she'd sat cross-legged on the pillow and worked to clear her mind, MacTee had taken her new proximity as an invitation to romp. He'd crept close, licked her face and generally made a nuisance of himself. Repeatedly discouraged, he now flopped on his own foam-filled mat when she lowered herself to her cushion.

Once she arrived home she tried, but meditation didn't help. The enlightenment she'd hoped for didn't arrive—she was unable to rid herself of Danson's image calling for help and urging her to hurry—that his situation was desperate.

On Monday morning, she flicked on her computer and read her e-mails before she dressed and attended to MacTee. Disappointingly, many of Danson's friends expressed concern, but no one provided new leads.

Chores done, it was chicken time. She wiped Danson from her mind and focused on the flock. First she rebuilt the listing chicken's armature then she prepared paste.

Pulling the paper strips through the paste, and smoothing them over the chickens soothed her. She loved watching the creatures emerge. Once she'd applied strips to the bodies, she built up the wings. She possessed a collection of found materials collected on her walks particularly on garbage nights when people threw out amazing things. Adorned with miscellaneous bits and pieces of metal, feathers and fabric, her animals became wondrous beings.

The doorbell rang as she mixed more paste. She peeled off her plastic gloves and sped down the three flights of stairs to open the door.

Jack Michaels, the new basement tenant, smiled.

"Would Candace mind if I parked behind her garage when I'm home during the day?" he asked without wasting time on pleasantries. "On the street, I get tickets."

"Go ahead, but be sure to okay it with her tonight," Hollis said to his departing back. Poppy's door flew open after he clomped down the stairs. She'd been lurking and listening. "Who was that?" she demanded.

Her interest surprised Hollis. She'd pigeonholed Poppy as a woman who only paid attention when people or things related to her life.

"The lacrosse player, Jack Michaels, who's staying in the studio apartment until he gets his own place." This was the perfect moment to ask Poppy more questions. "Did Danson mention him?"

Poppy twisted a strand of red hair around her finger and released the sausage curl as she shook her head. "I don't think he did."

"Candace said you couldn't remember what you and Danson talked about during those last three phone calls. Has anything jogged your memory?"

Poppy stared at Hollis for a moment before she dropped her gaze to her feet, where she rubbed the toe of her rhinestone-encrusted, turquoise satin mule on the carpet. "Do you really think something bad has happened to him?"

Hollis didn't think Poppy wanted an affirmative answer but felt it was her duty to ask.

"You know that I've been helping Candace search for him. Now that I know more about him, I have to say I think it's very out-of-character for him not to phone her. No one I've contacted has any idea where he might be. Yes, I think he's in trouble."

Poppy continued to slide her foot back and forth. Hollis guessed she was weighing the pros and cons of revealing information.

Finally, her foot slowed and stopped. "I suppose I should have told you this earlier, but I really didn't believe there was a connection. The lost article was in the personal column of the Saturday *Globe and Mail*. I don't remember the exact wording, but it had something to do with an anonymous person wanting other anonymous people to contact him or her about a particular Canadian stamp." She shifted. "I have some interest in stamps. Danson thought this article was important."

"You collect stamps?"

"I have a few," Poppy said.

"Do you own the particular one mentioned in the article?"

Poppy shrugged.

"I take it that means you do. Danson knew that and wanted you to call the number in the paper. What did you say?"

Poppy sighed. "I told him I didn't want to get involved. That whoever had put the article in was on a fishing expedition to locate those stamps. Although it said it would be to a person's advantage to phone, I wasn't born yesterday. I know a come-on when I read one."

"Why do you think Danson wanted you to phone?"

Poppy smiled. "When it comes to me, Danson worries that I'll be poor in my old age, and he thought this might be a way for me to make money. He gets carried away."

"How did you respond?"

"I said whatever it was, I doubted very much that it was good news. That's what crooks say to get you to respond. Think of those sweet Nigerian people who have your interest at heart, and if you send them a small amount to pay the costs, you'll end up with millions. I'm not stupid. There was no way I'd contact an anonymous person."

"What did Danson say?"

"He asked if I had any secrets he should know about." She wrinkled her nose and pursed her lips. "He's changed since Angie died. He's become a vigilante bloodhound always on the scent of returned bad guys. He's suspicious and nosy about absolutely everything. The darling boy loves us and wants to take care of us, but sometimes he goes too far."

"What did you say about your secrets?"

Poppy allowed herself to smile. "Every mother, particularly one who has led the kind of life I've led, has secrets. I told him that. He said, 'Poppy, you're right to question the reason the anonymous person put the ad in the paper. Checking it out may not be a good idea, but I could judge that better if you tell me what you think it's about.'" Her shoulders lifted, her head tossed, and she threw her hands up, palms flying. "Since I had absolutely no idea, I couldn't say. I didn't want to guess. I told him that." Her head, hands and shoulders dropped. "I still don't."

A dramatic performance, but Hollis felt like shaking the woman. Danson was gone. This was the last conversation she'd had with him, and she refused to make the connection, to worry that he might be in trouble because he had chosen to follow up on the newspaper item. Candace had said Poppy lacked the "maternal gene". She'd got that right, but there was no point in antagonizing Poppy by telling her what she thought of her total disregard for Danson's welfare.

"I believe that this mysterious stamp is connected to Danson. Now that I know precisely what I'm looking for, I'll root through my recycling box, and if I don't have that paper, I'll find it at the library. Then I'll contact whoever ran the notice in the paper."

Poppy shook her head and sighed. "Good luck. I probably should have told you sooner." She glanced at her elegant diamond-studded watch. "I'm off to the studio. Let me know what you discover."

Upstairs, Hollis riffled through the paper recycling bin without success and moved on to the rattan box where she stored the paper she used for her papier mâché. Newsprint topped the pile, but underneath she found *Globe and Mail*s. She flipped through them until she located the Saturday Life section she wanted. There it was—the notice that might have sent Danson on a dangerous mission.

She phoned. And listened to endless ringing.

She hung up and dialed Canada 411, searching for a

name to match the number, and learned it was unlisted. Hurling the phone across the room would serve no useful purpose. She faced that fact that she'd smacked into yet another dead end. That wasn't quite true. If the DNA matched Danson's, she'd pass the article on to the police who would identify the caller and the phone's location. She hoped the DNA wasn't Danson's, but either way, there was nothing to be done until the results came back.

She pushed the phone to one side and pulled her computer in front of her. George, Danson's Montreal friend, had answered her e-mail.

"Danson did phone me about a guy named Gregory. I was confused, because I couldn't remember giving anyone Danson's address, and I don't know any Gregorys. I didn't think much about it at the time. I remember how Danson always called his sister on Sunday, so if he missed phoning, it's a reason to worry. Without knowing Gregory's surname it'll be hard to track him down. I'll be downtown today, and I'll go to Concordia and see if they have a class list for the Sociology course. It's a long shot but the only thing I can think of to do."

Good news—bad news. Good that George was on the case, but it looked more and more that Gregory was bad news indeed.

While she thought about her next move, Hollis returned to her flock. She donned her gloves and began the soothing practice of repeatedly dipping, applying and smoothing paper strips.

*   *   *

On Monday morning when Rhona's alarm blasted the night's silence, she reluctantly rolled out of bed. She showered, tamed her unruly hair and applied makeup before she slipped into a red print blouse, a pressed, unspotted grey pantsuit and black cowboy boots with a red leather inset design. Ready for the day, she trundled to the kitchen, had a quick breakfast and fed her cat, Opie. He eyed her suspiciously and repeatedly stopped crunching through his kibble to cast sly sideways glances at her. Normally she pampered him on weekends, but this past one she'd rushed out first thing in the morning and fallen into bed exhausted when she returned late at night. Opie had noticed.

She felt guilty. "Maybe I won't be too late," she said.

What was she doing? Why should she feel guilty about leaving a cat? That's why people had cats—they were independent beings who needed to have their physical wants attended to but were quite happy to look after themselves. That was the theory. It might apply to some cats, but not to Opie. He always hung around when she was home. He did get lonely, and she did feel guilty.

"Treats. I'll give you treats when I get home," she promised and avoided his accusing gaze as she made for the door.

Homicide hummed with activity when she arrived at seven thirty. Ian, mug in hand, contemplated a pile of paper. The detectives spent much of the day fighting their way through piles of paperwork. Multiple copies of reports inundated their desks. They'd spent the weekend following new leads from anonymous callers, many of whom had claimed they suspected a neighbour or a coworker of being the killer, the wild man, the crazy person who wanted to kill every drug user. All their calls had been recorded, and detectives would have to follow up on the off chance they might identify the killer.

They'd made headway on the first stack of paper when a second mound arrived. Rhona flipped through the new reports. "You aren't going to believe this. *I* don't believe it. The DNA report is here," she said to Ian, whose desk faced hers.

"What magic button did we push?"

"Probably happened because the boss is frantic to make headway. The press is really on our case. I expect he pressured the lab to make this the absolute first priority," Rhona said.

"What does it say?"

Rhona sighed. "That I have a phone call to make."

"The DNA belongs to the Lafleur man?"

"It does."

They stared at one another. DNA didn't lie. Danson Lafleur lay in the morgue with his face smashed and his fingers removed.

"Time to talk to Candace. I don't have her office number." She grimaced. "And, even if I did, I don't like giving bad news in the workplace or over the phone. I'll leave a message that we'll drop over this evening. That will give her a clue that the news is not good. She'll guess that if it was, we'd phone her." She thought briefly of her promise to Opie, but cats definitely came second.

"Not a part of the job I enjoy," Ian said.

"I agree, but it's good we can identify the victim. It will be a terrible shock for the family, and it'll be even worse when Candace comes to the morgue. Even though the face is destroyed, we should ask her if she can confirm that the body is his. Maybe she'll recognize his body, his clothes or his personal effects. We can cover up the worst bit. I don't want to show it to her, because the image will imprint itself on her mind and be there forever."

A shadow of sadness crept over Ian's face. Should she ask or not? She didn't want to come across as hard-bitten or insensitive but also didn't want to be nosy. Ask—all he could do was say it was nothing.

"Something like this happened to you?" she said.

He nodded. "My younger brother was killed in an accident. I went with my mother when she identified the body. I see him in nightmares. I've seen a lot worse in police work, but when it's family, it's different."

"I'm sorry. How do you deal with it?" Rhona asked. Everyone dealt differently with trauma.

"I used to try to go back to sleep, but that didn't work because the dreams returned. Now I get up, make a hot drink and turn on TV. Sometimes Mom, who's a light sleeper and has her own nightmares, wakes up and joins me. We talk about Fergus, remember the good times and blot out his death. It helps."

He lived at home. Interesting. He had to be forty, but he still lived at home. Maybe he'd been married and divorced? Or never married? Or his mother was handicapped and needed him? If the appropriate moment came along, she'd inquire. Her attractive partner intrigued her, but he wasn't forthcoming, and she'd have to be skillful if she wanted to learn more.

"Maybe you can share your solutions with Candace Lafleur."

"Maybe, but I think finding the way out of the deep, dark pit is a solitary journey."

*   *   *

Later Monday afternoon, Hollis heard Elizabeth and Candace come home. Before she had time to clean up and talk to them, Candace pounded up the stairs and banged on the door.

A wave of apprehension swept through Hollis. Candace normally phoned, unless she'd been invited upstairs.

Candace, carrying Elizabeth, who still wore her pink outdoor jacket, rushed into the room. She set Elizabeth down unceremoniously. MacTee, carrying a stuffed toy, hurried to greet them and diverted Elizabeth, who wrapped her arms around his neck and buried her face in his fur.

"Detective Simpson left a message. They're coming round after supper. It can't be good news. If it was, they would have said so. Will you keep Elizabeth out of the way while I talk to them?"

Hollis opened her arms and hugged her friend. It was pointless to say that it might be a mistake, that maybe that

79

wasn't why they were coming, that DNA testing usually took much longer.

"Of course." Hollis squeezed her again and stepped back. "I'm sure you don't want to cook. Let me make your dinner."

Candace stood with a faraway look in her eyes, as if she were running an old movie tape or seeing something in the far-distant past.

With hours until the detectives arrived, it was time for a distraction, an alternative plan. "Elizabeth must be psyched about Hallowe'en tomorrow. At her day care they've probably talked about dressing up and everything that makes Halloween fun." She waited for a response but none came. "The Hallowe'en decorations in this neighbourhood are amazing." She grasped Candace's arm to pull her back to reality. "Why don't you take Elizabeth for a walk? Two blocks east on Belsize Drive, there's an electrified display, a white ghost that rises out of a huge orange pumpkin. It scares MacTee, but Elizabeth will love it."

Candace shook her head as if to close down whatever she was seeing in her mind's eye. "Sorry, I missed what you said."

Hollis repeated her suggestion.

"Good idea. I'll park her in her stroller and walk fast or even jog. Exercise is exactly what I need right now."

After supper, just as Hollis volunteered to give Elizabeth her bath, the doorbell rang.

Candace slid off the kitchen stool, straightened, threw back her shoulders, muttered, "Here goes," and headed for the door.

MacTee responded to the pealing doorbell as he always did. Golden retrievers love visitors, but do not like to meet newcomers without presenting a welcoming gift. He searched the floor for something to offer. His gaze fixed on one of Elizabeth's dolls that had fallen under her high chair. He scooped it up and trailed after Candace.

In the bathroom, Hollis ran the bath. Elizabeth permitted Hollis to lift her in. Hollis wished she were in the living room with Candace, but it was important to adhere to Elizabeth's routines and attempt to prevent transmitting their anxiety to her. After a happy ten minutes while the toddler filled and emptied various containers and allowed Hollis to wash her face and neck, Elizabeth eyed her speculatively. Not having bathed her before, Hollis didn't recognize the warning signs until a deluge of water splashed over her. She pulled back in surprise.

Elizabeth giggled. "Again?" she said and scooped more water.

"No." Hollis stayed her hand. "Time to get out. I'm sure you know you're not supposed to do that."

The child's guilty smile spoke volumes.

Hollis finally hoisted Elizabeth into her crib, kissed her goodnight and headed for the living room. When she walked in, Rhona stood up, said hello and introduced Ian Galbraith before she perched again on a sofa.

Hollis had expected to see Zee Zee, the Ethiopian-Canadian detective who had been Rhona's partner the last time Hollis had met her. She'd found it easy to talk to the two women and wondered how it would be dealing with this man.

Candace, face pale and eyes wide, was slumped on the other sofa.

Hollis didn't need a GPS system to figure out what she was about to hear, but until the words were spoken, she'd hope she was wrong.

Eight

The DNA is Danson's," Candace said in a voice totally lacking inflection.

"I'm so sorry," Hollis said.

"They," Candace pointed at Rhona and Ian, "have asked me to go to the morgue and see if I can identify his effects or. . ." she took a deep breath, "his body. I suppose it should be Poppy, but I'm not going to ask her to do it. Until there is absolutely no doubt that it's him I'm not going to tell her."

Given Poppy's indifference, up to that point, Hollis wondered what effect the news would have. Poppy might well rationalize the tragedy. Perhaps she was being callous? Surely no mother, no matter how detached, deals well with a child's death.

"Good idea," Hollis said.

Candace wasn't listening. She was reading from an internal script that didn't require answers. "These officers tell me his face has been..." she gripped one hand with the other and pulled them against her as if to hold herself together, "...badly disfigured. He's such a handsome man." She eased to her feet as if every joint, muscle and bone protested the action. "I suppose I'd better do it now. The job won't get any easier the longer I leave it."

"I'll take good care of Elizabeth," Hollis said. Looking at her friend's stricken expression, she thought ahead to what Candace was about to face. While the procedure at the morgue would be familiar—anyone who watched any

TV knew how it went—the reality would be something else. Until the last possible moment, Candace would hang on to the hope that the body would not be Danson's. Even when denial was no longer possible, one part of her brain would reject the truth.

*   *   *

"You're sure it's him," Candace said as Ian piloted the car to the morgue.

"It would be great to say no to give you hope, but DNA matches are hard to argue with," Rhona said.

This part of her job upset Rhona, no matter how she hardened her heart and tried to distance herself. The next-of-kin's meaningless, time-filling conversation as they steeled themselves for the ordeal they were about to face broke her heart. She preferred silence, but some people chattered. Others seemed frozen in a time warp where they wouldn't have to confront what lay ahead of them.

When the moment came and the attendant drew the sheet away to reveal the person they had known, many could only nod. Words deserted them. The body's reality shocked them, no matter what their relationship with the deceased had been.

Rhona knew it would be even worse for Candace, because the corpse was faceless. Without recognizable facial features, she would only have the man's hair, ears and general build to examine and decide that this once had been her living brother. If the sheet was pulled down far enough to reveal the bloody finger stumps, it would add to the horror.

Candace did not initiate conversation on the walk to the morgue. The squeak of her running shoes, the clump of Ian's brogues and the clicking heels of Rhona's cowboy boots accompanied them down the tiled hall to swinging doors that creaked open and allowed them in the viewing room. An attendant wheeled the body out.

Rhona heard Candace's sharp intake of breath as she viewed the devastation that had once been a man with an intact face and hands with fingers.

"If the DNA matches, I'll have to take your word that it's Danson, because I can't..." Candace faltered, shivered and turned away.

"We have his effects at the station. We'll show them to you now," Rhona said.

Ian drove. No one spoke until they'd entered the building and proceeded to a room furnished with a steel table and molded plastic chairs. Ian left to retrieve the effects.

"Why don't you sit down," Rhona said and gestured to the chairs.

Candace didn't hear or the words didn't register.

Rhona repeated the offer.

White-faced, with slack facial muscles and unfocussed eyes, Candace stared at her. She continued to stand.

Ian, carrying two bags, returned. "I'm sorry," he said. No matter how many times this happened, he empathized with the survivors. Their body language always brought back memories of the day he and his mother had identified his brother. The black bottomless sorrow in his mother's eyes and voice had imprinted themselves indelibly on his mind.

Two labelled clear plastic bags were on the table.

Rhona again invited Candace to sit down, but she shook her head. The two detectives also stood.

"These are the clothes he was wearing," Ian said pointing to the larger bag.

Rhona bent forward, withdrew and unfolded a grey poplin windbreaker, beige plaid flannel shirt stained with dried blood and tan cargo pants. She laid green, diamond-patterned socks beside well-worn, blue and white Nike running shoes.

Candace shuddered but didn't avert her eyes. Rather she snapped to attention. Her eyes cleared, and her jaw firmed.

"I've never seen him dressed like that." She pointed an index finger at each item of clothing. Her voice rang with conviction. "My brother hated plaid shirts like that. He said they marked you as middle-aged. Same thing for that jacket. He wore blue jeans, never cargos. He had extra-wide feet and always bought New Balance." She wrinkled her nose as if she smelled something disgusting. "I can't ever imagine him buying socks like those." Her eyes narrowed. "He was a cool guy. Unless he was trying to disguise himself, he would never, ever dress like that."

Her adamancy startled Rhona. "Thank you for telling us."

Candace lunged forward and grabbed a shoe. She yanked its tongue back and peered inside. "Eight narrow," she said and slammed the shoe on the table. "My brother did not wear eight and couldn't have squeezed his feet into this narrow shoe." She spoke firmly and with authority. "He wore twelve extra-wide. I know about the extra-wide because both my toddler and I need wide shoes. They're hard to find." Candace challenged the detectives. "You think I'm insisting these things don't belong to my brother because I don't want it to be my brother. I know what he wore. He wouldn't have worn those clothes, and he couldn't have squeezed his feet into those shoes."

"I'm not disagreeing with you," Rhona said. "We'll show you what this man was carrying." She opened and gently decanted the second bag's contents.

The first two items were a black comb with missing teeth and a ballpoint pen with a chewed end that transformed it from a standard to a poignant item. Rhona could picture the owner chewing pensively as he mulled over a problem or waited through a company's punch one, punch two and listened to "please stay on the line your business is important to us." Loose change. Subway tokens, a subway transfer, chapstick and a half-empty roll of Lifesavers. That was it.

Candace stepped closer to the table, bent over, and

peered at the items. "No wallet, no keys?" she asked.

"No. This is everything," Rhona said.

"If someone mugged him, that person could have cleaned out the apartment. We found no evidence that anything had been disturbed." Candace pivoted, paused and eyed the two officers.

Rhona suspected Candace had something to add but was wondering if it was wise.

"We're on the same side," Rhona reassured her. "If you know anything that will help our investigation, you should tell us."

Candace still hesitated.

"We don't care how you discovered whatever it is you know, but you must share information," Ian added.

Candace straightened, folded her arms over her chest and looked from one to the other. "Okay. Here goes. I have access to my brother's online banking. He withdrew money on the last Friday before he vaporized. No one has used his credit card. Although I don't believe the body in the morgue is his, I do think something bad has happened to him." She paused as if waiting for the detectives to comment, but they didn't.

"The chapstick from the person's effects would have traces of saliva. The comb might have hair—why don't you retest?" Candace asked.

"Candace, there is no doubt that after what you've told us we have serious questions about our identification. We will run the DNA tests again after we receive the dental report. I hope for your sake that we'll cross Danson off as the unidentified victim."

"How long will that take?" Candace asked.

"A few days," Rhona said and added, "I know that will seem like forever to you, but we must be absolutely sure."

"If that is Danson, may I ask how he was killed? Did his murderer do that to his face and hands before or after he died, and where did you find the body?"

86

"I'm sorry, but we aren't at liberty to tell you," Rhona said. She hated doing that—not knowing was always more excruciating than receiving the worst information. "I'd like to know more about your brother's life, but until we have the corroborating dental information, I'll wait to interview you. In the meantime, please make notes about the connections in his life that might help us in our investigation."

"We've already done some of that. Hollis and I checked out his apartment." Before the detectives reacted, Candace added, "We used gloves and replaced everything."

Rhona didn't smile. This wasn't a moment for levity, but it amused her just the same. Both Hollis and Candace would have known that if Danson had been a victim of foul play, the apartment would be sealed. If she was a betting woman, she'd wager Hollis had copied documents that she thought might help them find Danson or his killer. From experience, she knew Hollis wouldn't be content to sit back and allow the investigation to take its course.

"You do know that in a criminal investigation you could be charged with interference if you continue your investigation?" Ian said.

"Of course," Candace said, her voice lacking conviction.

"I'm sure I don't have to remind you that there are dangerous people out there. You don't want to do anything to make them think you know something incriminating about them."

"Would you like the keys to his place?" Candace asked in a conciliatory tone.

Rhona and Ian accepted the offer and Rhona recorded their receipt in her notebook.

*   *   *

After Hollis had tidied the kitchen, she boiled water for tea. Given the circumstances, tea, along with many hugs, should help. When the front door banged open, she hurried to embrace a white-faced Candace.

In the living room, Candace refused tea, folded herself into the sofa and tucked her feet under her.

"Want to talk about it?" Hollis said.

"Horrible, terrible," Candace shook her head. "Because the…" she inhaled sharply, "they weren't going to show me his face. They had it covered, but I insisted. I thought it couldn't be that bad, and I might be able to tell if it was Danson. But I shouldn't have done that. Oh God, it was awful. It was destroyed. I couldn't tell if it was Danson. The hair looked right, and the man was tall and in good physical shape, but the other evidence, the clothes, particularly the shoes, which were the wrong size, didn't belong to Danson." She clasped her hands together and lifted her eyes. "Although everything—his clothes, the stuff he was carrying—is wrong, it's hard to argue with DNA."

Hollis joined Candace on the sofa and swung to face her. "What a totally awful experience." No point dwelling on the horror, they had work to do. "What did he have in his pockets?"

Candace listed the items.

"No wallet, no keys?"

Candace shook her head as tears leaked from her eyes. She took a shaky breath. "You know what really undid me?" She answered her own question. "A pen with a chewed end." She choked and put her face in her hands. "It's too much to deal with," she sobbed. "I don't believe it's Danson, but maybe I'm fooling myself. Even if it isn't Danson, it's a man someone must love, must be worrying about."

Poor woman. Time for more TLC, Hollis thought as she moved closer and put an arm around her friend. "It's something no one should have to deal with. Since working helps both of us, we'll get on with the tasks we set for ourselves," she said and squeezed Candace's shoulder.

Candace covered her mouth with her hand. "I gave them my second set of keys and told them we'd left everything as we found it, but I forgot about the computer." Her eyes anxious, she examined Hollis's face, "Have you returned it?"

"Yes, I forwarded every file I thought we might need to my computer. I have a mass of information."

"What can I do—we're supposed to be a team. You're doing all the work."

"We are a team. Your task is to pry more information from Poppy."

"Oh my God—Poppy has to be told." She straightened her legs, put her feet on the floor, half-rose then sank back. "No." She clenched her teeth and narrowed her eyes. "No. She doesn't need to hear until the identification is absolutely positive, absolutely one hundred and ten per cent positive. Imagine going through the grief then having the police say, 'Oops, we made a mistake.' It's bad enough that I have to go through this—there's no way I'm telling Poppy."

"Good decision. Since you're not convinced, there's no point in burdening her."

Candace nodded. "They'll soon finish with the dental records. I'm sure they will. They said they wouldn't release his name until I've told everyone. I'll continue with life as usual—go to work—carry on." Her eyes widened. "I nearly forgot. Tomorrow is Halloween. I have to send Elizabeth to daycare with a costume and leave work early to see the kids' parade in their outfits. Then we snack on Halloween treats. Thank goodness I didn't volunteer to make anything. I'm taking cut up pita and hummus."

"Elizabeth is a hummus fanatic. She'll be pleased."

"Dealing with Halloween will take my mind off the waiting won't it?"

"If you're taking Elizabeth out, I'll answer the door."

"Two and a half is too young to go trick or treating. We'll dispense the candy. I'll allow her stay up until seven thirty then turn out the outside light to discourage any more visitors."

Denial came in many forms, and if this was how Candace wanted to handle the situation, who could blame her? Certainly the difference in shoe brands and sizes had to be significant. Hollis also depended on New Balance for shoes. Anyone who knew her would confirm that. For many people, brand loyalty was important.

*　*　*

"What do you make of what Ms Lafleur told us?" Ian asked after they'd seen Candace out and were on their way back to their desks. "She was positive the shoes and the clothes didn't belong to him. Hard to argue with the shoes."

"How do you explain the DNA? It definitely matches. Maybe it wasn't his hairbrush, maybe he entertained a visitor who borrowed it." She shrugged. "I don't have an explanation."

"Even if it isn't his, we're further ahead, aren't we?" Ian said.

"We are. The body in the morgue is someone who spent time in Danson's apartment and used the hairbrush. We don't know who he is, but it does give us a jumping-off place."

"Seems to me we should dig into Danson's life before we hear about the dental records," Ian said. "On the other hand, this isn't the only murder we're dealing with. If it isn't him, we'll be wasting time."

They went to their respective desks. After Rhona sat down, she leaned back carefully—she didn't want to stress her painful hip—and continued the conversation. "Given that Hollis Grant is involved, and she'll be meddling in everything, we'll open a file. I expect she's copied what she considered relevant information. My worry is that she'll plunge ahead and get herself in trouble. She nearly died the last time she tried that."

"Don't you think she'll be smarter this time?" Ian asked.

Rhona shook her head. "It's the third time I've been involved with her. I can tell you I don't have much faith in her common sense. Once she thinks she's on to something, get out of the way. She's as determined as racehorse heading for the winner's circle."

Ian laughed. "As a track aficionado, I like the picture."

Rhona added this piece of information to the Ian jigsaw she was assembling. "It's an added challenge. We'll have to work smarter and faster than Hollis."

*　　*　　*

Discouraged—that was how Hollis felt. What else could she do? She thought of movies where the person choosing to disappear took evasive action to prevent anyone from locating him. Had Danson done this? Had someone been hunting him and forced him to go to ground? If that was true, he wouldn't have contacted Candace or Poppy in case his pursuer pressured them to reveal his address. Having lost Angie, he'd never endanger his family. Given that he chased dangerous offenders, it was a reasonable assumption.

Or, had Candace and Poppy's involvement in his life been smothering him? Nothing Hollis had heard or seen had given her that impression. Nevertheless, this too was a possibility.

Evaluating the situation rationally, his life appeared to have stopped cold almost immediately after he'd visited Poppy and discussed the possibly of phoning what had turned out to be an unlisted number. But Poppy was not helping.

She had no time for her chickens. Danson's papers came next. She swept them into a pile and sorted through them, cross-stacking each time the topic changed. This time-consuming chore finished, she glared at the document tower and sighed. When you didn't know what you were looking for, it was difficult to pinpoint anything odd. Certainly he'd led an interesting segmented life with many contacts in

91

each slice. Some were stand-alones. Others overlapped—she'd cross-reference those. The task was daunting. First she'd clear away the dead wood, the files she judged to be irrelevant. After that, a chat with Danson's boss or his colleagues might provide shortcuts to vital files.

Halloween probably wasn't the best of nights to visit the Starshine, where he worked. She suspected costumed hordes would revel until dawn but if she arrived early before the crowds she'd have a chance to talk to the staff. Candace would flip off her outside lights at seven thirty, freeing Hollis to trek downtown. Should she call first or arrive and hope surprise would elicit information? Difficult to explain her mission on the phone—better to show up unannounced.

First, Halloween. Shortly after she heard Candace and Elizabeth arrive home, she went downstairs.

Candace, tightlipped and tense, answered the door. "It's been an awful day," she said. "I go over and over my doubts and wonder if I'm kidding myself when I say it isn't Danson. I keep seeing his terrible mutilated face and fingerless hands."

"Some days seem endless," Hollis commiserated. "Remember that you're not giving up hope until you learn what the dental records show."

Candace slumped against the door frame. "You're right. But I can tell you it would be easier if I didn't keep seeing the corpse, hoping it isn't Danson then feeling guilty."

Elizabeth, decked out in a polka-dot clown suit with matching makeup, emerged from behind Candace. "Tee," she asked clutching Candace's leg with one hand and peeking behind Hollis.

"He's upstairs. Halloween scares him."

Elizabeth frowned, "Scares?" she said in a puzzled voice.

Oops, she shouldn't make Halloween out to be really frightening.

"He doesn't like it when the doorbell keeps ringing," Hollis said.

"Why?"

Quick thinking required. "Because he always wants to bring a present to the person at the door and he doesn't have that many toys," Hollis said. It was a lame explanation, but it was the best she could do.

Elizabeth digested the information. "Okay," she said.

At that moment the doorbell rang. Candace glanced at her watch. "Five thirty. Trick or treaters getting a head start." She straightened, removed Elizabeth's hand, darted back into the apartment and reemerged swinging an orange plastic pumpkin brimming with miniature chocolate bars. "Come on, Elizabeth. We'll see who's here."

Moments later, Elizabeth shrieked, "No, no, don't like," then wailed. Hollis hoped her comments hadn't triggered Elizabeth's reaction. Apparently MacTee wasn't the only one who didn't appreciate Halloween. Hollis went upstairs, collected MacTee and returned. "I'll answer the door," she said to Candace and reached for the candy-filled pumpkin.

"Thanks. Witches and goblins are too much for her," Candace said.

Downstairs, Hollis, not a fan of Halloween, did her best to respond cheerfully to the excited children and smile over their heads at the shepherding parents who hovered behind them. When she'd been a child, her parents wouldn't have dreamed of accompanying children, but those innocent days were gone for good.

Her pumpkin gradually emptied.

At the grocery store earlier in the week, she'd grabbed two boxes of her favourite Sweet Marie bars knowing even as she bought them that she'd earmarked them for her own consumption. Once a year she did this. After she'd pigged out, she vowed not to fall into the same trap the following year, but she always did. This year she'd have to share. She trotted back upstairs. The phone rang as she opened her door.

"My name is Carol Usher. You e-mailed me about Danson."

Hope flickered. "Thanks for calling. Do you have any information that might help?"

"I work for a not-for-profit group that helps immigrants," Carol said and summarized what the group did.

Hollis, aware that she hadn't locked the downstairs door, wanted to hurry Carol along but restrained herself and made encouraging sounds.

"He was interested in learning how the Russian immigrant community organizes. Two weeks ago he wanted to know if I knew if there were any fronts, any legitimate organizations that fronted for the Russian mob."

Hollis fingers twitched. This could be it. "What did you tell him?"

"Nothing. That isn't the sort of information that I know. But I thought you'd want to know what he was doing before he disappeared."

Hollis thanked her, replaced the phone and reluctantly refilled the pumpkin from her stash, setting aside four bars for her own consumption, and raced back downstairs.

By seven thirty, mobs of half-grown youth who jostled and shoved as they angled to fill their shopping bags and pillowcases had replaced the small children. Time to close down.

She flicked off the outside light and headed upstairs. What to wear to the Starshine? It shouldn't matter but it did—she wanted to look serious but not conspicuous. Since clubbing didn't play any part in her social life, she visualized the front page of the tabloids she studied at the supermarket checkouts. Immediately she pictured thin young women with long, shiny hair, usually blonde, short skirts set off by very high heels and low-cut shimmery tops. None of these items languished in her wardrobe.

Black silk pants, white silk shirt and short black velvet jacket—that should do it. She dressed, regarded herself in the mirror and decided she resembled a waiter. Too bad. At eight o'clock, no swinger worth his or her reputation would be there and anyway, why did she care?

Shouts from downstairs. What was going on? She stepped out on her landing and listened.

"I repeat. Someone has been in my apartment. You must have left the front door open. How could you be so careless?"

Poppy's shouts could have been heard on the street. Nothing wrong with her pipes.

"Of course I didn't," Candace replied in a lower tone.

"Someone has been in."

"Maybe it was Alberto. He has a key, doesn't he?"

"He was with me."

"Danson. Could it have been Danson? Maybe he's come back from wherever he is."

Hollis recognized the excitement in Candace's voice.

"Not too likely. He would have come and seen you. If it wasn't Danson or Alberto or you, who was it?"

"How do you know someone came in? Was something taken?"

"No. I always leave the phone pad exactly aligned with the phone. Now it's on the other side of the desk."

"Poppy. You could have done that yourself. Alberto could have done it. Relax. No one was in your place."

Hollis, listening intently, thought of the moments she'd spent upstairs talking to Carol and refilling the pumpkin. Surely there hadn't been time for anyone to enter the house, search and leave. Should she go down and confess the security breach? What good would a "mea culpa" scene do? Instead, she collected purse, coat and car keys and set off.

The Starshine nightclub's glittering marquee and brightly-lit entrance promised patrons an exciting evening. Located on Richmond Street in the heart of the entertainment district, it was well-positioned to draw in the crowds, but when Hollis arrived, no lines snaked away from the entrance. In fact, the only other person in the vicinity was a panhandler plunked on the pavement with a worn-out cap containing a few coins set on the sidewalk in front of him. Hollis didn't give to beggars—she preferred to make her donations to homeless shelters and food banks—nevertheless the pathetic wrecks appealing to her goodwill made her feel guilty that she didn't provide loonies and toonies. She met his gaze and smiled at him.

"Have a nice night," he said.

She felt even worse. Why couldn't she deal with her problem and accept her decision? She shook her head and entered the foyer. In the ticket booth, a woman with jet black hair, white makeup and a witch's hat watched her.

"We don't open for half an hour," she said.

"I'm not here as a…" Hollis paused, groping for the right word, "…patron. I want to talk to the manager."

The young woman ran her eyes over Hollis. "You're not here about the waitress job, are you?"

That would be the day. She could only imagine how much she'd hate working here. She'd waitressed during her college summers and ranked high on the inefficient, ineffective scale. Time would not have improved her coordination. She shook her head.

"Sam should be in his office. Go in, turn right and up the stairs. First door."

Hollis followed directions and tapped gently. Told to enter, she obeyed.

The office could not have been more businesslike if it had been located in a downtown office tower. No glitz here. The swarthy man behind the desk wore a dark suit with a dark shirt and tie. If he was supposed to resemble the mobsters in movies about Vegas, he carried it off well. Maybe this was a Halloween outfit?

"What can I do for you?" he asked but didn't rise or invite her to sit down.

"I'd like to ask you a few questions about Danson Lafleur," she said.

He said nothing for a moment as his gaze ran up and down her body like a stockyard buyer estimating a steer's value. "You don't look like a cop or smell like a cop, and you would have showed me your badge if you were a cop.

96

Ditto if you were a PI. So who are you and why should I talk to you?"

Nice guy.

"I'm a friend of Danson's sister. She hasn't heard from him for two weeks, and she's worried. I thought you might have an idea where he'd gone."

"If I did, I don't know why I'd tell you. As it happens, I don't. Friggin' asshole left me in the lurch. Didn't show up for work. Didn't call. Nada. No, I don't know. Since he's no longer on my payroll, I don't care." He pulled a file toward him, opened it and lowered his gaze. Clearly this was dismissal time.

"One more question." Hollis addressed the top of his slicked back hair, thinking he should use dandruff shampoo. "Did he ever talk to you or anyone here about his private life?"

The man snorted, making the sheet of paper in front of him flutter. He stared at her. "Lady, he was the bouncer. I'm not on intimate terms with my bouncers. Talk to Spike. He's the other one. Maybe he knows something."

Hollis wended her way back to the foyer to talk to the ticket seller.

"When does Spike get here?" she asked.

"He's out back in the kitchen," the woman replied. "Go through the club then the door to the left of the stage."

Would the bouncer be more helpful than the manager? She had to hope. She was running out of leads.

Hollis moved to the kitchen of the Starshine Club to talk to the bouncer. She felt sure she'd found her man when she spied a massive, heavily muscled, bald man leaning in the kitchen door frame, drinking a can of Red Bull and chatting with a scantily clad waitress. When he smiled at Hollis, she noted his gold-capped teeth. "You want the boss?" he said.

"Actually, if you're Spike, I came to talk to you," Hollis replied.

Spike's smile evaporated. "What about?" His heavily accented voice had turned unfriendly.

"About Danson Lafleur, my friend's brother," Hollis said.

Spike sighed and his lips twisted into a rueful grimace. "Sorry, I'm suspicious of people." He shook his head. "This sometimes bad scene."

"I'm sure. That's why I'm here. You know Danson has disappeared?"

Spike shook his head and waved the Red Bull can. "Surprised boss fire him. Never know he had problem."

"When he didn't show up for work, the boss left a phone message that he was fired. Did he talk to you or did you hear that he was in any kind of trouble?" She clutched her handbag to her chest as she waited for his reply.

Spike's furrowed brow and pursed lips gave Hollis the impression he was thinking, and it wasn't an easy process.

"We talked. Sometimes ended up in kitchen before or after work. Friendly guy. Never told nothing private or anything." He continued to frown. This conversation appeared to be taking a toll on his mental abilities. "Except once, long time back. I remember, 'cause he was interested."

"What did you talk about?" Hollis tightened her grip on her bag. She needed something significant, something to give her a lead.

"After shift, sometimes three or four, I get hungry. There's all-night souvlaki place down King Street." He grinned, "Three o'clock in morning—interesting people. Anyway, maybe can't tell from name or accent, but I'm Russian."

English clearly wasn't his first language, but Hollis hadn't picked up on what his first might have been.

"Anyway, I kinda like to know what bad guy Russians do." He hesitated. "Some into bad things. I try keep nose clean." He grinned again. "To do, you have to know what they do and who they are."

This sounded interesting, Hollis thought.

"Anyway, like I say, was eating souvlaki, minding own business, when I seen guy come in alone."

Hollis felt her eyebrows lift. Why would he be surprised to see someone come in by himself? What significance would it have?

"I see I said wrong," Spike said. "Guy's connected to," again he paused before he breathed the word, "mob."

She nodded, as if talking about the Russian mob was something she did every day.

"Anyway, mob go in packs." He frowned. "Suppose that's why they call them mob?"

"Must be," Hollis agreed.

"Anyway, guy comes in. I recognize him except I don't. He got same triangle face of mob guy that got caught, sent to pen and deported. Rest of him different."

"How so?"

"Hair brown—was black, eyes dark—were blue, big glasses—never had before, and is thin—used be fat and was never alone. Never knew him to talk to. Don't stare, 'cause, if same guy, is dangerous. Take second look when I think it okay. Either deported guy is cousin or is same guy but changed. Strange."

Immediately, Hollis thought about Danson's tracking activities. "Did you tell Danson about him?"

"Yah, I did."

"What had the Russian done to be sent to prison and deported?"

"Something I know nothing about. Think they call it company, no, not right. What they call those places where there are many companies? Whole bunch off Highway 400 and Highway 403?"

"Industrial parks."

"Right. Russian guy charged with industrial something."

"Espionage?"

"Right. Also suspected of murder, but not able to prove. Anyway, told Danson 'cause that kind of thing important to him." His brow furrowed. "Didn't some guy that came back whack girlfriend?"

"Yes."

"Guess that's why he interested."

Hollis suspected Danson had not told Spike that he searched these men out and did his best to get them thrown out of the country again.

"When did you have this conversation?"

"While ago. September?"

"That was the last time you really talked to him?"

"Couple weeks ago he asked if I do double shifts if he's away. Something he had to do. Wanted to keep job. Would be okay if we fixed it between us." He smiled, obviously pleased he'd dug out this information. "That what you want to know?"

"Exactly," Hollis said, wanting to praise this big, slow guy and make him feel useful. She wondered when he'd come to Canada—he didn't talk as if he was a product of the Canadian school system. She'd ask.

"How did you end up here?" she said, loosening her grip on her purse and hooking it over her shoulder.

"Here?' he gestured at the kitchen, at the waitress filling salt shakers and listening to their conversation.

"No. In Canada."

"Long story." He scrutinized his watch, a massive affair with a black, stud-crusted band. "Got time." He resettled himself against the door frame. "Father die in Russia. Mother bring me and brother."

"Brave move to come to a new country," Hollis said. Anticipating a lengthy tale and seeing nowhere to sit, she'd moved into the kitchen and leaned against a counter.

"Not good. Nurse in old country. No job here. She clean offices to feed us. Very mad," he frowned.

"You went to school?"

"No, too old. Went to work. Younger brother, Boris, go to high school. Mother wanted more, but he quit," he sighed. "Sad story."

"What happened to him?"

"Dead." He crossed his arms on his chest. "That how I know about mob—Boris work for them. Deal drugs. Guy kill him."

"Your poor mother. To bring you here and have that happen."

"Very bad." Spike tapped his forehead. "She go cuckoo." He shrugged, but it was a gesture of helplessness, not indifference. "I try to help, but she cuckoo."

Hollis wished she hadn't pursued the topic since the subject made Spike unhappy. Maybe she could help? If his mother hadn't plugged into the mental health system, it wasn't too late. She still could. There was help available.

"Does your mom live in Toronto? Is she seeing a doctor?" she asked.

Spike shook his head like a bull shaking off a cloud of unwelcome flies. "No help. Doesn't want."

Time to change the subject. "I am sorry. To get back to Danson, if you could tell me where he was going, that would be perfect, but I don't suppose he told anyone." She smiled again as Spike crunched his drink can and tossed it in the garbage. "Spike, that was great, thanks." She proffered an up-to-date card she'd printed on her computer. "Take this, and if you think of anything else please call me."

The waitress, who'd been following their exchange as if it were a ping-pong game, approached timidly. "I talked to Danson a lot," she said.

Hollis stuck out her hand. "Hi, I'm Hollis, a friend of Danson's sister, Candace."

"Molly," the girl replied, shaking the proffered hand then plunging her hands deep in the pockets of her apron. "He liked to talk to me because he said I reminded him of his girlfriend, the one who was shot. Danson always wanted to make sure I was okay. I think he worried that guys in there," she withdrew her right hand and pointed through the swinging doors, "would come on to me, but it isn't like this is a strip club. They come in couples or bunches and stick together like glue." She leaned forward, pulled her hands

101

from her pockets, clutched them together and lowered her voice. "I did call his place when he didn't show up, but I got the answering machine. I've been worrying about him—it wasn't like him not to show up for work."

According to Candace, Danson responded to those in need, and Molly looked as if her life had been hard and probably still was. Thin to the point of emaciation, she needed dental work to correct an obvious overbite. Heavy makeup failed to cover a poor complexion, and her brittle blonde hair needed conditioning and loving kindness. She radiated concern when she spoke of Danson.

"His family is worried too," Hollis said. "Can you think of anything he said that might give us an idea where he might have gone?"

"I talked to him the last day he worked, the Saturday, and he said he'd just figured out that someone was jerking him around, and he wasn't going to stand for it."

"Did you ask him what he meant?"

Molly nodded and twisted one of the many silver rings on her fingers. "He said the less I knew the better. That he was playing in the big leagues where they didn't mess around."

Exactly what she'd feared. The hunter had become the hunted. Somehow the pursued had fingered Danson, who was now in big trouble.

"I wish I'd asked more questions, tried to make him tell me what had happened," Molly said as she increased the speed of the twirling ring. "I knew our talk was upsetting him. He was always nice to me, and I didn't want to do that." A tear glistened and slid down her cheek. "He was the greatest guy. I always envied his girlfriend. Imagine having someone like Danson love you." She shook her head. Her smile was rueful. "Actually, I can't imagine it. I attract the creeps. It's like I have a sign floating over my head that says I'm an easy mark, a pushover, a sucker."

"Molly, I'm sure you did everything you could. Don't be hard on yourself. We don't know for sure that something bad has happened to him." As she spoke, she had a picture of Candace's face when she'd returned from the morgue. DNA didn't lie. But no point in upsetting Molly until they knew for sure what had happened.

A maverick thought floated into her mind. What if the body in the morgue belonged to the elusive Gregory? It could have been his hair brush? Had they ever told the detectives about Gregory? She searched her mind but didn't come up with an answer. What if Gregory was the person who'd jerked him around, and Danson had dealt with the problem? She didn't know him well enough to say if he could be violent. Who knew what circumstances would drive a person over the edge?

This was not a happy thought.

If he'd murdered Gregory, Danson would have had a very good reason to vanish. It would also explain why he hadn't contacted Candace.

"You will call and tell me when you find out, won't you?" Molly said. She scrabbled in her white frilled apron pocket and pulled out an order form and pen. After she'd written her name and number, she tore off the sheet and handed it to Hollis. "Don't forget. Good or bad, I want to know."

Hollis promised.

As she left the club, she noticed that the panhandler remained but was no longer alone. Costumed patrons lined up halfway down the block. They ignored the man as if he was an inanimate object, a garbage bag set on the sidewalk. Spike, busy vetting and letting in the crowd, waved and winked at Hollis as she passed.

103

Nine

The next day, a dog walker stumbled upon another body.

Reportedly the victim had been yet another marginal drug user, and he'd been stabbed. Again the corpse was in a back alley near Sherbourne and Carlton. Like the other victims, the man showed no signs that he'd struggled with his assailant. Whoever the killer was, the victims had not considered him a threat until it was too late.

Rhona and Ian, along with others on the task force assigned to the case, were told to recanvass neighbourhood residents for information.

"We're missing something," Rhona said. "I know we've run a canvass through here before. This time let's make sure we talk to all the neighbourhood regulars—the moms with their strollers, the people who feed the pigeons, those who walk their dogs, the winos drinking rotgut out of paper bags and anyone else who spends time in Allan Gardens. "

"Then we'll cross the park to the Salvation Army Mission," Ian said.

Rhona glanced up at the wall clock. "It closes after breakfast—everyone has to leave—and doesn't reopen until dinner time, but you're right, it should be a good spot to talk to people. Regulars hang around outside and across the street at Moss Park Arena." She gathered her belongings. "I like walking through the gardens. Have you ever been in the—what do they call that glassed roof building? The conservatory?"

"No. I'm not into plants," Ian replied without giving her any indication of what he was "into." Rhona liked to know details about a partner's private life, of their likes and dislikes. Ian was not "into" revealing and sharing.

After they parked, they walked along Carlton Street and chose one of the diagonal paths that cut through the park's green space. A woman sitting on a bench ignored them as they passed. She pushed a sleeping baby in a stroller back and forth with one hand as she read a book. When addressed, she frowned and pointed to her lips. "He sleeps very lightly," she whispered.

Rhona whispered her questions. "No idea," the woman murmured and returned to her book.

They next encountered two middle-aged women zipped into nylon anoraks and lugging shopping bags who smiled at them.

"Could we have a word?" Ian said as he showed his badge.

The two looked at one another before they nodded their agreement and indicated a nearby bench, empty except for an old man perched on the end clutching a paper-wrapped parcel with an open, green glass bottle protruding from the bag. The women set their carryalls down.

"Police," the shorter of the two said, and her eyes were bright.

Whatever these women's backgrounds, unpleasant run-ins with officialdom had not played a part. "Do you live in the area?' Rhona asked.

The second shopper waved an arm toward Sherbourne Street. "The Rackley Arms apartments," she said.

"We're investigating the deaths of several murdered men," Rhona said. "We're questioning people who live in this neighbourhood."

After an unspoken communication passed between them, the short one spoke. "Druggies. There are druggies everywhere. Too many." Her brow furrowed, and she lowered her voice. "They'd kill you for a quarter just to buy drugs." She leaned toward Rhona, "We don't go out at night. Never."

It was unlikely that the men had been murdered in broad day light. Possible, but not probable.

"We don't know nuthin' about murder. Just two old women trying to stay alive," her companion stated, hooking her hand through her bag's handle and pulling it toward her.

"Sorry." The short one adjusted her head scarf and shrugged. "She's right—we mind our own business."

The detectives next encountered a dogwalker attached to five canine charges and armed with a large plastic bag filled with more plastic bags. Obviously the pack's alpha dog, she led the way and the assorted dogs trotted along side by side, intent on their outing. When Rhona approached her, the woman waved her away, "No time to talk. Can't stop. Have to get these dogs home and pick up the next crew."

Further inside the park, a man of indeterminate age, wrapped in a filthy, once-beige greatcoat, lay sleeping on a ragged tarp laid under a tree. When Rhona and Ian approached, the combined smell of alcoholic fumes, unwashed clothing and neglected personal hygiene forced them to catch their breath.

"He's out of it," Ian said. "Doubt if he can tell us his own name, let alone who killed the men. Maybe we can talk to him later."

Rhona agreed, and they marched on. Not far from the man, they saw a woman with a red bandana covering her hair occupying a bench. She had spread her long, voluminous red skirt and positioned herself and a large flowered carpet bag featuring vivid pink peonies to make it impossible for anyone else to sit without asking her to move the bag. A tall, thin man of indeterminate age who had been talking to her slunk away before the two detectives reached the bench.

Knitting needles clicked and a purple scarf grew longer as they watched.

Rhona flashed her badge. "We're police officers, and we'd like to speak to both of you," she said to the man's departing back. If he heard, he didn't acknowledge Rhona's request but kept walking. Rhona thought about following but decided against it. Instead, she focused on the woman.

"We'd like to speak to you," she repeated.

"What about?" the woman answered in a heavily accented voice.

Might as well get to the point. "About the men who've been murdered in the neighbourhood," Rhona said.

"I know nothing," the woman said, swinging away from them and rummaging in the carpet bag.

"We aren't finished." Rhona moved to stand directly in front of her.

The woman continued to dig in the bag's depths.

"How often are you in the park?" Rhona persisted.

The woman mumbled something.

"I didn't hear you. What is your name?"

"Katerina," the woman shouted. "Police persecution. All the same. Czars, Communists, KGB—stinking rotten rats." At this, she raised her eyes. "Arrest me. Beat me. They did."

Rhona stepped back. "Madam, this is a murder investigation. We expect citizens to cooperate. We are not the KGB, we are ordinary Toronto citizens like you."

"They say that. Not true. Not true. I know what you do." Her eyes narrowed. She pressed herself back against the bench. "I know. You go after woman like me. Not criminals, not drug dealers, not Mafia. I know nothing." She sank back.

"Madam, if you are here in the park every day, you may have seen more than you think you have. We want to know who else is here regularly. Are there nurses or social workers who come to the park and help people?"

Katerina grabbed the half-finished scarf and pointed both needles at them. "Social workers—they try put me in home. To give me pills. I tell them—go to hell."

Clearly this woman wouldn't give them information,

although she likely could identify the park's regulars. Given the references to pills and social workers, Rhona categorized her as one of the many mentally ill people who drifted through the neighbourhood caught up in their delusions. Her references to the KGB told Rhona that the woman's experiences had given her a grudge against the world in general and police officers in particular. Maybe asking her what she did with the knitting would calm her down.

"That's a lovely scarf. Do you make many of them?" Rhona asked.

"Why tell you?" Katerina shrugged. "Yes. I make and give away. People need, and I give."

"They must be very happy to have them. Thanks for talking to us. If we come back, you'll remember that we are citizens just like you, won't you?" she said.

Katerina, whose needles flew again, said nothing.

Their approach to the pigeon feeders sent clacking crowds of birds heavenward and annoyed those scattering bread and seed on the ground. Neither the bird lovers nor anyone else frequenting the park offered anything like a lead.

"The daytime people aren't too helpful," Ian said. "We should come back at night."

"Definitely a park with a bipolar personality."

"Benign by day, dangerous at night," Ian added.

Few men hung around outside the Salvation Army hostel, and fewer still had anything to offer.

"Let's come back when there's a big crowd, just before they open the dining hall for dinner," Ian said.

"Good idea," Rhona agreed.

"Right now we've got time to visit Danson's apartment," Ian said as they drove toward the station.

"Yes, we need to figure out how his DNA got on the brush if the body isn't his. His apartment may tell us."

"Do we have time to eat?" Ian said. He added, "I'm always hungry. Always have been. My mother used to say I had a tapeworm." He patted his stomach. "Doesn't matter

108

how much I eat, I never gain."

Rhona envied his ability to chow down like a stevedore and remain rail-thin. She agonized over every morsel she put in her mouth and fought a constant battle to maintain a reasonable weight.

"The cafeteria's open. You can eat a revoltingly calorie-laden meal, and I'll have a salad."

Ian laughed. "Don't hold me responsible for my genetic makeup."

After a quick lunch, they set out for Danson's apartment. Inside his front hall, they absorbed the ambiance.

"Wasn't he tidy?" Ian said.

"Candace was right—the perp wasn't a mugger, or he would have been in here cleaning out the place before Danson hit the ground. I'd say we can remove robbery as a motive," Rhona responded.

They did a walk-through.

Ian opened the door of the second bedroom. "Fuck," he said.

Rhona peered into the room. "Jesus, I'm not admitting to anyone that we never asked if Danson lived alone. What the hell were we thinking? No wonder the DNA doesn't match."

"Well, his sister never mentioned anyone, and initially we didn't seriously think her brother might be the murdered man, did we?" Ian responded.

They looked at one another. Without a word being said, Rhona knew neither one would admit they'd missed asking the right questions.

"His sister was right, wasn't she? She'll be a happy camper, even if she doesn't know where he is," Ian said.

"Maybe, maybe not. Since the DNA originated here, maybe we can assume it belonged to this other guy, whoever he is. If he's dead and Danson's disappeared, where does that lead us?"

"With Danson in the frame as the killer?"

"Certainly a possibility. Let's find out who the other guy is."

"One second." Ian flipped up his hand, palm towards Rhona. "This is my first case in homicide. We have Candace's permission to search for info about Danson, but not about this guy. Is that okay?"

"A technicality. She gave us the keys."

"As long as we aren't compromising evidence," Ian said. "I've had enough experience, and so have you to know how important it is to go by the book when collecting evidence."

"Right now we're not after evidence, we're trying to identify the second man and see what connection he has to Danson. All straightforward and above board." Rhona raised her shoulders and spread her hands. "We don't even know if whoever lives in this room is a guy."

Ian opened the cupboard door and waved an arm at the contents. "Unless it's a cross-dressing woman, I think we can assume it's a male?" He left the door ajar and swung back to face Rhona. "I don't want to be a pain in the ass about this but hasn't the situation changed? Now that we know about Mr. X and can presume the DNA is his, shouldn't we get a warrant to search? His sister did provide the keys hoping we'd locate her brother. Now he's a 'person of interest'."

"Exactly right. We're even more anxious about finding him. In order to do that, we need to know all about his life," Rhona said. Was Ian going to be a nit-picker, a do-it-by-the-book kind of guy? It would be understandable—he didn't want to blot his copy book on his first case, but it would be tiresome.

Ian shifted from one foot to the other. "I'm not sure you're right. But if we do turn up something incriminating, we are out of here and back with a warrant." Ian's tone of voice told her there would be no question about this.

Moving away from the cupboard, Ian plucked the shaving kit from the bureau. He rifled through the contents. "Take a gander." He held up drug paraphernalia. "Maybe

110

it's the lead we're looking for. The identified dead men had a connection to the drug trade, didn't they?"

"True. Small-time users and no mutilation. Doesn't seem likely there was a link. We need to know why the guy's face was smashed and his fingers clipped. It's odd that our man left without his stuff. Maybe he didn't intend to be gone long. We should be able to get confirming DNA from something in there." Rhona tapped the shaving kit.

"Nothing with his name on it," Ian said.

"No. Let's try the computer."

But as Hollis had, they found they needed a password.

"It won't be a problem downtown," Ian said as he shut it down.

"His computer will provide information, but whether it's relevant, only time will tell," Rhona said. "While we're here, let's see what info we can root out about Danson and this other man. I'll do the bedroom, you take the living room."

In Danson's bedroom, she zeroed in on the cell phone plugged into its charger. She punched the keys, read the screen and called to Ian. "Candace phoned a number of times. We'll follow up on the phone book entries—see who he contacted frequently. I'd like to pull his cell phone and his regular phone bills—and take them along, but to be on the safe side and make you happy, we'll get a warrant." She left the phone and strode to the living room, where she tried Danson's computer but found once again that she needed a password. They'd take this machine as well as Gregory's to the techies.

Ian, bent over an open drawer in the filing cabinet, raised his head. "What about telling Candace her brother might not be the victim—it's cruel to leave her believing he's the dead man."

Rhona's phone rang. She snapped it open. "You're sure?" she said before she thanked the caller and snapped the phone shut.

Ian raised a quizzical eyebrow.

"The lab. The dental records don't match Danson Lafleur's."

"More good news for Candace," Ian said.

"If he was involved with the murdered man, it isn't good, but we'll allow her to enjoy the relief of knowing the body in the morgue isn't her brother. She won't be home from work. First, we'll case the Salvation Army dining hall. After dinner we'll drop in on Candace and share the good news."

"We'll also see what she knows about the roommate we didn't know existed."

"Without confessing that we should have asked if he had one," Rhona said with a grin.

Back in the car, they headed downtown to the mission. This time Rhona drove, even though her hip continued to hurt. She was glad police cars had automatic transmissions —cops had enough to think about without having to change gears. In city traffic, that wasn't much fun.

Her own car had manual—she'd chosen it because she loved shifting up and down, accelerating from zero to who knew what in minimum time. In her weaker moments, she pretended she was a race car driver and, when she was alone, made appropriate noises and commentary as she drove. She shook her head—sometimes when she thought about the things she enjoyed and those that amused her, she wondered if she wasn't suffering a severe case of continuing adolescence. "An overgrown kid—that's what I am."

"What did you say?" Ian asked.

Rhona realized she'd spoken aloud. "Just thinking that in many ways I haven't grown up. I enjoy the same things I did when I was seventeen."

"Like what?"

"Driving fast. Pretending I'm on a race track."

"I'll never admit I said this, but I still get excited when we turn on the siren and drive like crazy. It isn't cool, but I enjoy the adrenalin rush, knowing something serious is going down," Ian confessed.

Conspiratorial grins flashed between them.

Rhona could have double-parked outside the mission but chose to slot into a small space on Queen Street. They walked back to the Queen and Sherbourne intersection and waited for the light to change. She'd been right. A kaleidoscope of men formed and reformed outside the hostel.

Pausing gave them time to examine the crowd. What stories these homeless men could tell, from simple bad luck, lack of education to mental illness and drug and alcohol addiction. With a helping hand, a tiny minority climbed back to the working or middle class. These few were men with a sense of self-worth, who believed they had something to give, that they'd had a bad break. Others had no illusions. This would be their life until they died.

Rhona hated the laws that forced the mentally ill onto the streets, where they didn't take the meds that offered them hope for a more mainstream life. She knew the stinking, noisy tenements where they lived. The exploitation they endured. Vocal liberals screamed that no one should be forced to take medication or be kept in institutions. These poor souls had freedom of choice.

Big deal. She'd bet the majority of righteous liberals had never seen what their determination to defend individual liberties did to these helpless, unmoored souls. Enough. They were here to see what they could learn. These men, many of whom were addicted to drugs and alcohol, had to be unnerved by their peers' deaths.

They surveyed the crowd, now shuffling into a ragged line. Time to ask a few questions.

Rhona approached a clean-shaven young man. She'd bet he'd once been a carpenter or skilled tradesman. "Excuse me, we're looking for information."

The young man met her gaze. "Sure."

"What talk have you heard about the men who were murdered in the area? We're eager to know if there are rumours circulating about the killer?"

113

He shook his head. "Only been in Toronto a couple of days. Been up in Kirkland Lake looking for work. Can't help you." He edged forward then stopped. "A guy named Preacher Peter might tell you something—he knows everyone."

The next man in line was swathed in a dirty khaki military overcoat that was far too hot for the autumn evening. Matted grey hair straggled over the collar. He pushed a tattered hockey bag ahead of him with a worn-out boot. Rhona tapped him gently on the shoulder.

"Fuck off," he muttered without knowing who was behind him. Ian cut off a tiny man shambling toward the line and put his hand on the man's sleeve. "Excuse me, can you help us?"

He froze. "Cops," he said.

Ian didn't deny it. "Where can we locate Preacher Peter?"

"Don't know nuthin'," he said, shrugging off Ian's hand.

"This isn't productive," Ian said to Rhona. "Let's talk to someone on the staff."

"Okay. They hear about what's going on. Unfortunately, even though they have information, they don't always pass it on when they should. Protective instinct or something."

At the head of the line, the crowd surged forward, pressing those at the front against the door. Rhona refused to be squashed in the crush.

"Might as well let this mob go in before we try," she said over her shoulder.

The two stepped away from the steps to the sidewalk's edge.

"What a mess," Rhona said, surveying crumpled paper bags, cigarette butts, orange peels, candy wrappers—the flotsam and jetsam washed up by the tide of men who lived on the street.

"The smell of unwashed and malnourished bodies jammed together reminds me of my previous life. It's strange how smell triggers memories," Ian said.

Another clue and an interesting one. He'd given her an

opening. "Where were you before? What were you doing?" Rhona said.

Ian's expression told her he wished he hadn't made the remark. "Vancouver's lower east side," he said.

She'd try one more question. "Working?"

"Doing this and that."

His tone said "keep out", and Rhona respected this. Everyone harboured secrets they didn't care to share. Nevertheless she was curious.

The doors opened, and the human tsunami swept into the building. Once they were gone, Rhona and Ian followed.

A harried worker sitting behind the reception desk surveyed them. "Who do you want now?" he said in a tired voice. His thin brown hair pulled across his forehead, faded eyebrows and soft brown eyes belied his tart remark. One of the world's meek, he no doubt suffered frequent verbal abuse without complaint. In Rhona's opinion, workers and volunteers in hostels and soup kitchens deserved medals of honour.

"Bad time to come, but we need information about a guy named Preacher Peter who works in this neighbourhood. Can you describe him, tell us where we can find him and anything about him?"

"Preacher Peter." The man's lips tightened, and he drummed a finger on the scarred desk. "I can tell you lots. He doesn't have a last name, at least not that anyone knows." He sniffed. "I expect he's wanted for a dozen crimes. Probably extortion is the least of them."

Rhona cast a quick glance at Ian, who had the alert look of a bird dog ready to work.

"What does he do?"

"Preys on the weak, the gullible, the mentally deranged. Takes what money they have." He paused and almost hissed, "To pave their way to salvation." He stopped drumming, opened pudgy hands, spread them wide and leaned forward. "I myself heard him say that. More likely pave his own way to hell."

115

"Does he have an actual church?" Ian asked.

"A storefront just around the corner on Queen. However, he's out on the street most nights."

"How would we recognize him?" Rhona asked.

"Tall, thin, long nose, frightening eyes."

"Frightening?" Rhona felt her eyebrows rise.

The man nodded. "Some guys here have the same look. As if they see something you don't, and it's right there behind you. Mostly the mentally ill. I'd guess they see disembodied spectres that go with the voices they hear. Peter," he snorted, "I'm not going to dignify him with preacher, looks messianic. That appeals to some poor lost souls."

A rumble of agitated voices came from the dining hall. The man half-rose. "Sorry, got to go. They may need help." A malevolent smile, at odds with his meek demeanour, curved his lips. "I hope he's done something that you can charge him with."

Outside again, Ian took a deep breath, although downtown Toronto air didn't have much to recommend it.

Rhona didn't comment on his obvious relief to be outside and away from the crowd. "Let's walk west on Queen and search for Preacher Peter."

When they found the storefront, it was locked. A badly painted and spelled sign, "Salavation is for Everyone", graced one window and "Repent before the End" the other. Spelling wasn't one of Peter's strengths. Rhona wondered if anyone had pointed out to him that he was saying "drooling is for everyone."

A hand-printed sign on the door informed them that Preacher Peter would be present every afternoon from three to five and on the streets with "His People" every evening. Peering through the dirty glass, they saw folding metal chairs set in two rows, a chalkboard at the front beside a table covered with a white cloth and topped with a wooden cross. Bare bones for sure.

"What next?" asked Ian.

"We'll see the sister first. Then we'll come back and cruise around."

* * *

When Hollis piloted her battered truck into a small parking space half a block from Candace's house, she glanced up and saw two people marching toward the house. They reminded her of Mutt and Jeff, old fashioned comic strip characters, one very short and one very tall. She could have jockeyed the truck closer to the curb, but the need to learn what news the detective brought outweighed her urge to park more neatly. She left the vehicle stranded a foot from the curb.

She rushed to arrive at the front door of the building before Candace opened it for the two detectives. The four of them crowded into the front hall. Hollis moved to stand beside Candace.

"Well?" Candace said examining the officers' faces. She didn't invite them to move upstairs to her apartment.

"Good news," Rhona said without warmth.

Hollis noted that both officers eyed Candace speculatively. Something had altered dramatically since they'd last spoken to her.

Candace didn't notice the change. Her eyes widened as she processed the two important words. "It isn't Danson?" she whispered.

"It isn't. Why didn't you tell us he didn't live alone?" Rhona said.

A puzzled frown and a shrug. "I guess I never thought about it. Gregory only moved in a few weeks ago. I never met him and know nothing about him. I was so worried about Danson that Gregory dropped right off my radar. I should have put two and two together, but I didn't. I guess that's why it never occurred to me to tell you."

This had to be the explanation for the changed atmosphere,

117

she thought. "It's Gregory's DNA? He's the murdered man?" Hollis said.

"Seems likely," Rhona said. "What can you tell us about him?"

"Why don't we go upstairs and sit down in the living room?" Hollis said. It wasn't her house, but Candace, nurturing a small smile, wasn't listening.

Upstairs they chose seats. Rhona, her face reflecting physical discomfort, cautiously lowered herself into a chair.

Hollis, aware of Candace's continuing inattention, answered the question the detective had posed downstairs. "I read Danson's e-mails. Gregory contacted Danson, saying they'd been in a sociology class at Concordia and Danson's friend, George, had suggested that he speak to Danson about renting him a room in his apartment. But when I e-mailed George, he had no idea who Gregory was." She paused. "George promised to go to Concordia today and see if he could locate a class list for the Sociology course. I can run upstairs and see if he had any luck?"

Rhona waved Hollis on her way. Hollis took the steps two at a time. Inside her own apartment, she briefly patted MacTee, who'd rushed to the door with a battered tennis ball. She sat down and clicked on her e-mail. As she waited for the download, she wondered if Danson had murdered Gregory. If the detectives thought so, this explained their changed attitude.

George's response popped up. "Sorry. No info. Is there anything else I can do?"

She e-mailed a quick thank-you, saying she'd contact him if she thought he could help.

Three heads swivelled when she entered the room. "George couldn't find any info on Gregory." She slipped into the chair nearest the door. From here she could watch everyone.

The detectives perched on the sofa. Candace, back straight and hands folded in her lap, had picked one of two slingback IKEA chairs facing the two detectives.

118

Rhona, favouring her hip, winced as she leaned forward and addressed Candace. "We need to talk about your brother," she said.

Candace appeared to be paying attention although Hollis wouldn't have bet on it. The news that the DNA did not belong to Danson seemed to have unhinged her.

"Did Danson have a history of violence?" Ian asked.

"Violence?" Candace's eyebrows rose, and she looked from one detective to the other. "Violence?" she repeated as if she couldn't process the question's implications. "You think Danson had something to do with Gregory's death?" Her rising voice along with her widened eyes expressed her incredulity.

"It is a possibility, isn't it?" Ian asked.

"No, it isn't," Candace snapped. "It definitely isn't. Danson is a passionate man. He cares deeply about people. You have no idea how he protects our family. He's always worrying about us. He can be tough, single-minded even. He plays a rough game of lacrosse, but he would never, absolutely never, do what that man's killer did. Absolutely never." She crossed her arms and scowled. "Never!"

"Has he ever been in trouble with the police?" Rhona asked.

Candace shook her head. "Never. You're on the wrong track. I can see why you might think that he'd be involved, but he wouldn't ever kill anyone." She shivered. "I saw the body. He would never, ever do that to another human being."

Rhona pulled a notebook from her large black leather handbag. "We need to know everything about your brother. We need a recent photo—even better would be two different up-to-date ones. Before you go, tell us what he drove?"

Candace stared at Rhona. "Drove?"

"What make and model of car," Rhona said in the tone of voice she might have used to address a small and not-too-bright child.

"I don't know. I'm not into cars. It was a silver sports car,

119

"not expensive, and he leased it."

"Do you know the company he leased it from?"

Candace shook her head.

Rhona worked through a list of questions. Candace scrunched smaller and smaller, as if to protect herself from the barrage. She did not volunteer one iota of information. She did not tell them about Danson's passion for tracking returning criminals, about his murdered girl friend, about the newspaper article. She responded to each question Rhona asked but offered nothing else. Surely the detectives could see that she was deliberately not helping? Perhaps they attributed her reticence to shock, to her inability to picture her brother as a killer.

While Rhona posed the questions, Ian watched Candace. He reminded Hollis of a predator waiting to pounce on unsuspecting prey.

Finally, Rhona levered herself to her feet. "Please get the photos."

Hollis stood, bent over and offered Candace her hand. Candace's mouth opened. Her hands rose as if to defend herself. She clenched her fists.

Time to intervene. Hollis grasped Candace's hands in her own. "Photos. They need the photos," she said firmly.

While Candace went to search for photos, Hollis showed the detectives to the front door. They hovered.

"I didn't know which ones to bring, but here are two copies of three from this summer," Candace said extending the photos.

"We won't need the duplicates," Rhona said.

Candace handed three pictures to Ian, who held them up to catch the light from the wall sconce. He didn't comment but passed them to Rhona, who also examined them.

"I see the family resemblance," Rhona said.

Candace shook her head. "We aren't alike. He's tall and graceful like Poppy."

"Poppy?" Rhona said.

"My mother."

"We'll need to talk to her too. Does she live in Toronto?" Rhona said

Candace flipped a finger toward the stairs. "Right below me."

"How much does she know about the situation?" Rhona said.

Candace jammed her hands in the pockets of her dark grey slacks and rocked back on her heels. "Of course she knows he's missing, but I didn't tell her about the body in the morgue."

Rhona's eyebrows rose.

"Would *you*?" Candace demanded, her jaw jutting forward. "Would you tell your mother her only son had been murdered and mutilated unless you were absolutely sure it was true?" She paused as if waiting for an answer. When none came she said, "I think not. If you're a decent human being, you spare those you love."

Ian nodded.

"Poppy is involved in her own world, and she's great at denying unpleasant things," Candace continued. "Anyway, she's away. I'm sure by the time she's back, Danson will have returned and explained why he was gone."

This was a barefaced lie. Poppy and Alberto would leave tomorrow.

"I hope you're right," Rhona said. "Thanks for your help. Tomorrow we will have obtained an official search warrant for Danson's apartment. I know you gave us permission, but the situation has changed." She addressed Hollis. "It's a crime scene," she paused, "and it's absolutely out of bounds."

Once they'd left, the women returned to the living room. Before she sat down, Candace stopped and stared at the photos in her hand as if she could bring Danson back as he had been in the summer.

Hollis thought her friend might stand forever in the same position, locked in disbelief or wishful thinking.

"Sit down," she said as, hand under Candace's elbow, she shepherded her to her chair. Time to reclaim Candace from never-never land. No better way to do that than to talk of specifics, of work needing to be done. "We were serious before, now we have to redouble our efforts," Hollis said.

"I thought we were," Candace murmured, shuffling the photos and staring at each one.

"Not as a wanted man. The longer he's gone, the more likely it is the police will believe he killed Gregory."

Candace shook her head. "He never would have done that."

"You know that, but they don't. It's time to put our brains in gear and see what ideas we come up with. To use a tired cliché—think outside the box."

Candace pried herself away from her morose fascination with the photos. She ventured a half-smile. "Okay, I'm thinking."

"Where else could Danson have gone? Maybe a friend's cottage up north? Back to Montreal?" Hollis said.

"You e-mailed his friends. No one had heard that he was planning to go anywhere. He's a city person. It's late fall. Cottages are closed for the winter." She stopped. "You're saying he might hide where we are unlikely to look?"

"Right. We've explored the obvious answers. Now we have to take other paths."

Candace pursed her lips. "Cottage. Who do we know with a cottage?" She tapped the photos on her knee. "It would have to be an old-fashioned, seasonal one that didn't have an alarm system. Let me think."

Hollis allowed the silence to lengthen, glad that she'd drawn Candace into the search.

"He's been up to Emory Crabtree's family cottage on Lake of Bays. He told me it was an old-timer that they'd chosen to keep that way. I think it has a hand pump in the kitchen, and that's their source of water. A privy outside. Really primitive. Danson said it reminded him of the cottages in *Hansel and Gretel*."

"Sounds like a perfect place to hide out. What about this Emory Crabtree? Could we tell him we're wondering if Danson could be hiding out there?"

"Absolutely—he's a great guy. I'll do it this minute," Candace said leaping to her feet.

While she was on the phone, Hollis formulated more questions.

Candace returned, shoulders sagging. "Emory says they have workers repairing the dock—Danson wouldn't be there. Any more ideas?"

"What about Montreal? Might he go to ground there?"

"Who knows. E-mail George and see if he has any ideas?" Candace's voice reflected her discouragement.

Time to discuss the interview and discover why Candace had behaved as she had. "You didn't volunteer any information to the police," Hollis said.

Candace straightened, crossed her arms over her chest and leaned forward. "Let them do their own work," she said.

"You didn't even tell them about the link to Poppy and the newspaper item."

Candace's lower lip jutted forward. "No."

"I don't agree with keeping things that secret." How could she convince Candace that amateurs didn't have the resources, that not cooperating was a crime? "We should at least give the police the phone number in the article. When I tried it, I didn't get an answer, then I found that it was unlisted. They have the wherewithal to trace the number. That could give them a lead."

"I don't want them to have a lead. I want us to do it," Candace said. Eyes narrowed and lower lip thrust out, she resembled a sulky, obstinate ten-year-old.

Hollis squeezed her friend's shoulder. "Be realistic. We don't have the resources. We should tell them everything we know."

"No. I agree that we should, but not yet. Let's set a time

limit." Candace paused. "Let's give ourselves till the end of the week. We'll succeed. I know we will." Her eyes widened. "It's really important to get to him before the police do."

Hollis could see that Candace believed Danson might have been involved in Gregory's disappearance. No matter what argument she used, Candace wouldn't buy it. She wanted them to search. But it was wrong to withhold information, particularly if Danson had been involved.

"I don't know if I can continue the search unless we pass on the information," Hollis said.

"Not even until the end of the week?" Candace asked.

It wasn't very long. It went against Hollis's principles, but Candace looked so woebegone that she didn't have the heart to refuse.

"At the end of the week, we turn over everything to the police. Agreed?"

Candace nodded.

Hollis wondered whether to make the next remark but, if they were going to go on, she had to do it. "Have you considered that Danson has run away? That something, maybe Gregory's murder, scared him, made him think he would be the next victim?"

Candace straightened, lifted her gaze and ventured a tiny smile. "Victim—that's it. I was trying to think why he wouldn't have contacted me. That could be the reason. He's afraid whoever killed Gregory is after him. He wants to make sure there is no connection to Poppy, Elizabeth and me." Her tiny smile grew into a grin. "You've found the answer. He's protecting us."

"Maybe. It might also mean he's implicated and is on the run. Either way, it may be dangerous for us to continue the search."

Candace's smile faded. "You mean we should sit back and wait for him to contact us or for the police to locate him?"

Hollis nodded.

"You know what the police do to suspects, don't you?" Candace said.

"Bring them in for questioning and release them if they had nothing to do with the crime," Hollis said steadily and with conviction.

Candace glared at Hollis. "In a pig's eye. They twist the evidence to convict. Think about Steven Truscott, Guy Paul Morin and plenty of others. For all we know, hundreds of innocent people are rotting in jail. What happens if the person they're trying to apprehend runs or appears to reach for a weapon? They grab a taser gun or shoot him with a real gun. Afterwards, they claim they thought he was armed. No sir, I don't want that to happen to my brother." She reached forward, eyes locked with Hollis's and pointed at herself then at Hollis. "*We* are going to succeed."

Hollis admired Candace's determination, but being adamant wasn't giving them any leads. "Okay, okay, I get the message. The question is how, how are we going to do this?" she said.

Candace's shoulders slumped. "I don't know."

"Maybe our brains will hit on a solution while we sleep," Hollis said.

*   *   *

"What did we learn?" Rhona asked as they pulled away from Candace's house.

"We know what he looks like, what colour of car he drives and that the vehicle is missing. His car lease details should be in his apartment." Ian flipped his wrist to allow the streetlights to illuminate his watch.

"Flip on the car light," Rhona said.

"I can see. It's too late tonight to contact the companies. We'll get on it first thing," Ian said.

"I'd guess he's long gone to who knows where. We'll issue an APB. His sister wasn't exactly frank. She knew a lot more than she was saying," Rhona said.

"Right on. She answered our questions but didn't volunteer any information. Tomorrow we should also know what the techies uncover in the two computers. We'll have a lead to Gregory's identity and maybe know what links him to Danson."

"Now we locate Preacher Peter."

They parked on Carlton Street. Ian pointed to the brightly coloured Akenasis van positioned under a street light. A motley collections of souls waited beside it.

"They do a great job for the First Nations people, don't they?" Ian said.

Rhona assumed someone had told him she was part Cree. If not, this was the time for her to leap in and do so in case he harboured racist sentiments. It would be truly awkward if he made remarks he later had to apologize for.

"They do," Rhona agreed. "Because of my Cree heritage, I've considered volunteering at their drop-in street space. If I did, it might help the police image. Up to now I haven't done anything about it. The trouble with volunteering is you have to turn up regularly and with our schedules that's impossible."

Was she telling the truth? Was it possible she didn't want to associate with the down-and-out First Nations people who depended on the service. She hoped that wasn't the reason, but the worm of doubt twisting in her mind made her believe it might be. When this case ended, she'd face herself and her hesitation.

"You'd be a role model," Ian agreed.

Problem averted. Furtive movements deep in the park. Drug-dealing probably. Not their business tonight. Ahead, a swarm of people jostled and pushed.

"Something going down?" Ian asked as they strode forward and before they saw the truck dispensing free food.

Rhona's shoulders, which had been hunched around her ears, dropped to their regular position. Regular massages alleviated the knotted tension that accumulated in her shoulders, and she constantly ordered herself to relax, to deal with stress some other way. Not that it did much good, but she tried. Rhona tapped the arm of a man who'd snagged a snack and stepped away from the truck. "Have you seen Preacher Peter?" she asked.

Oversize jeans and a tattered T-shirt draped the tall body. Unshaven, with long hair that badly needed washing, the man sized her up. "Cops," he said. It was a statement, not a question. How did officers go undercover? Hollis didn't think she and Ian looked particularly different from others in the neighbourhood, but maybe they gave off a warning scent or stood a certain way. She'd like to ask this man, who didn't look unfriendly, how he'd known. She would.

"How can you tell?"

He shrugged. "Just can."

"We're looking for Preacher Pete."

"Saw him down outside Moss Park Arena half an hour ago. Collecting a flock. Creepy bastard." Conversation over, he swung away and unwrapped his sandwich.

Outside Moss Park Arena, young men lugging hockey bags and trailed by girls or family traipsed into the arena. The lively, healthy young crowd pouring into the building contrasted with the sad, sorry men loitering outside the mission across Sherbourne Street.

"He won't be at the hockey game. We'll walk west on Queen and see what we come across," Rhona said.

Minutes later they came upon a crowd forming in the open area behind the arena where the local dogwalkers let their animals run.

"Drugs or salvation?" Ian said.

"God offers you salvation. It's a brave man who turns him down," a hoarse voice exhorted.

A man elevated above the crowd was planted atop a white metal step-stool. His almost skeleton thinness and crown of curly white hair increased the impact of his height, as did his outspread arms. A silvery cloak over a gleaming white suit heightened the drama. His audience's nondescript dark clothing acted as a foil, and the overhead streetlight highlighted him as effectively as a spot light.

"Isn't that a presentation? He's like an archangel, isn't he?" Ian whispered.

Men and women pressed closer. Unlike the chatting, murmuring crowd at the food truck, these people's silence underlined their intensity. These were the believers.

Rhona and Ian, careful not to invade anyone's personal space, lingered on the fringe listening to Preacher Peter.

Ian folded down, placed his mouth close to her ear and whispered, "He does have crazy eyes."

Rhona, keeping her voice low, replied, "Scary, very scary. Let's move back."

They shifted away from the rapt audience, none of whom marked their passing.

"I don't think we can justify breaking this up to ask him questions when all we have is a cranky observation from the official at the shelter," Rhona said.

"He thinks the guy is a messianic charlatan, which is no doubt true. Let's wait a few minutes to see if Preacher Peter takes a break. Be ready to move in and tell him we'll talk to him at his office at ten tomorrow."

They edged into the rapt audience until they were close enough. When Preacher Peter grabbed a water bottle from one of his supporters, they delivered their message then backed quickly away.

"Enough for tonight," Rhona said as they headed back to the car.

"He's charismatic. Probably a charlatan but he may have insights about the murderer. He clearly moves with the masses. Maybe he's on a crusade to eliminate the slackers himself, the men who refuse to hear his message?" Ian said as he slid into the driver's seat.

Ten

On Wednesday morning, wind-whipped maple and oak trees showered the still-green grass with red, orange, yellow and brown leaves. The brilliant blue sky added contrast to the dazzling coloured shower. Exhilarated, Hollis burst from the house and drew in great breaths of air that sparkled and effervesced like nature's champagne. She and MacTee ran their usual route and returned for breakfast. Hollis prepared her usual blueberry and oatmeal breakfast. A creature of culinary habit, she loved the anticipation of a predictable meal. As she enjoyed her berry-laced cereal, the phone rang.

"I saw you come back. We're on our way out, but I thought you should know that I had another call at two this morning," Candace said.

"Tell me."

"'Are you looking for Danson or his body?' the guy whispered, then he gave this insane giggle. It was horrible. Whoever he is, he knows something," Candace said.

"Maybe, maybe not. As I said before, it may be some sadistic bastard who knows Danson's missing and gets his kicks out of tormenting you," Hollis said. "Did you call the police this time?"

"No."

"They could put a trace on your line. Candace, I really think it's time to turn everything over to the police."

"You promised," Candace said.

129

"I did, and I'll keep my promise, but the minute the time is up, we go to them," Hollis said. She hung up.

Minutes later, she heard Elizabeth in the downstairs hall.

"No day care. Stay with Tee," Elizabeth shrieked. "Stay home. Lizabet stay home."

A murmur. Candace had to be persuading Elizabeth that remaining at home was not an option. Elizabeth didn't protest again.

Then Hollis heard the front door slam. Had Elizabeth won? Was Candace about to enlist her and MacTee as babysitters? She stood up and walked to the window, expecting to see the Volvo parked at the curb. Instead she saw Alberto lugging Poppy's large, brightly-patterned suitcases to the curb where what must be his small black bag already sat. They were leaving for Vancouver. Alberto dropped the bags, stepped into the street and craned his neck, staring toward Yonge Street. Poppy said something to Alberto, who patted her shoulder. At that moment an airport limousine pulled up, and they climbed inside as the driver hoisted the luggage into the trunk.

How could Poppy leave Toronto knowing her son might be in terrible trouble? How could participation in a dance competition override maternal worry? A puzzling question. Given that Candace had not told Poppy that a body in the morgue might be Danson's, perhaps her lack of concern was understandable? Poppy knew he was missing but had avoided the terrifying emotional roller coast ride Candace had survived.

After the couple left, Hollis finished her cereal and settled down to work on her flock, to think about Danson and to decide what their next move should be.

No more than twenty minutes later, her buzzer rang. She wasn't expecting anyone and felt slightly uneasy as she raced downstairs.

"Yes," she said without opening the door to the front vestibule.

"Hi. Sorry to bother you. It's Jack Michaels."

Hollis opened the door.

"The toaster oven won't toast," he said abruptly.

"You'd like me to see if I can figure out why?" Hollis said. Jack nodded.

In the basement apartment, Hollis checked the oven.

"You have to set this dial to toast and use the timers," she said as she demonstrated. The machine's light lit up, and it hummed into action.

"I should have figured that out," Jack said.

Privately, Hollis agreed. Had this been a ploy to get her downstairs to his depressing subterranean lair? Why would he do that unless he simply wanted company? She'd do the neighbourly thing.

"I haven't finished my breakfast coffee. Would you like a cup?" Hollis offered.

"I would, thanks," Jack said.

Upstairs, after Jack had survived MacTee's rush to greet and present him with a well-chewed toy, she invited him to sit down, poured two mugs, offered cream and sugar and sat down.

"How's your job search going?" she asked.

Jack stared at her as if she'd asked him a question in ancient Urdu. "My job search," he repeated. "Sorry, I was thinking about something else. I start at the Tim Hortons coffee shop near here on Yonge Street next week. They know about my lacrosse and will work out the shifts." He lifted his mug. "I'll smell fresh coffee and baking bread every shift—probably gain ten pounds from inhaling."

"Glad you found an accommodating employer. Any luck on the housing front?"

"No. I haven't done any more than go online. Really depressing how much everything costs. Since I got a job near here, I'd like to live in this area. Lots of apartment buildings but all pretty expensive."

"Starting over in a new city is difficult."

131

Jack nodded and leaned forward. "I saw the police car here last night. What happened? Have they found Danson?"

So, the toaster oven had been a ploy to extract information. No doubt the whole lacrosse community wanted to know what had happened to Danson, but Hollis wasn't about to share the man in the morgue story. "No."

"Really weird the way he just went. Not like him, was it?" Jack said. He added more milk to his coffee. "You're friends with his sister, aren't you?"

Hollis nodded.

"She must have an idea what happened to him. Does she know much about his life? "

"Candace sees him often."

"It's the beginning of lacrosse season, and it's totally weird that Danson would go away when it's starting."

Maybe she could turn the tables and pick Jack's brains about Danson's life. "It does. What do his teammates think about the situation?"

Jack swallowed a swig of coffee and shrugged. "I'm new. Most of them have played together before."

What did being new have to do with anything? "They must talk in the locker room," she persisted.

"Everyone has a different theory. Some think he's in serious trouble and has run away. Others think it's a woman and he'll be back. Most have no idea. They say they don't care why he's gone, but they wish he'd get back," Jack said. "I don't know any more. To change the subject, did I see the lady on the first floor leave this morning?"

Did this young man do nothing but stare out the window? "You did. She and her partner went to Vancouver for a big dance show."

"I didn't know people as old as them did that," Jack said.

Tactful lad, but at Jack's age anyone over twenty-five was ancient. Well-preserved though she might be, Poppy would seem decrepit to Jack.

"Well, they do."

"I guess that's a specialized world, like lacrosse. Not many people know about lacrosse."

"You're right. The whole world must be filled with people with passions that consume them but are little-known to their fellow citizens. There's a shop on Mt. Pleasant. . ." How would he know where that was when he came from Montreal? "That's a shopping street that runs parallel to Yonge Street. George's Trains, a store devoted to model railroaders, has been there for decades. I went in once. There's an amazing board there. I don't know if you know, but I certainly didn't that they have conventions everywhere in North America. The devotees are totally passionate about their trains," Hollis said.

"There are collectors of almost anything you can name. Old hockey cards—you wouldn't believe what they're worth," Jack said.

"On a smaller scale, things like stamps fetch millions at auction," Hollis said thinking of her mysterious conversation with Poppy and the strange notice in the paper. "What it is that makes people want to collect? It's not a gene I possess. It's difficult for me to imagine the time and money collectors devote to acquiring their treasures." Hollis smiled at Jack. "What about you?"

Jack shook his head. "Not me." His gaze rested on the half-made chicken flock. "I bet people buy one of those and then want to collect them. They're neat."

"You're right, they do. After I finish the chickens, I'm making a bulldog for Elizabeth, the little girl downstairs."

"She's cute, I bet she'll like it," Jack said. "I'd better go. Thanks for the coffee."

What had Jack really wanted to know? Hollis puzzled over his comments and questions and dismissed him as a nosy young man who lived in the house of a missing person and wanted to know where he'd gone.

But now it was time to finish the chickens.

Even throwing herself into a task she enjoyed didn't take her mind off of Danson. What else could they do?

If she'd been in a silent movie film, she would have clapped her hand to her forehead when the eureka moment occurred. How could she have forgotten the sheet of paper she'd found in Gregory's book?

Where to go to for a translation? Someone at Balalaika, the long-established Russian restaurant on College Street, would have a person who could do it. Even as she thought about it, she remembered the movie *Eastern Promises*. It had been about the Russian mob in the UK. The chief villain had been the charming proprietor of a well-established Russian restaurant. In that movie, the heroine needed to have a dead girl's diary translated and took it to the restaurant owner. Because of her eastern European background, she knew the Russian Mafia operated in London, but it never occurred to her that the genial restaurateur would be part of the mob.

This was Toronto, not London, but maybe she wouldn't go to the Balalaika. Where else could she go? The University of Toronto, Ryerson or York must have linguistics departments. Surely their professors would be above board.

She booted up her computer. Online she discovered Slavic Studies departments in all three universities. Not that familiar with the city, she located a city map in her backpack, unfolded and spread it on the kitchen counter. York was north and west of the city centre, far from the last subway stop. She could drive there, but why do that when both the University of Toronto and Ryerson were subway rides away? To park anywhere downtown was not only difficult but hideously expensive. Before she could change her mind, she called U of T.

"We often get requests like that," a sympathetic receptionist responded when she'd explained the situation. "Come in this afternoon. Professor Andrnovich has a class at one and a tutorial at four. He should be in his office by two thirty. I'll tell him you're coming."

What would the paper say? Would it give her another lead?

*   *   *

Wednesday morning. Rhona wandered into her kitchen and appeased her sullen cat, Opie, with treats before she prepared for the day. She chose a charcoal pantsuit and black cowboy boots with red trim, slapped on a modicum of makeup, grabbed a black car coat as the weather woman promised a chilly wind, and this was the day they interviewed Preacher Peter.

Homicide hummed with activity, and Ian already sat ensconced behind the usual pile of paperwork.

"Ready for the good preacher?" Ian asked. "I ran his name through the computer, but nothing came up. If I'd used fingerprints, I'd likely have found a file."

"Too true," Rhona agreed as she readied herself for work. "I don't suppose knowing his background is important just yet. We'll see how he responds to our questions. I can't think of any reason he'd murder the men, but you never know and he fits the bill."

"How's that?" Ian leaned back, ready for a discussion.

"Men would trust him. Whoever did the killing was known to and not feared by the victims. If he's messianic, he may believe he's on a mission to recover lost souls and eliminate those unwilling to follow his path." The theory sounded good to Rhona.

"That's not so far-fetched. Thousands of people have lost their lives in the name of religion," Ian agreed.

After more than an hour's desk work, they drove to Preacher Peter's storefront operation.

The wind, scuttling a downtown city street's trash against the shabby storefronts, added to the dishevelled rundown air. The harsh morning sun highlighted flaking paint, peeling posters, and dirt on Queen Street's premises. Tired and dispirited, the street awaited the white painters. When the bell over the door tinkled to announce their arrival, Peter emerged from the back room.

"Right on time," he said. "What can I do to help?" While his words indicated his willingness to cooperate, his hooded eyes, hands folded over his chest and his stiff posture told a different story. He didn't ask them to sit down.

Throughout her career, Rhona had learned to compensate for her stature. She wasn't about to allow this human skyscraper to loom over her. "Please sit down," she said, indicating the row of chairs.

Peter didn't move.

Rhona waited. "Perhaps we should conduct this interview at the station?" she said conversationally.

"That won't be necessary," he said and sat, carefully positioning himself with his back to the sun streaming through the dirty glass storefront windows.

Rhona remained on her feet, moved to minimize the light's effect and dug out her notebook. Ian too continued to stand.

"Now, for the record, what is your legal name?" she began.

"What difference does that make? I thought you wanted to ask me questions about my congregation."

"We need to know something about you as well," Ian said.

A long pause. Rhona realized, as surely as if he'd spelled it out, that this was a man with a record. His nickname hadn't checked out, but his fingerprints surely would. She'd bet money on it.

"Peter Graves."

"How long have you run this storefront operation?" Rhona didn't call it a church.

"About a year."

"And before that?" Ian said.

"I was in..." a pause, "Montreal."

Archambault prison perhaps.

"We're investigating the men murdered in this neighbourhood. Since you're out proselytizing every night, you may have seen or heard something that would help us," Ian said.

Again Ian had used a word she wouldn't have expected. Apparently Peter hadn't either, for he blinked at "proselytizing". But he'd understood the rest of the question and gave a good imitation of a man reflecting seriously.

"I talk to many troubled souls trying to bring them to Christ," he said in the deep and sonorous tones they'd heard the night before. "Trying to help them find their way out of their sinful lives into the light and blessing of the Lord's grace and forgiveness." He eyed them to see how his spiel was being received.

"I'm sure you do, but that isn't what we're asking," Rhona said.

"I wish I could help, but even if someone had confided in me, I wouldn't be free to share that information with you. Professionally, what a minister hears is confidential."

"A minister," Rhona said drawing out the word. "Tell us what denomination you belong to and where you were ordained?"

Peter's chin rose. He contemplated them as if to take their measure as adversaries. "My calling was personal and direct," he stated flatly.

"In that case, there is no clerical privilege. You are an ordinary man like other men and are required to share any information you may have," Ian said.

Peter's eyelids lifted. He produced a wide-eyed guileless stare and sighed, "I know nothing about the murders. No one has told me anything that might be useful to you."

Checkmate. Probably a matter of principle not to tell the police anything. They would have done better not antagonizing him. How to regroup and enlist his help— that was the question. Time to try.

"I can see that even if you had heard something, you wouldn't want to share it if someone had spoken in confidence. We've heard that you have a real connection to your flock, that you empathize with them," Rhona paused. Empathize had not been the right word. "Are you familiar with the details of the crimes?"

"As much as anyone sees on TV," he said, his voice noncommittal.

Rhona leaned toward him and lowered her voice. She wanted him to feel he was privy to inside information. "Not one of the victims put up a fight. This is remarkable, isn't it?"

Preacher Peter unconsciously mimicked her forward-leaning stance and lowered his voice. "It is. I didn't know that."

"What do you think it means?" Rhona continued.

The tall man rocked back and raised his eyes to the ceiling, perhaps hoping for heavenly inspiration. "Whoever committed these terrible crimes knew the men, and they knew the killer. It was someone they trusted or didn't fear."

Rhona too leaned back and smiled at him. "Exactly right. You know this community well. What sort of person would that be?"

Head cocked to one side, hands clasped in front of him, Preacher Peter said, "A social worker, a church volunteer—someone who helps in the community. I can't think of anyone in particular, but," he stopped and his gaze moved from Rhona to Ian and back, "the men in my mission are frightened. Some have chosen God and prayer to save them from this murderer. I would like to be able to tell them that I am helping. I will ask for their help."

"You will contact us if anyone tells you anything or even says they're suspicious of a particular person?" Ian said, handing him a card as they prepared to leave.

"That was useless," he said as they walked along Queen Street.

Rhona pulled her coat close, glad that she'd brought it.

The chill wind reminded her of winter's approach. "We'll see. There's no doubt he's a fraud, but since we stopped asking him about his background and gave him another reason to look good in the eyes of his congregation, he might help. Meanwhile, we won't write him out of the script."

Earlier that morning, Rhona had supplied the provincial police force with Danson's name and the license number she'd obtained from the leasing firm. They had found the info about the car in the apartment. Back at her desk in the overcrowded homicide department, an OPP memo awaited her. She showed it to Ian. "The OPP's answer," she said.

"That was fast. What does it say?" Ian said.

Rhona scanned the report. "Two days ago, the parking attendant in a Niagara Falls hotel worried about a silver Camaro parked in the garage for almost two weeks. When he called the hotel front desk he found that no one had cited that license plate when registering. The manager phoned the police and provided the vehicle's license plate number." Rhona waved the paper. "Even more odd, when the police arrived, they found the car unlocked. A parking ticket marked Monday night, a ring of keys and Danson's wallet were in the glove compartment."

"Strange," Ian said.

"Moreover, there was no luggage in the car."

"Raises interesting questions, doesn't it? Did Danson flip across the border and melt away into the good old US of A?" Ian ticked the fingers of his left hand with his right index finger. "Since we hadn't issued an APB, he wouldn't have had a problem getting across." He lowered his hand, frowned and made a notation on the pad in front of him. "Is his passport in his apartment? Since his ID was in the glove compartment, he couldn't have crossed without a passport. If he did, why did he leave his wallet and ID?"

"Maybe he had documents for a new identity," Rhona said.

"Could he have rendezvoused with someone and taken on a new persona?" Ian said.

"We could also hypothesize that he threw himself over the falls, couldn't we?" Rhona said.

"Or did he leave the wallet and the keys as red herrings designed to mislead?"

"Wouldn't that be a stupid thing to do? Wouldn't it lead us to ask the very questions we're asking?" Rhona said.

"It's a puzzle, isn't it?" Ian tidied the papers in front of him. "Should we call his sister and tell her?"

"First, let's interview the hotel staff, scrutinize his wallet's contents, and see what keys he left behind." Rhona glanced at the clock. "Less than two hours to Niagara Falls. I'll okay it with the boss, and we'll cruise over." She eased to her feet—favouring her hip. "Before we go, I'll see if the Niagara Falls police or the OPP have fished any unidentified bodies from the river in the last two weeks."

"I'll make copies of Danson's photos," Ian said.

Leaving Toronto on the Queen Elizabeth Way, they veered left outside Burlington, arced over the Burlington Skyway and drove towards Niagara Falls. White-capped Lake Ontario lay on their left and an undulating line of almost continuous subdivision snaked along on the right. Ian waved at an expanse of raw bulldozed land staked out for a new one. "When I was a kid my family had a spring tradition of driving to the falls and enjoying the blossoms. In those days, the developers hadn't gobbled up acres and acres of prime agricultural land. There were miles and miles of orchards and vineyards. I can still hear my mom oohing and ahing and making my father stop several times for us to pile out and inhale the wonderful smells. Can you imagine brilliant sunshine and warm air saturated with perfume? I've never forgotten it." He sighed. "And now? All that beauty and wonder replaced with cookie-cutter housing. Why did we accept this," he waved again, "as progress?"

"People have to live somewhere," Rhona said.

"Maybe, but whoever allowed those greedy developers to do this should be held responsible? Maybe thrown in jail?" He laughed. "Maybe that's extreme, but it was beautiful."

"I never saw the blossoms, but the end products, the peaches and pears, were good too," Rhona said. "It isn't all gone. Still many wineries around here. Some of the world's best wine comes from Niagara."

"It won't last long," Ian said gloomily. "The developers will buy the land."

"I hope not," Rhona said. They negotiated their way through the town of Niagara Falls and located the hotel without difficulty. Rhona showed Danson's picture to the young man at Sunny Crest hotel's front desk. His name tag identified him as Brian.

"Do you remember checking this man in on Sunday evening two weeks ago?" she asked.

"I don't, because I wasn't on duty. If you leave the picture, I'll make sure the other front desk staff see it," the young man said. As he spoke, his prominent Adam's apple shot up and down and his head bobbed. He gave the impression he was eager to be helpful and excited to have an interruption in the day's tedium. "If he registered, especially if he was alone, Jenny or Corinne would remember him," he said. "They're both single," he confided, "and they notice the single guys, although you can't always tell these days."

Other than looking for a wedding ring, it was hard to imagine how the girls separated single from married. Certainly Rhona didn't find it easy. Never mind, she felt sure that Brian would do his best to determine if Danson had registered.

"How far away are the falls?" she asked.

"An easy ten minute walk. That's one reason people like to stay here. Enjoy," he chirped as they left.

Outside the hotel, listening to the distant thrum as thousands of tons of water crashed over the drop, Rhona felt deeply disturbed by her reaction to the fall's pull. If she stood above it, she knew she'd have to fight a compulsion to throw herself into the turbulent water. "Could have been a suicide," she said "Even though the police forces don't have any unidentified DOA's at the moment, they don't always find jumpers' bodies. I suppose they get trapped under water in the rocks at the bottom."

At the nearby police station, they introduced themselves, and the front desk clerk smiled at them. "We've been expecting you." She buzzed them in and made a call. "A constable will be here in a minute to take you to the evidence room."

Once there, they pulled on gloves and slid Danson's wallet and keys from the evidence bag. Ian opened the wallet and sorted through the contents. "Driver's license, Visa, health insurance card—everything you'd expect," he said.

Rhona nodded. She'd picked up the keys. "Do these seem too new and shiny to you?" she said to Ian.

Ian examined the proffered keys. "The car key's metal is dull."

"Agreed, but the others should be somewhat worn, and they aren't." Rhona addressed the constable. "We'd like to sign this stuff out."

The young man didn't argue but opened drawers until he found the right form.

While he did this, Rhona jingled the keys. Once they had the evidence, she thanked the officer and they headed toward the car. Ian drove.

After she'd arranged herself to minimize pressure on her hip, Rhona spoke. "I want the sister to examine these keys." She rummaged in her bag and pulled our her cell phone. "I'll call and tell her we're coming to see her tonight." She shifted, searching for an even more comfortable position. "Although if she reacts to our news the way she did the last time we told her something, we may not be able to get much useful information."

Ian, flashing his lights at a car hogging the passing lane and driving well below the speed limit, took a moment to respond. "Don't you think she reacted that way because of the joy she felt that it wasn't her brother's DNA?"

"True, and also because we implied he might have been involved in the tenant's death. But this situation will upset her too. When we break the bad news, she'll be as shocked as she was before and maybe just as unable to…"

Ian, passing the plodder, who'd finally moved aside, interrupted, "Can we really say it's bad news?"

"True. I'm jumping the gun. All we know for sure is that we've found his car and his possessions. Telling her that will raise unpleasant questions, which she may or may not want to face. Once that's over, we'll ask her if she can identify the keys."

"Who's Gregory? That's the big question. Since we found the brush with DNA in Danson's apartment, it must be Gregory's corpse. As his sister says—it could be totally innocuous—Danson could simply have rented a room to a friend of a friend. We'll have to keep an open mind until we know more about Gregory X."

"On the other hand, maybe Danson has disappeared because of the connection," Rhona said. It seemed like the more likely of the two scenarios. "Gregory's computer should tell us something."

Back in Toronto, Rhona hotfooted it to the lab. The computer specialist, whose down-turned lips and hostile eyes reflected his long-term dissatisfaction with life, mumbled an acknowledgment of her arrival.

"Any ID from the computer?" Rhona asked.

"Really busy here. Haven't had time to really try," the man said.

"This is a priority case," Rhona snapped. "I don't want to pull rank, but it's exceedingly important we get into that computer. Make time. Get back to me when you've found the answers," she said, pivoting on the heels of her cowboy boots without giving him a chance to reply. Had he been slow because she was a woman and he had issues with female police officers, or did he respond to everyone the same way?

"He hasn't done it yet," she reported to Ian.

"What's his problem?"

"He's good at what he does, but he's a slacker with a bad attitude. If we don't have the info by tomorrow, we'll haul in the heavy guns." Rhona glanced up. "Five o'clock. Time we had something to eat. Candace expects us at eight."

Eleven

Hollis located the Slavic Studies department and introduced herself to the receptionist.

"Professor Andronovich expects you," the woman said, gave directions and sent her on her way.

Invited to enter, Hollis stepped inside Professor Andrinovich's office.

A tall young man stood up at she entered. His sandy hair, beard and dark eyes reminded her of a cuddly Teddy Bear, and his warm smile added to the impression. It made her want to know him, to find out what made him tick, why he'd chosen linguistics. One step inside the room, and he'd enchanted her. This was ridiculous, she told herself.

"I understand you have a mysterious missive for me to translate," he said. His deep, warm voice matched his appearance. Legions of female students must have fancied themselves in love with this man. He'd captivated her in a few seconds. She couldn't imagine how you could sit in a classroom without fantasizing about him. But she was being silly. No doubt he was happily married to another professional—a physician or teacher—and had a mob of curly-haired offspring.

"Thank you for doing this," Hollis said and proffered the paper.

Professor Andronovich waved her to a grey, molded-plastic chair facing his desk and settled himself in a state-of-the art ergonomic model. He anchored the paper with large, competent-looking hands and read.

She'd always loved men with generous, workmanlike hands. Hollis dragged her eyes away from him and glanced around the room.

Bookshelves crammed to overflowing filled the walls. Framed diplomas hung one above the other on the one space not occupied by shelving. Piles of books and papers threatened to collapse a flimsy table set in front of the window. It curved in the centre, as if the weight was too much to bear. It was such a typical academic's office, it was a cliché.

"Where did this come from?" Professor Andronovich demanded. A frown had replaced his smile.

"Why?"

"It's a serious, even a frightening, letter. Tell me about it."

"Serious? What does it say?"

"First, I need to know who you are and how you obtained this paper."

No help for it. "I'm a painter, recently moved from Ottawa. I found this in a book."

"In a book." He sat back. "That is an enigmatic remark meant to mislead me. What book? What does this letter have to do with you?"

Anxiety and alarm jolted through her. She didn't want to confess that Gregory, the owner, might be dead or that the police suspected that her friend's brother, who had disappeared, had murdered Gregory.

"It was in a book belonging to a friend of a friend, and we're worried about…" she paused. Maybe better not to say they were afraid for him. "…about what it may mean."

Professor Andronovich pulled a pad of legal-length, yellow-lined paper from his desk drawer. "Although I will write you a translation, your explanation is fuzzy to say the least. I'd like to know exactly where this came from."

Should she tell him? No, she shouldn't. Candace would not want the professor or anyone else to hear that there was a possibility that her beloved brother might be a killer. While

Candace desperately wanted to know Danson's fate, she wouldn't want the message shared with anyone but the police.

"When I see what it says, I'll know if I should tell you or anyone else," Hollis said. A stalemate.

The professor considered her thoughtfully before he bent his head over the paper, scribbling away and pausing occasionally to reread what he'd written. Finally, saying nothing, he passed the pad to Hollis.

She read the message.

> *I cannot overstate how vital your job is. It is a critically important assignment.*
>
> *Memorize the contents and destroy this letter.*
>
> *1. The plan's success rests on anonymity. I cannot emphasize this enough.*
>
> *2. Not only must you find out 'who' and 'what' he has, you also must make sure all information is destroyed, along with the investigator.*
>
> *3. It must appear to be an accident. There must be no police investigation.*
>
> *4 Five and Seven must be protected at any cost. The others are expendable, but Five and Seven are not.*
>
> *5. Do whatever you judge to be necessary.*
>
> *You have done this before and always very well, but we feel you may have lost your edge after the unfortunate Super Bug incident. Put that behind you. Focus on the task at hand.*
>
> *Do not fail us.*

She sorted through the words. The investigator must be Danson. Why else would Gregory be in his house? And Danson had disappeared. Had Gregory accomplished his mission? Why hadn't he destroyed the note? Had something happened to him before he was able to memorize it? She still didn't know his surname.

Super Bug—that might provide a lead. She realized the professor was speaking to her.

"I'm sorry. I didn't hear what you said."

"I asked if you planned to tell me what this is about and where you found this paper?" Professor Andronovich said.

"No," Hollis sighed. "I can't. It's complicated. Thank you for translating it for me." She stood up and reached for the original.

"You're meddling in dangerous matters. If it didn't sound wildly improbable, I'd say that this," he flapped the paper, "is a directive from unknown person A to unknown person B to do two things: to kill someone and to protect the identity of at least two or more other people." He too rose. "If that's the case, I hope you'll contact the police immediately." He examined her face and must have concluded he needed to say more. "I'm assuming, and it may be a false assumption, that you aren't one of the bad guys. If that's true, I have to advise you that whatever mess you're in, get out now. This could be very dangerous."

It touched her that he would be so concerned about an unknown woman who'd wandered into his office with a mysterious paper.

"Thank you for the warning and for caring. I'm sure it's nothing as serious as that. I promise to go to the police if I think there's any danger."

Professor Andronovich reached into his desk drawer, extracted a business card and extended it. Before Hollis could take the card, he said, "You look anxious. I have an hour and a half before my next tutorial. Would you like a coffee?"

Now that was a surprise, a pleasant one. "I'd love a coffee," Hollis said, accepting the card.

In the cafeteria, they collected thick white china mugs filled to the brim with steaming coffee before they found an unoccupied and relatively clean table. After small talk about the university and its growth, the professor leaned toward her.

"Why don't you call me Willem and tell me about yourself," Profess Andronovich said. He placed his elbows on the table and waited.

Willem. It had a lovely sound and matched his expressive, concerned face. "That's an open-ended invitation. I will if you agree to reciprocate."

"Agreed," he said and sat back. One hand toyed with his cup, the other rested on the table.

"First, tell me why your name is Willem—isn't that Dutch?"

"Good diversionary move. Long story, but one of my ancestors fleeing the Russian revolution ended up in Holland and married a Dutch girl. Ever since, we've had Willems in every generation."

This was an opportunity for a segue to uncover more personal data. "Do you have a Willem?"

A faint grin on his face told her he realized what she really wanted to know.

"Not a Willem, and not a wife, so, for the moment, there's no prospect for this generation unless my sister chooses to be a single parent and have a male child."

Caught out, she knew she should feel embarrassed. Instead she felt a surge of pleasure. He was single. Inside, she laughed at herself. Half-an-hour after meeting him, and she wanted more. Time to keep her end of the bargain and provide a synopsis of her life. Carefully, she omitted saying where she lived or mentioning Candace or her family. She did share the leap she'd taken when she decided to try to make it as an artist.

"Brave move." He paused. "We may be birds of a feather."

Now that was a happy thought. Didn't birds of a feather flock together?

"I'm restless too. I may go to law school."

Hollis felt her eyebrows rise.

"You're surprised. You should have heard my parents." He grinned. "To quote them, 'After the years you spent in school, why would your give it up when you have tenure and a secure future?'" His smile faded. "I understand. They've worked hard for everything. Typical immigrant story. They pinned their hopes for the future on me. My sister too, but for them a successful son was the be-all and end-all. To witness me tossing aside my professorship will be incredibly difficult for them."

"How did you explain yourself?"

"I gave them the 'greater good' speech."

Willem intrigued her more with each word he uttered. She watched expressions flit across his face. The love he felt for his parents was evident.

"What is the greater good speech?"

"That when I died, I wanted to believe I'd contributed to making the world a better place. I'd have a much better chance to do that as a lawyer than I ever could as a linguistics professor."

"I don't see the connection."

"Nor did they."

"Most lawyers that I know want to do something quite different. I have to say, the general opinion is that many lawyers are scuzz bags. What kind of law would you practice?"

"There's a huge need in the immigrant community. Most lawyers who defend Russian immigrants don't speak Russian, and they're forced to use translators. Those they hire don't always get it right."

"How do you know?'

He pointed out the window. "We're not far from the courts in old city hall. I work there part-time as a translator. Many Russians have court-appointed lawyers, and they aren't well defended."

A chill spiralled up her spine. Had she chosen the wrong person? Would she have been better off to have gone to the Balalaika? She'd entrusted the paper to a man who frequented the courts and believed accused Russians deserved better lawyers. Could the Russian mob be supporting his bid to return to law school? Thank goodness she hadn't told him the paper's background. She wished she hadn't revealed so much about herself. This wasn't the moment to let him know his confession had alerted her to the possibility that he might be on the other side, whatever that was.

"Will you do it, or is it a pipe dream?" she said.

"There's nothing to stop me. I'm not in debt, not married and not too old. No reason not to do it."

"Convincing arguments. What did they say?"

Willem shook his head. "You don't want to know. Let's just say they weren't happy. They like having a son who's Herr Doktor Professor." He grinned. "The only thing they would accept as a valid reason to change careers would be a decision to become a real, a medical, doctor."

"That isn't likely to happen?"

Willem threw his head back and laughed a deep, contagious laugh.

Before he could enchant her further, she pulled her jacket from the back of the chair and stood up. In an instant he was behind her ready to help.

Jacket on and belongings collected, Hollis held out her hand. "Thank you for your help."

"I'd like to see you again, but I don't know how to reach you." He paused. "Your expression tells me the feeling isn't mutual."

Having someone read you accurately was disconcerting. Although his references to his court work had alarmed her, she did find him attractive and would like to go out with him.

"My life is…" she searched for an appropriate word and found one she'd used before, "complicated." She dug in her handbag and extracted an old business card with her Ottawa address. "This is out-of-date, but my cellphone number is the same," she said and gave it to him.

"I accept that. Will you call me if you need anything else translated or need any help?"

She nodded.

"You do know that there are thousands and thousands of Russians in Toronto, and the Russian Mafia is also here?" he asked.

Again she nodded.

"They are not a force to be trifled with. Amateurs should stay out," he said.

"How do you know?" she asked.

"I have many connections in the community. Believe me, I know," he said. "From your reaction or rather your lack of reaction, I think you know something about this message. I'm concerned. You shouldn't try to solve this puzzle, whatever it is, by yourself. Go to the police."

Although she thanked him again, she made no promises. If she'd inadvertently walked into a hornet's nest, she'd have to do her best to avoid trouble. One way would be not to tell him any more and not to see him again. On the way home, she reviewed what she had told him. At least she hadn't said where she lived and hadn't mentioned any members of the Lafleur family.

Before going home, she pulled into the Loblaws parking lot on St. Clair Avenue and rushed inside to load a cart with easily prepared food she could share with Candace and Elizabeth. She'd remembered her carry bags, proudly refused plastic and helped the clerk pile frozen pizza, lasagna, macaroni and cheese, along with several desserts and salad bags into the black cotton bags. This stock should provide a few meals.

She and Candace, holding Elizabeth's hand, arrived at the house simultaneously.

Elizabeth brandished a drawing. "Tee," she said proudly.

"She painted a portrait of MacTee," Candace explained.

Hollis bent down and examined the wild scribbles. "Terrific," she said to Elizabeth and peered up at Candace. "I bought a ton of quick and easy food. Let me bring dinner down."

Candace nodded. "That would be very welcome." She ruffled Elizabeth's hair. "The detectives are coming tonight at eight. I was out of the office, and they left a message. I hope it's good news, but I'm not optimistic."

Should she share the contents of the note that Willem had translated before or after the police came? Maybe after. If Danson was a suspect, this note could be damning. She wouldn't keep it back forever. That would be tampering with evidence. However, she'd wait until she heard what they had to say.

Upstairs, she collected MacTee, and they walked through the neighbourhood meeting and greeting other dog-owners out for an after-work walk, along with children returning from school and day care and men and women straggling home from the office. Toronto, at least in this neighbourhood, was a walking city. Although it was November and the shadows were long as the days shortened, it remained relatively warm. Pedestrians trotted along with jackets half-zipped, savouring the mild late afternoon. MacTee, always friendly, allowed her to talk to his many admirers. It was a welcome respite from the tensions of Candace's home.

Back from the walk, she prepared a salad, microwaved the pizza, set both on a white plastic tray and went downstairs. This time she made sure MacTee, the canine babysitter, accompanied her.

"Tee, Tee," Elizabeth shouted. She hugged the dog, clutched his collar and dragged him to the refrigerator. "See, see, Tee," she said to him. "See. It's Tee."

Candace and Hollis exchanged amused glances. MacTee did not respond. Having his portrait painted did not impress him. However, when Elizabeth offered him her half-chewed carrot, his tail wagged rapidly. After he'd munched it, he and the little girl began their usual games.

Hollis busied herself portioning the pizza and adding a balsamic dressing to the salad.

Candace uncorked a bottle of red wine. "Let's have a drink." She moved to the oven and turned it on at its lowest setting. "Leave the pizza in here for a few minutes. I need to unwind and fortify myself for whatever the police are going to say."

The two women perched on the kitchen chairs, raised and clinked glasses.

"To better days," Hollis said. She sipped. "Nice wine, not too rough."

Candace exhaled, pushing the air out noisily. "I hope they come right at eight. I want to get this over with. I'm running out of 'coping' steam."

"Not knowing is always hard. Any knowledge, no matter how horrible, is better than uncertainty."

"After that terrible visit to the morgue and the endless hours during which I thought it was Danson, I'm not sure about that." Candace gulped a large mouthful of wine and made a rueful face. "I'd better not suck it down, or I'll be stoned when they get here. Seriously, I'm not so sure knowing is better. I continue to hope Danson will turn up with a rational explanation for everything that's happened."

"Since we don't know anything for sure, that could happen," Hollis said. She reached for the bottle and topped up Candace's glass.

"Did you find out any more today?"

"I did. I trekked over to the University of Toronto linguistics department, and a professor of Russian translated the note."

Candace set her glass down with a thunk that sloshed wine over the rim. A worried frown creased her forehead, and she bit at her upper lip. "What did it say?"

"Nothing very helpful. Didn't bring us any closer to knowing who Gregory was or what he was doing."

Not exactly true, but it seemed wrong to give Candace the translation until the police visit was over. She could only absorb so much information at once. Time for diversionary tactics.

"He was one cute guy," Hollis said.

"The professor?" Candace said with a note of incredulity in her voice.

"They aren't all old and stodgy, you know. He was about my age, and we went for coffee."

Candace had risen, ripped paper towel from the roll, and was mopping up the spilled wine crumpled the paper. "My God, that was fast. Did he ask you out?"

"How did you know?" Hollis gave what she hoped was a mischievous smile.

Women and sometimes men always obsessed about their single friends meeting the "right" partner. To this point, Candace, who was also single, had not evinced any interest in Hollis's dating life; however, it was a gambit that usually worked, and again it was doing the job.

Candace raised her eyebrows as she tossed the balled up paper towel at the waste paper basket. "And?"

"I put him off, but I have his card."

"Why did you do that if you thought he was attractive? Single men our age aren't that plentiful." Candace looked at Elizabeth, who was draped over MacTee. "Believe me, I know."

Was this a reference to Elizabeth's father, the never-mentioned man, or to the general lack of men in Candace's life? The opportunity couldn't be ignored.

"What happened in your life?"

Candace shook her head. "Long story, and dinner awaits before Elizabeth has a meltdown."

Good lateral move. Obviously an off-limits topic.

Elizabeth protested when Candace bent to pick her up.

"You can play with MacTee after we eat," Candace said. She pointed to the dog, who had positioned himself next to the high chair. "He's going to sit right beside you."

Mollified, Elizabeth allowed Candace to hoist her into her high chair.

Time in the oven had not improved the pizza.

"Olives," Elizabeth said joyfully when Candace set her

155

plastic plate in front of her. She carefully picked up and ate each morsel. Once she'd stripped the olives, she lifted the slice and chomped into it.

"You should give the note to the police," Hollis said.

"I haven't even seen it, and you said it didn't tell much," Candace said.

That would teach her to minimalize. "I don't think it relates to Danson, and it could be helpful to them."

"You don't know that for sure, do you?"

"No."

"You promised we'd wait until the end of the week," Candace stated.

It *was* Candace's brother. And she *had* promised. "Okay, but I think it's a mistake. I'll push off right after dinner," Hollis said.

"No, you won't," Candace snapped. Her arrow-straight body and out-thrust jaw emphasized her determination. "You're not going anywhere."

"What?"

"You're staying right here. Whether it's bad news or good news, two pairs of ears are better than one. After they've gone, I'll need to talk about whatever it is they're coming to tell me."

Hollis smiled. "I did promise to help you. If this is one step in the process, I'm with you. I'll stay as long as you want."

After Elizabeth was in bed, they marched to the living room.

"This reminds me of the sinking feeling I had when I was called to the principal's office. I remember sitting in the waiting area stewing over what sword hung over my head. It didn't matter if I'd done something bad or not, having the principal boom my name over the classroom loudspeaker always chilled me," Candace said.

"The principal could be telling you about a prize you'd won or passing on good news—it didn't matter. Now that we're grown-ups, it's exactly the same. Any occasion where you wait for critical information is horrible," Hollis agreed. "I remember when I defended my thesis, and they sent me outside to await the verdict. It took a long time, and I'd convinced myself they'd rejected me when they finally came out and passed on their congratulations."

"Let's hope this is one of those good moments," Candace said.

Twelve

The doorbell rang. "The moment has arrived," Candace said over her shoulder as she headed for the door. "Ready or not, we're going to learn something—good or bad."

Rhona and Ian refused offers of coffee and sat side by side on the couch facing Candace. Hollis had tucked herself into a second chair out of their line of fire.

"Have you found Danson?" Candace asked.

"No. We located his car," Ian said.

"Where?"

"In a hotel parking lot in Niagara Falls."

"Niagara Falls, you're kidding," Candace said. "What in god's name was he doing in Niagara Falls?"

"Did he have any connections there? Anyone he knew?" Ian asked.

Candace shook her head and softly repeated, "Niagara Falls."

"Is there a lacrosse team there or in Buffalo?" Hollis interjected.

Both detectives turned to her.

"Candace told me he often scouted players for the Toronto team," Hollis explained.

"Hollis is right, but there are no teams in that area," Candace said. Her gaze flipped from one detective to the other. "Do you have any idea why he was there?"

"There are several possibilities," Rhona said.

"And they are?" Candace said.

"He could have been staging everything. Leaving his car

in a hotel parking garage would give him time to run and be far away before it was found."

"Why would he do that?"

"If he was involved in Gregory's death," Rhona said. Both detectives watched Candace, and Hollis realized they were weighing her reaction.

"Well, he wasn't," Candace snapped. Her rigid upright posture and the tight line of her lips revealed her unwillingness to entertain this possibility. "Do you have other ideas?" she said.

"He could have committed suicide," Rhona said.

Candace's head rose, her lips parted and her eyes widened. Clearly this was not something she had contemplated. "Suicide? Danson. Not a chance." Her brow creased. "Something made you think that. What was it?"

"We found his wallet and his keys in his unlocked car."

Candace said nothing. Colour drained from her face, and she slumped back against the cushions.

Learning where they'd discovered the car had surprised Hollis, and the implications of this information shocked her.

"All his important cards were in his wallet, along with money. His passport was in his bureau drawer in his apartment."

Candace said nothing. She licked her lips and closed her mouth. Her shoulders hunched forward, and she shrank into a protective stance.

Whatever they'd been expecting from the detective's visit, this hadn't been it. What a bombshell. If it wasn't suicide, Danson might have been involved in Gregory's death. Grim news either way.

"I'm sorry to provide such distressing news. But I can't leave it at that. We have a task for you," Rhona said.

Candace nodded.

Hollis saw the unmistakable signs that her friend was in shock. Whatever Rhona wanted Candace to do, it would be hard for her to collect her thoughts and pull herself together.

Rhona withdrew an evidence bag from her shoulder bag.

She dug deeper, pulled out latex gloves and handed them to Candace. Then she dropped the keys onto the coffee table. "These are Danson's keys, or at least they're the keys found with his other effects. Please tell us what doors they open."

Candace stared at the gloves.

"Pull them on and check the keys," Hollis said quietly.

Candace, operating on automatic pilot, fingered the first key that everyone could see was a car key. She puzzled over the next small brass key, before she said, "His bicycle." The third one was easy for her and for the others—a safety deposit key.

"I didn't know he had a box," Candace said. "What do you suppose he keeps in it?" She frowned. "I've seen his key ring many times, but I don't remember noticing it. I don't think it was there." Her head lifted and tilted. "Maybe it belongs to someone else. Is that a possibility?"

Gregory's name popped into Hollis's mind. Had Danson killed Gregory for this key? A chilling thought.

Candace focussed on her assignment. "This is the key to his mailbox." She dropped it and fingered a silver key. "I haven't got a clue about this one. Maybe it's for the club or for the lacrosse team's locker room. I don't know."

She reached for the last key, flipped it and stopped. "This is wrong," she stated flatly. "Wrong, wrong, wrong."

She had everyone's attention.

"Danson and I have had funny rituals since he was a little boy." Her eyes filled with tears that spilled down her cheeks. "Something is terribly, terribly wrong," she gulped and began to cry—noisy, hacking sobs.

"What? Tell us what," Hollis said as she reached into her jeans pocket, extracted a crumpled tissue, stood up and pressed it into her friend's hand. "Candace, hang on. Come on." She patted Candace on the back. "It's terrible. We know it is, but we have to know what's so wrong that it's done this to you."

The three waited while Candace fought to control her

sobs. Several ragged breaths later, she quavered, "I'm okay."

Clearly she wasn't. She scrubbed at the leaking tears with the back of her hand. Another deep breath. "Okay, I'm okay," she said in a shaky voice.

Hands clasped tightly together, she turned inward as if pulling a memory from a storage depot deep in her brain.

"All families have private rituals," she began then frowned. "They do, don't they? I'm sure we weren't unique."

"They do," Ian reassured her.

"We had two major ones that we've used ever since Danson was little. The first one," she paused, "doesn't have anything to do with keys, but it was important."

"Tell your story any way you want," Rhona encouraged.

"I was sometimes afraid to open the door when someone knocked or rang the bell." She was looking back in time, not at the other people in the living room. "Danson would be out, and if I was home he didn't always remember to take a key. He knew I was afraid, and he always whistled 'Alouette', when he approached the door. It got to be a joke, and he's done it ever since." Speaking of Danson and the familiar ritual, she choked up.

"It's okay. We understand," Rhona said. "We'll wait until you're able to tell us about the key."

Candace reached into her pocket and pulled out shreds of the crushed tissue Hollis had given her. After she mopped her eyes and blew her nose, her lips continued to quiver.

"I'll get you a glass of water," Hollis volunteered.

Candace sipped the water, and the detectives waited. Finally she regained control. "When Danson was young, he went to babysitters. In grade school, maybe Grade Four, I trusted him to come home and let himself in. He stayed alone for a couple of hours until I got home from high school." Her gaze swung from one to the other. "It wasn't exactly legal. He was too young, but I didn't know what else to do."

"My mother also did that. She had to work, and she had no one to leave us with after school," Ian said.

Relief washed over Candace's face. Even though this had happened eons ago, Candace wanted to know that what she'd done had been okay. It must have bothered her for years.

"I wanted him to be able to march right up to the door and quickly let himself in. I always had nightmares about pedophiles following him or someone intent on burglarizing the house. I needed to visualize him scooting to the door and whipping inside. The problem was that he had a bicycle key, a school locker key, the outside door key and the apartment key. He had to fumble through them for the right one."

"A lot for a kid to manage," Ian said sympathetically.

"I had to think of a way to make it easy," Candace said. "It was vitally important."

Hollis noted that they nodded in unison.

"One evening when I was doing my nails, Danson suggested I splash a dab of nail polish on both sides of the outside door key. He said only he would know why I'd done it." Her smile was that of a proud mother. "He was a smart boy, and he's a smart man." No past tense here.

"Anyway, we moved frequently in those days. Colouring the door key became a ritual. When Poppy tossed us keys for a new place, Danson would laugh and say, 'What colour nail polish are you using?' I remember the year silver was in," Candace said. "Do you remember? All the lipsticks and nail polishes were frosted."

Again they nodded as one.

"I was worried that it wasn't bright enough and went out and bought red. Danson wouldn't allow me to paint the key with it, because our ritual was that it should be whatever colour I was using at the time. Even when he went to Concordia, he brought his keys home, and we did them. Every time he moved, we tagged the outside door with nail polish. Like I said, it was a ritual."

Candace picked up one key and showed them both sides. "This is for the outside door to his place. Nothing." She rubbed it with her latex-covered finger. "There never has been." She laid the key down. "This key is shiny and new, but it's an old building. I imagine the locks are original. Danson's key was old and worn."

She picked up the ring and moved from one key to another. When she fingered each one she raised her gaze.

"Besides the fact that the house key doesn't have and has never had nail polish, there's one more thing wrong with this ring."

"Tell us," Ian said.

"There's one key missing," Candace said. She wasn't equivocal or tentative—this was a statement of fact.

"Which one?" Ian said.

"The key to Poppy's apartment."

"How can you be sure?" Ian said.

"Poppy is extremely, almost fanatically security-conscious. Her key has a distinctive square top. It's made by a company called Medico that numbers and registers its keys. To get an additional key, you have to jump through hoops and pay major bucks. Her key isn't here."

"Why would your brother have had it?" Ian said.

"Because he takes cares of her plants and sometimes, when she travels, he feeds her cats." Candace crossed her arms over her chest. "I don't know what's going on. I'm afraid it's something terrible. I can tell you as surely as the sun will be in the sky tomorrow these are not Danson's keys. At least not all of them."

Hollis digested what Candace had said.

"You're an astute observer," Rhona said, laying the keys on the table. "Let's start with the car key and work our way around. You identify each one, and we'll make a record."

They worked quickly. When they finished, Rhona tucked the keys back in the bag and stood up "I don't dispute what you're telling us. It adds even more complexity to the case. Thank you for the information. We'll get back to you when we know more."

"Have you found out who Gregory is?" Hollis said.

Rhona frowned. "You know I can't discuss an ongoing case," she said.

"Why do you want to know?" Ian asked Hollis.

"Everything pivots around Gregory, the mystery man. I haven't found anyone who knows him. Because I needed a password, I couldn't open his computer. You have experts to do that, and I thought the least you could do would be to tell us who he was," Hollis said.

"We can't," Ian said, and that was that. The detectives left.

Once they had the apartment to themselves, Candace shook her head. "I hope they figure that out. Let me see the translation."

"Of course," Hollis agreed. "I'll go one step better and make you a copy. Then, together, we'll see what we make of it."

Upstairs, she checked her messages.

"Hi, it's Willem. Your mysterious message is driving me crazy. If you insist on pursuing this yourself, I have a couple of ideas for you. Come to lunch tomorrow. Twelve thirty at the law society restaurant. In case you aren't familiar with it, just look for the historic old red brick house on the corner of University Avenue and Queen Street. The food's great. Hope you're available and decide to join me. Since I couldn't reach you, I made a reservation. Let me know."

She might not be the most sophisticated woman in town, but she wasn't totally naïve. Without looking in a mirror, she knew she wasn't such a flaming beauty that she'd swept him off his feet. His line about worrying didn't ring true. More likely he wanted to know something. She shivered. The best thing to do would be to ignore his invitation. But what if he really did have an interesting insight to pass on? Wasn't her allegiance to Candace and Danson? If she didn't follow up on every lead, she'd be letting them down. Nine thirty. Not too late to call.

Willem's phone rang six times and clicked to a message. The first words were in what she presumed was Russian.

Then it switched to English. "If you didn't get that, it's okay—not everyone speaks Russian. Leave a message, and I'll get back to you."

After the beep, she identified herself, thanked him for the invitation and said she'd see him at lunch.

She made two copies of the translation, took the sheets downstairs and handed one to Candace, who was sitting at the kitchen table.

"Willem phoned," Hollis said, pulling out a chair and flopping down.

"Willem. Who's Willem?"

"Professor Willem Andronovich, the linguistics specialist I went to see."

"That was fast. You must have made quite an impression."

"He asked me for lunch tomorrow. Said he'd had thoughts about the translation that he wanted to share."

"Not a bad pickup line," Candace said. She smoothed the paper. "No more conversation. I'm dying to read this." She read and reread it before she raised her gaze. "What do you think it means?" she said.

"Before we get to that, doesn't it strike you as odd that Gregory would have stashed it in a book? The letter specifically instructed him to destroy it."

"You're right." Candace studied the letter before she spoke. "How about this scenario? He receives it in the mail, reads it, but doesn't have time to commit it to memory because he has to go somewhere in a hurry. When he gets wherever he's going, he's killed."

Hollis reviewed the scene Candace had set. "Here's another possibility you're not going to like."

"You're going to say Danson had a role, aren't you?"

"Right. What if Danson intercepted the message or walked into Gregory's room and somehow read it and killed Gregory because he knew what the message meant?"

Candace laughed. "Good try. A for effort, but Danson couldn't read Russian. He wouldn't know what it said any

165

more than we did. Furthermore, I'm sure the police have already swept the place for traces of blood."

"Maybe yes, maybe no, but they wouldn't have told us, would they?"

"Point taken. Okay. Let's agree that it's puzzling that he didn't destroy the paper and get on with figuring out what it means. What do you think?"

Hollis leaned forward and rested her elbows on the table and steepled her fingers. "It's a letter of instruction. Gregory had an important job to do for someone. He has to find out something, get the information, and kill the investigator."

"And you think the investigator is Danson?"

"It would explain why Gregory wanted to move in with Danson."

"Five and Seven?" Candace asked.

"People, I'd think. Maybe moles, agents." Hollis shrugged. "Who knows."

"It's a mysterious message and has scary implications. Don't you wish we knew what the Super Bug did?" Candace searched her friend's face. "Do you think your professor is involved?"

"That's too far-fetched. However, I didn't tell you that he volunteers or is paid to attend court as a translator for Russians who don't speak much English. That affords him a window into a larger segment of the Russian community than he might normally meet."

"The criminal element," Candace said slowly and paused before she spoke again. "I've read the Russian Mafia is big in Toronto. Could Gregory have been involved with them?"

"Could be. Willem would know who they were, even though the criminals would hire top notch criminal lawyers and have their own translators. I expect Willem translates for recent immigrants who aren't major players. Nevertheless, with those contacts he may have dug around and have an idea what this letter is about."

Candace inhaled a quick sharp breath. "Did you tell him about us, about Poppy, Elizabeth and me?"

"I didn't tell him anything about your family. I also didn't say where I lived, and I don't plan to reveal any of that information tomorrow. He said he had something to share with me. I promised nothing. I intend to enjoy a delicious lunch at his expense." Hollis yawned. "Now, if you're satisfied that that's all we can do tonight, I'm walking MacTee."

Candace rose and banged her right fist into her left palm. The resulting smack startled both women. "I'm sick of this. I want Danson home, cleared of any involvement in Gregory's death, and I don't know what else we can do."

Hollis, who'd opened the door, said, "Hang in there, kid. We don't know anything for sure, and as long as that's true you have to believe he's alive and innocent. Maybe the best case scenario is that he's hiding out because he's afraid he's opened a can of worms and doesn't want to drag his family into the mess."

"Speaking of cans—I forgot to feed the cats."

"Cats are independent. Can't they wait until tomorrow?"

"No. Poppy gives them fresh canned food every day. I'll go and do it. Poor things, they'll be hungry."

"Want me to come down with you?" Hollis offered.

"You're thinking someone might be there, aren't you?" Candace said.

Hollis shrugged.

"What about Elizabeth?"

"If you're worried, I'll stay here. I'd offer to go, but you may be able to tell if anyone else has been there."

"Stay here in the doorway. That way you'll hear either one of us."

At that moment, the phone rang.

Thirteen

Ian, who was driving, half-turned to Rhona. "So what do you make of her key explanation?"

"She may be grasping for anything to help her believe her brother is okay, but her story rang true."

"If it is, what does it mean?"

"Someone wants us to think Danson jumped in the falls or ran away. If that person murdered Danson, his body could be anywhere. If this is what happened, the killer drove Danson's car to Niagara Falls and left Danson's wallet and keys."

"Why make new keys?"

"To have continuing access to Danson's and his mother's apartments. Danson was last heard from two weeks ago. The killer had time for a leisurely search. I assume whoever made the duplicates didn't know how close Danson and his sister are. He wouldn't know that Candace would know so much about Danson's keys. From that we can figure that whoever this person is, he wasn't intimate with either of them. Since the missing key is for the mother's apartment, we'd better talk to her."

"Didn't Candace say she was away?"

"Right, we'll do that as soon as she's back."

"It's about time the techies opened Gregory's or Danson's computers," Ian said.

"It had better be done by now, or I'll raise blue bloody murder," Rhona threatened.

At the station, the computer expert had left. The computer's mysteries remained unsolved. Rhona filed a complaint with her superior. She hated to do it, but the job came first, and knowing what was in the computers was vital to the case. Once she'd done that, her head lifted. "Ian, did we ask Candace if she knew her brother's password?"

"No. Don't tell me we've done it again?" Ian said. "We assumed she wouldn't know it and passed both computers to the techies. Now that we're aware of how close she and her brother are, it figures she may have the information. I'll call her," he said.

A moment later, he replaced the phone's receiver. "Angie—that's the password," he said.

"Time for a quick scan. I'll collect the computer," Rhona said.

With Danson's laptop planted on her desk, she glanced at Ian, "You or me?"

"Go ahead. There'll be enough information for both of us to analyze. Forward any relevant files," Ian said. He pulled paper from his in-basket. "I have work to do."

Rhona centred the computer on her desk, tapped in "Angie" and clicked on Danson's e-mail. She downloaded the new messages—more than a hundred—and slogged backwards from the newest to the oldest. When she lighted on one she thought might relate to Danson's disappearance or to Gregory, she forwarded it to Ian.

Then she focussed on his files. "I'm outraged," she roared.

Ian's head jerked up as did every other officer's. "What. What is it?" he said.

"For *three years* Danson has tracked criminals returning illegally to Canada. Neither his sister nor Hollis thought to mention this to us." She banged her fist on the desk. "Can we charge them with obstructing justice? That's the question. I'd like to. Imagine how helpful that information would have been."

"You think they knew?" Ian said.

"*Knew.* It explains why his sister has been panicking, doesn't it? She must have been well aware that he operated

169

in dangerous territory. Returning perps don't like being fingered and turfed out. I imagine if we'd talked to the guns and gangs bunch, they'd have known about Danson. Just wait until I see those two women. What else have they hidden or not told us?"

"Candace didn't volunteer any information, did she? We'll go after them again. What's in the tracking files? Ian said.

"I'll send everything along. Take a break and read it."

Ian affixed a yellow sticky note to indicate where he'd stopped in the report he was working on and laid it to one side. He opened his computer. "What are you reading?" he asked before he read the information she'd sent.

"I'm inspecting the mail folders, mainly because I sometimes inadvertently file stuff in the wrong folders. I've already found three or four. Hard to say if he did it on purpose or was just careless."

"I see that in his most recent file he refers to tracking a Russian involved in industrial espionage," Ian said. "Possibly whoever was running the espionage agent clued in to Danson's activities and arranged for Gregory to live with him and keep an eye on what he was doing."

"That would explain things, wouldn't it? I'll print the relevant info and take it to the specialists—the team that deals with Eastern European criminals."

*   *   *

Candace moved to answer the phone, but Hollis waved her back. "Let me. If it's the prankster, I'd like to hear his voice."

"Where's Danson? Wouldn't you like to know," the caller whispered and hung up before Hollis could respond.

"It was him, wasn't it?" Candace said.

"It was. I don't know whether to take the call seriously or not. I still think you should tell the police."

"I will if we haven't found Danson by the end of the week," Candace said.

170

Hollis regretted again that she'd agreed to keep everything secret for that long, but a promise was a promise.

"Feed the cats," she said and leaned against the door frame. When Candace returned, "Someone has been up there. I know they have."

"How do you know?"

"It feels different."

"Come on. No one could get in. You're imagining things."

"You're not very sympathetic," Candace said.

"No. I'm not. I'm tired, and I'm going to bed." Hollis stomped upstairs, wishing she'd never got herself involved in the search for Danson Lafleur.

Next morning she woke long before the sun rose. She lay in bed mentally sorting puzzle pieces. Why had Danson's car and effects showed up in Niagara Falls? Why had someone tampered with the key ring? Who was making the phone calls, and might the person know where Danson was or what had happened to him? She couldn't come up with any satisfactory answers. Perhaps the police, now that they had the password for Danson's computer, would find something significant that she'd missed.

She rose and readied herself for the day. She leashed MacTee and decided they both needed a long run. The repetitive, rhythmic activity cleared her mind, soothed her spirit and sometimes relieved her depression. November's short days and frequent cloudy grey skies and the depression she often suffered made her wonder if she had Seasonal Affective Disorder.

They began in the crisp, lavender-tinted predawn. Gradually, as the sky lightened, trees shaded from black to grey to vibrant autumn shades. The thin November sunshine failed to warm but did cheer as they tracked over a carpet of crisp leaves and headed north and east toward Sherwood Park.

Inside the park that curved and flowed for miles along one of Toronto's many ravines, she unleashed MacTee and maintained a steady pace along the trail through half-bare

171

trees and over a sometimes slippery, leaf-covered path. Her spirits lifted as the kilometres flew by. When she reached the point where she usually stopped and drank from her water bottle, she checked her watch and reluctantly turned back, realizing she'd need to shower before her lunch with Willem.

Back on Belsize Drive, she slowed to a walk as she cooled down. Near the house she recognized the figure approaching. It was Jack, the lacrosse player. He'd unlocked and climbed into a dark blue Ford van which pulled away from the curb ahead of her before she could say hello. Probably on his way to practice, she thought.

While she luxuriated in the warm water coursing over her body, a question occurred to her—why did Jack's van have Ontario plates if he'd been living in Quebec and driven from Montreal?

*   *   *

Rhona hurried to her desk at eight fifteen on Thursday morning. Having slept through the alarm, she'd fed Opie, grabbed clothes, thrown them on and rushed to her car without breakfast. In the parking garage under police headquarters, she tidied herself up and saw that the pants she'd thought were black were actually navy. They did not go well with the black-striped blouse which had a stain on the front. Dishevelled, disorganized and at least three-quarters of an hour late, she'd hoped to make an inconspicuous arrival. No such luck. She shared the elevator from the parking garage with her boss, who peppered her with questions—most of which she failed to answer to his satisfaction. The elevator mirror reflected a face needing makeup and hair looking as if she'd been standing in a force nine gale. Once in the office, she fished through her in-basket.

"Your memo to the chief must have done the trick. The techies have Gregory's computer open," Ian said, breezing past her.

"Do we know who Gregory was?"

"Not his name. Everything is in Russian. They've sent the machine's hard drive for translation. We'll know more later."

"Russian. Danson was tracking a Russian criminal. If we'd given the dentist a chance, he could have told us that. At least he would have known the dental work was done by an Eastern European. Ever wonder how they know?"

"I went to a forensic dentistry seminar once. You'd be amazed at what teeth tell about a body," Ian said.

"I know about age, sex, etc, etc, but I'd like to know how different nationalities do dental work," Rhona said. She touched the pile of work in front of her. "That's not our issue. Did Danson know Gregory's real identify? That's the next question."

"And one we won't be able to answer until we get the translations. It's back to Preacher Peter and the addict murders for us, isn't it?"

"I had a thought about that," Rhona said as she slapped a form in her printer and pressed copy.

"Which was?"

"We may have been on the right track when we interviewed the people in the park. The fact that not one of murdered men fought back has to be as important as the fact that they were addicts. Those men knew the killer."

"What kind of person would that be?" Ian said.

"A nurse, doctor, social worker, a neighbourhood friend."

"What are we waiting for? Paperwork can wait. Let's track down a living, breathing person and ask the *right* questions."

From his emphasis on right, Rhona realized that Ian still smarted from their failure to ask Candace if Danson lived alone.

They grabbed their coats.

Ian offered to drive, and Rhona, whose hip continued to pain her, accepted. As they travelled the short distance across College and Carlton streets, he spoke. "Any particular

173

way to identify a likely druggie other than making him roll up his sleeves or take a urine test?"

"No easy way. Since it's early in the day, the girls on the stroll will be eating. I could do with a coffee. They'll pass on some names if we assure them we have no interest in the men except as information sources. I'm sure they're as eager to root out the killer as we are. And cooperation may pay off if the next serial killer targets prostitutes like Pickton did in Vancouver. How many women died before they finally arrested him? The police weren't too swift there. In Edmonton a killer has been murdering prostitutes, and no one has been arrested. Dealing with nut cases is a prostitute's nightmare."

Inside the coffee shop they surveyed the room before Rhona led them to a booth occupied by two young women.

"You're cops," said one, who had café latte skin and tightly braided corn rows.

The metallic bracelets on her arms jangled as she raised a hand and gestured dismissively before reaching down to adjust her tiny white leather skirt and low-cut black top.

Her companion, a thin girl who looked no more than fourteen, radiated alarm. Her legs were bare, and she wore what could have been a private school kilt. No makeup, blonde hair pulled back in a ponytail. Dressed to attract the guys who were pedophiles at heart, who liked the girls as young as they could procure them. The younger girl pulled her grey hoodie tight to her body.

"We are. I'm Rhona, and this is Ian. We aren't here to trap you, or to bring you in for any reason." Not quite true. She'd like to see the young one's ID, but this wasn't the time. "We want to talk about the murders."

"Don't know nothing," the black woman said, gathering up a black leather bag studded with faux stones.

"Your name is?" Ian said.

"Alicia," she mumbled.

"And your name?" Ian said to the younger girl.

"What difference does it make what my name is?" she squeaked.

"If we're having a conversation, it goes better with names."

"I don't want to tell you."

Rhona and Ian waited.

"Call me Tiny."

"Okay, Tiny, order something to eat, then we'll ask you a couple of questions," Rhona said. She and Ian squeezed in on opposite sides of the cigarette-scarred red arborite table and effectively blocked the escape route.

"Anything?" Tiny said.

"Anything you fancy." Rhona beckoned the waitress.

With her gaze fixed on Rhona, the young girl spoke fast in her clear high voice. "A large cherry coke and..." She paused to see how Rhona had reacted.

"Go ahead," Rhona said.

"Coconut cream pie," she said and smiled.

She had braces on her teeth. Someone had cared enough to pay for expensive dental work.

"Coffee," Alicia said.

The two detectives ordered coffee as well.

"We want to stop the killer before he strikes again. We need users' names and where we can find them," said Ian.

"Why do you think we'd know?" Alicia said.

"We don't. We hope you will, because the faster we reach these guys and talk to them, the better our chances. We think he may have targeted other men that he didn't manage to kill. Probably something interrupted him or they ran. Anything you can tell us could be helpful. We intend to stop him before he strikes again."

"Spider Jones maybe could help you," Alicia said. "He's a crackhead, and he's really spooked about the killings. In the daytime he hangs out in the park near the Sally Ann. I've seen him there." She shrugged. "Good luck with him."

*　　*　　*

175

The crowded restaurant buzzed with conversations as Hollis told the hostess whom she was meeting and was shown to a small white linen-covered table in a far corner. Willem rose as she approached. He pulled her chair back and waited for her to seat herself before he too sat. A bottle of white wine ensconced in an ice bucket waited beside the table. The wine steward hurried over, poured a smidgen for Willem who sipped, savoured and said, "Very nice."

Their glasses filled, Willem said, "Today the specialty is roast beef."

"I'm a vegetarian."

"If you eat fish, they do a superb seafood bouillabaisse If not, their spaghetti primavera is also good," Willem said.

After they'd ordered, they exchanged polite remarks about the weather.

This was getting them nowhere, thought Hollis. Time for the preemptive strike. "We're here to discuss the paper you translated. You said you have information?" she said.

Willem steepled his fingers and regarded her in silence for a long time. "I think you're over your head and involved in something that could be very dangerous," he said.

Hollis didn't like his tone. "Why?"

"I did a little sleuthing."

Alarm. Whom had he spoken to? What had he been? "You shouldn't have done that. I asked you for a translation. I didn't ask you to investigate the contents." Hollis tried to control the tremor in her voice but didn't quite succeed. She didn't know if anger or fear or a little of both caused the quaver, anger that Willem had taken matters into his own hands. Dread that Danson had left to protect his family, and her meddling might have brought danger to their doors. If she had, she'd never forgive herself.

"Take it easy." Willem reached across and patted her hand.

She withdrew it immediately.

"I told you I had contacts in the Russian criminal community. I've represented good people, but I know about the others, the not-so-goodniks. I flew trial balloons. Said I'd heard something about the Super Bug and wondered what it was and if it was still around. I can't tell you who I talked to, but I can say he's in the mob and owes me a favour or two."

Oh, God. This was worse. The mob. What had he said? Had he given her name?

"Where did you say you'd heard the name?" Hollis said. Her stomach muscles clenched, and she held her breath.

Willem straightened and positively smirked. "You won't believe how canny I was," he paused, obviously wanting to prolong his moment in the sun.

"How canny were you?" she said, wanting to reach across and smack him.

"On the subway. I said I'd overheard two men speaking Russian on the subway, and they mentioned the Super Bug. The man talking to me became very upset, demanded I describe the men, asked if I'd recognize them if I saw them again. Wanted to know where they got on, where they got off."

"What did you say about these imaginary men?" Hollis said. She hoped she didn't sound as outraged as she felt.

"Told him I hadn't paid much attention because I'd been eavesdropping and didn't want them to notice me. Said they got off at Union Station, and they both had suitcases." He grinned. "Wasn't it a good idea to get them out of the city?"

"The Super Bug. Did this 'friend' tell you what it was about?"

Their lunches arrived. The bouillabaisse lived up to it's billing, but it could have been warm tap-water as far as Hollis was concerned. She kept thinking of Candace and Elizabeth and praying she hadn't endangered them.

Willem, who'd ordered the roast beef, spooned horse-radish and hot mustard on his plate before he replied. "That's what I'm here to tell you. He said it was dangerous stuff, nothing to meddle with. To forget I'd ever heard the name and mind my own business." He forked a large portion into his mouth.

Worse and worse. She was no further ahead. Willem didn't know, and his acquaintance hadn't been prepared to tell him.

"I should have ordered red wine to go with my beef," Willem said.

"Never mind the bloody wine. Why wouldn't he tell you what the Super Bug was about?"

Willem tapped his finger on the table. "No need to be testy. Because it would be dangerous for me to know. Given the contents of the paper I translated, I think you should back off whatever it is you're doing. If it's in the same league as the Super Bug, it's dangerous to you and to anyone else involved." He took another mouthful.

Hollis had no appetite. She should leave, should go directly to police headquarters and pass on the translation, along with Willem's warnings. "I'm upset that you took it upon yourself to do this," she said coldly as she watched him chewing vigorously, apparently unaware of her fury. "Since you have, I think you'd better stick your neck out and try other sources. I need this information."

Willem, impaling a chunk of beef, stopped. "Now wait a minute. You won't tell me where this came from. You say it's, what's your word, complicated, yet you expect me to continue poking my nose into this business. Are you crazy? Why would I do that?"

Why indeed. Did the person who poked the stick in the hornet's nest hang around to see how many stings he'd receive? "Because you notified the mob that the Super Bug was attracting attention. Now they're on alert. Where does that leave me? Even though I don't know anything, you've probably endangered me."

Willem carefully placed his fork on his plate and angled his body toward her. "You have no idea, absolutely no idea, how dangerous the mob can be." He'd lowered his voice.

178

She mimicked his attitude and spoke quietly. "Oh—yes—I—do. Don't ask me how, but I do."

"Hollis, why can't you go to the police? They have special task forces to deal with gang stuff. If what you told me about your background is true, you have no experience. You're a nice middle-class woman. Go to the police."

"Eventually, I will. Meanwhile, it's critical that I learn what the Super Bug was or is."

Both pulled back simultaneously. Stalemate. Neither spoke.

"Okay." Willem tapped his finger on the table. "I don't agree with you, but I do have one other source. I'll see him and stick to my subway story." He brushed bread crumbs off the table and mumbled, "I just hope you don't read in the *Globe and Mail* that they've fished my body out of Lake Ontario."

"Surely no one gets killed for asking. However, if you think it's that dangerous, maybe it would be better if you didn't do it."

Willem worked away at the crumbs and shook his head as he said, "It *is* dangerous. Whatever Super Bug is, they're threatened when the subject comes up. I'll try to ask without attracting attention."

The waiter arrived and left after he examined Willem's half-eaten and Hollis's almost untouched meals.

Willem gestured at his plate and at Hollis's. "Since this may be our last supper or my last supper, let's eat and make pleasant conversation. I'll have something nice to remember when they chop off my fingers or my hands, likely while I'm still alive, before they shoot or stab me and toss me in the lake to improve Lake Ontario fishing."

He wanted her to lighten up, to smile. As much as she wanted to be lighthearted and pleasant, it didn't happen. He'd hit close to the mark—she remembered Candace's description of Gregory's body. Looking at Willem's warm brown eyes, she wavered. Even though he'd initiated the investigation, she didn't want him to end up like that.

Maybe she should go immediately to the police. Tempting, but her first responsibility was to Candace and to Danson. If she gave up the chase, Danson might never be found.

"That isn't very funny. Okay, I acknowledge that it may be dangerous. Let's put a time limit on your search. Twenty-four hours. Call me on my cell tomorrow afternoon. If you haven't learned anything, we'll forget we ever had these conversations."

"Then will you go to the police?"

Hollis shook her head. "Depends what information you get, but either way, your involvement will be over."

Willem again covered her hand with his. This time Hollis didn't withdraw. The heat of his fingers sent pleasant messages to various nerve centres in her body.

"I'd like to see you again," he said, tightening his grasp. "When whatever this is ends, maybe we could have coffee or run in High Park and treat ourselves to lattes afterwards?"

"When I talked about running in the ravines with my dog, you didn't say you were a runner."

"I'm a triathlete."

Triathlete. She'd never aspire to do that. Even thinking about what was involved—running a marathon, pulling on a wet suit to swim a huge distance then biking for endless kilometres—exhausted her. He must be in great shape and have drive and persistence if he did this. He wasn't suggesting she join him. Running she could handle. "I'd love to. I'm new to Toronto. I'd like to explore more ravine trails. I'm leery about doing that by myself unless it's midday on Saturday or Sunday."

"It's a deal. We'll talk tomorrow."

They finished lunch, vetoed dessert or coffee and left together. On the sidewalk, Willem grasped her sleeve. "I will do my best," he assured her before they parted.

His warnings had frightened her. She'd promised that he wouldn't be involved when the twenty-four hours ended, but it was time to rethink her own commitment. She'd give it until noon tomorrow. If Willem hadn't come up with useful information, she'd pass the paper on to Rhona. Somehow knowing there was a time limit comforted her.

Nothing else to be done until she heard from Willem. She'd fill the hours with work. Not the gold painting. Its uninspiring surface dominated the apartment, but she refused to work on it until she had a better idea of where it was going. Instead she'd finish the chickens. After she flipped open the paste container and donned gloves, she couldn't bring herself to work. She needed downtime. Caught up in the investigation, she hadn't taken enough time to meditate, to centre herself.

Twenty minutes later, refreshed and calmed, she set to work. Blue eyes or green eyes for the leader? Maybe red to sympathize with the difficulty any leader faced, particularly a chicken when there was no rooster to strut his stuff.

She rummaged through her eye collection and picked two glowing crimson eyes.

The phone rang. "Hollis Grant?"

Whose voice? She'd heard it recently but couldn't quite place it. She acknowledged her identity.

"I got idea for you."

Spike, the bouncer. This could be good news.

"I'm glad you called. Tell me what it is."

"You know I say mother cuckoo. She hate Russian mob 'cause my brother die?"

"I remember."

"When I tell Danson, he say he know Russian mob. He going to get them."

Verification of their suspicions. After her conversation with Willem, she didn't know whether to rejoice or weep.

"That's helpful. Anything else?"

"Yes. Mother do need help. Will you talk to her?"

She hadn't expected this. What could she do? She didn't have connections to the mental health facilities in Toronto. "Does she speak English?"

"Yes."

"Where does she live?"

"She not want anyone to know." He paused, as though realizing it would be hard to help without meeting her. "She go to park every day. She knit and knit."

"Which park?"

"On Carlton. Greenhouse in middle. East, past Jarvis Street, before Sherbourne."

"She goes there every day?"

"Every day. She leave apartment, take umbrella or she wear coat. She knit and knit."

"Why do you think she'll listen to me?"

"Because you not social worker. You woman like her."

"How is she with dogs? I'd like to take my golden retriever, MacTee, with me. If she likes dogs, she'll love him." Dogs often broke through barriers. Alzheimer's patients, depressed withdrawn elderly patients—a long list of damaged people responded to dogs. A friendly golden ranked high on the appealing dog totem pole.

"Dogs good. She little girl in Leningrad in siege. Still feel bad they eat dogs."

Great, a deranged woman with a knitting fixation who felt guilty because she'd had to eat her dog. Not too many women got an opportunity like this. "Spike, if you think it'll help, I'll go this afternoon."

"Thank you. Call, tell me what she say?" he said and gave her his cell phone number.

She dropped the phone in its cradle and whistled to MacTee. "We're on a mission. You'll be a therapy dog this afternoon."

Before she left, she pocketed dog biscuits and her cell. You never knew when you'd need either one.

Bucketing along in her beat-up old truck, she tried to map out a scenario for the encounter ahead. Nothing came to her. It would have to be improv.

In the park, MacTee sniffed the trees and attempted to

lift his leg higher at each successive one. Very large dogs must use this park, and MacTee was working to establish his place in the hierarchy.

She spotted Spike's mother. Knitting furiously, hair covered with a bandana and her possessions spread on the bench, she commanded a strategic spot at the junction of several paths, where she could monitor approaches from several directions.

Hollis released MacTee, who moseyed along, nose to the ground, collecting olfactory information. As he neared Spike's mother's bench, his head lifted. He stopped, raised his nose even higher, and sniffed.

"Sausage. I got Polish sausage," Spike's mother said to Hollis.

"He's great at smelling good things," Hollis said.

MacTee sidled close to the bench and fixed the women with a pleading gaze.

"Is he hungry?" the woman asked

"No. It's an act. He's a ham…"

A puzzled look.

"I mean he's an actor. He pretends he's hungry hoping you'll share your Polish sausage with a starving dog who isn't starving." Hollis smiled. "May we join you? Is that going to be a scarf?"

The women peered at Hollis through narrowed eyes. Hollis continued to smile.

"Okay. You sit," the woman said and moved her flowered carpet bag to make room on the bench.

"I'm Hollis, and my dog's name is MacTee," Hollis said and held out her hand, which she regretted as the woman held knitting needles in both hands.

The woman laid the knitting in her lap and offered a chapped red hand. "Katerina."

"Lovely name. Is it German?" Hollis said and wished she could haul the words back into her mouth. She'd known Katerina was Russian but thought it would make the woman suspicious if she zeroed in too soon. German? Was she out of her mind? This woman had survived the more than nine-hundred-day siege of Leningrad.

"German." Katerina spat on the ground. "If Katerina German—I change it. I hate Germans. Buy nothing German. Name is Russian."

MacTee nudged Katerina's flowered carpet bag and stared beseechingly at her.

"Can I?" Katerina asked, pointing her needle at the bag.

Wagner's "Ride of the Valkyries" blasted from Hollis's handbag. Wagner, the quintessential German composer and inspiration for Hitler—bad choice. She grabbed for the phone, pressed talk and said hello.

"It's Willem. I found some info for you," he said. Hollis heard suppressed excitement in his voice.

"That's terrific."

"I don't want to…" he stopped abruptly.

"What the hell. Who are you? What are you doing? Get out of my office," Willem said.

Hollis heard fear in his voice.

A rumbling, menacing voice speaking in a foreign language.

Willem replied in what must be the same language.

A crash. What was happening?

More talk. This time it sounded like an order. Short staccato speech.

"Call 911," Willem shouted.

Another voice speaking heavily accented English. "Get the fucking phone. Under desk."

Silence.

Fourteen

Hollis snapped to attention and punched in 911. "Willem Andronovich was talking to me when men broke into his office in the Slavic Studies department at the University of Toronto. They're attacking him. Send the police. It's an emergency." She identified herself, gave the address at the university and, instructed to stay on the line, did not hang up but held the phone in her hand.

"Willem Andronovich," Katerina gazed at her with raised eyebrows and head cocked to one side.

Hollis focussed on the woman. "Yes. Do you know him?"

Katerina's eyes brimmed with tears. "He good man," she said. Hollis wanted to pursue this, to learn how Katerina knew Willem, but not now. Although she knew she shouldn't hang up, she had a call to make. Rhona's number was in her cell's phone book. She pressed in the number. Why, oh why hadn't she believed Willem when he'd said how dangerous it was to ask questions? This was her fault. She should have shared the information with Rhona as soon as Willem had translated the message.

"You have reached the extension of Detective Rhona Simpson. I am on the other line or away from my desk. If your call is urgent, call 911. If not, please leave a message."

Damn, the woman was never there. What message should she leave? Over the phone, she wasn't about to admit she'd withheld evidence. They charged you for that—it was a serious crime. "I hope you're in the office. I'm bringing in evidence that links Danson to Gregory to the Russian mob."

As she spoke, Katerina stood up and moved close. She planted herself inside Hollis's space and loomed over her.

"You!" Katerina thrust a knitting needle into Hollis's arm.

It hurt. Hollis yanked her arm back and slid along the bench out of reach of the grey metal skewer.

"You connected to mob? To drug dealers? You came to get me? Trap me?" Spit foamed on her lips. She breathed in short, oxygen-deprived gasps.

MacTee, hovering close to the sausage bag, backed away in alarm and skulked back to Hollis.

This woman was crazy. How had she got herself in such a mess?

"No. No. I have nothing to do with drug dealers or the Russian mob. Nothing. Believe me—nothing."

"Why you talk about evidence and mob?" Katerina panted.

"Because I know someone who is involved, and I'm trying to help," Hollis said.

"Help. You help mob?"

"The police. I'm helping the police," Hollis shouted. She had to force this dense woman to understand.

"Why you come talk to me?" Katerina moved threateningly near. Her quiet intensity frightened Hollis.

The truth. "Your son suggested it."

"My son," Katerina stopped and stepped back, mouth open. Clearly she hadn't expected this response. She calmed down a bit. "How you know my son?"

"Long story, but I do. He's worried about you and asked me to make sure you were okay," Hollis said.

Katerina clutched her knitting and rocked back on her heels. "Something happen to him." Her voice high and thin, she dropped her knitting and grabbed for Hollis. "What is wrong?" Her hands clawed at Hollis's jacket. "Why he not come himself?"

Hollis detached the grasping hands and stepped back. "Because he's a friend of mine, and he…" She paused.

What line would work best with this woman? Inspiration struck. "He thought you and I might be friends because he worries that you don't have enough friends."

"You lie," Katerina said flatly. "You not know my son. He never sent you."

"He did."

"How I know that?" Her eyes narrowed. "What is his name?"

"Spike."

"Hah, I have no son name Spike. Venedikt is my son. You lie."

"It's..." how to explain nicknames? "That's what he told me his name was."

Katerina's chin jutted. "What does this Spike do?" There was a note of triumph, of "now I've got you" smugness in her voice.

Hollis sighed. She didn't want to be having this bizarre conversation, she wanted to be in her truck driving to the university searching for Willem.

"He works at the Starshine Lounge," she said.

Katerina's face revealed her displeasure at being wrong, that Hollis did know her son and did know where he worked. She deflated as fast as a punctured balloon. Hollis lightly touched the woman's shoulder. "I do know Spike, and he did ask me to come and talk to you. I have to go, but I'll be back."

Katerina didn't try to stop her. She subsided on the bench without even picking up the knitting lying on the path. "Okay," she mumbled. "Okay."

Hollis hated to leave, but she'd come back.

In the truck, she drove as fast as she dared and left her vehicle in an outrageously expensive parking garage close to Willem's office. Out of the truck, she and MacTee ran to the building and up the stairs. When she reached the office, the door stood open. The office was empty. Willem's overturned chair provided mute evidence that something had happened. She knelt down and examined the floor. No blood stains—that was good.

"What are you doing?" a voice behind her demanded.

She stumbled to her feet. A petite, dark-haired, neatly attired woman stared at her.

"I was looking for Willem," she said.

"Under the desk?"

"No. He was talking to me on the phone when men broke into his office and attacked him."

Hands on her hips and head tilted, the woman sniffed. "That's hard to believe. I work here, and I saw him walk out with two men. He wasn't making any fuss or anything. Minutes later the police stormed in, and I told them I'd seen him leave. They checked a bit and left. Said someone must have phoned in a crank call." She peered at Hollis. "Were you that someone?"

If only she hadn't hung up, she could have confirmed that Willem had been abducted.

"I was. You'll be glad to know that you may have endangered Willem's life by telling the police he left voluntarily," Hollis said.

Thinking of where Willem might be, and what might be happening to him, filled Hollis first with horror and then with rage.

"I don't suppose you noticed that the men walked very close to Willem? You couldn't see but I'll bet they had a gun or a knife poked into his side, and that's why he walked quietly."

The woman glared at Hollis. "You're making that up so I'll feel bad," she said, her tone petulant.

"I'm not. I wish it had been a message so I could play it back, but you'll have to believe me.," Hollis said.

The young woman studied Hollis for a moment. "If it's true, I'm sorry, but how was I to know. This is a university, not a place where professors are abducted at gunpoint."

"I agree, but it did happen."

"Oh my god, poor Willem. Is there anything I can do?"

"If the police come back, tell them you were wrong,"

Hollis said as she redialed Rhona's number.

Rhona still wasn't there. She left a message relaying what had happened to Willem.

While she talked, the young woman leaned on the door frame. "I'm so sorry," she repeated.

Hollis felt contrite. There had been no need to lash out the way she had. "I'm sorry I said what I did. There was no way you could have known," Hollis said.

MacTee trailing after her, she retraced her steps. In the truck she sat and thought about what she should do next. Katerina's distraught image flashed into her mind. Perhaps she could undo the damage she'd done there and uncover the woman's connection to Willem. Maybe Katerina would have an idea where the men had taken him. She didn't want to think about what they might have done to him and shivered at the thought of Gregory's smashed face and fingerless body.

*　*　*

"Let's go find Spider Jones in Allan Gardens," Ian said.

Inside the park, they carefully examined the pigeon feeders, the strollers, the brown bag drinkers.

"Katerina's here again," Ian said, looking ahead to the spot where three paths converged.

"Something's wrong with her," Rhona said.

Katerina paced around and around the bench, talking to herself and gesturing with her knitting. A purple trail measured her circles and isolated her like an agitated spider in its web.

"Katerina," Rhona said softly as they slowly approached the bench.

The woman stopped as if the sound of her name had been a brake. Her head, which had been lowered as she paced, came up, and her neck stretched long and flexed back like a cobra about to strike. She flicked her gaze from side to side, finally fixing on Rhona's face.

"You," she hissed. "They sent you." She raised her eyes and bobbed her head. "They will never get me. No, no, no, never, no." The litany went on and on as she resumed her measured tread around the bench. She shot glances their way but didn't slow her pace or stop the monotonous drone.

"Who do you think sent us? What are you saying no to?" Ian said.

Katerina ignored him.

"No one sent us. Can we help you?" Ian said.

Katerina acted as if she hadn't heard.

"I don't like to leave her like this," Rhona said.

"I don't suppose she's dangerous, is she?"

"No. We're here to talk to drug addicts but…"

Hollis, who'd entered the park shortly after the two detectives but had hung back waiting to see what was happening, recognized their impasse. She wanted to corral Rhona and pour out her story, tell her about Willem and what had happened. It was time to cooperate.

"Maybe I can help," Hollis said, tapping Rhona on the shoulder.

Rhona jumped and whirled around. "What are you doing here?"

Her voice penetrated Katerina's preoccupation with denial. She stopped and lifted her head. A puzzled frown creased her forehead. "You with them," she said in a flat voice.

What was Spike's real name? She needed it, like a blessing. That was it—Venedikt.

"Your son, Venedikt, sent me."

"Why he not come?" Katerina said.

"Because he had to work," Hollis said.

"Now I remember. You say Willem. Then you run away. How you know Willem?" Katerina's frown deepened, and her eyes narrowed. She didn't resume her walking. Instead she stared at the sky as if looking for inspiration. Then she lowered her head and glowered at Hollis.

"You with them." It was a flat statement. "I know you." She waved the knitting needles at the two detectives. "You.

190

All come from them. Come to get me. To put me away." She shuffled backwards, clutching the knitting to her chest and trampling the strands lying on the ground.

"No, we haven't," Hollis said wondering if it was true, if a woman as obviously agitated as Katerina should be taken somewhere where she'd be safe from her demons.

"I get them. One by one I get them," Katerina said. Her voice rang with conviction and triumph.

An alarming statement. Who was she getting and why? Hollis felt uneasy. Since Katerina had responded to her and not the detectives, she posed the question. "Who? Who do you get?"

A sly expression crept across the woman's face. "Them. Soon I get them all." She glanced down at the tangled purple skein on the ground, yanked the strand coming from the ball she carried in her pocket to her lips and bit through it. No longer attached to the purple mess tangled with fallen oak leaves, she pulled her knitting close to her chest, moved back to the bench and scooped up her flowered bag. "Go now," she mumbled and edged away.

"How do you know her?" Rhona said to Hollis.

"Her son, Spike, is a bouncer at the Starshine club where Danson worked. When I talked to him, he asked me if I'd come and make friends with his mother and try to get her help, because she needs it. He says she's crazy and obsessive and suspicious of nearly everyone."

"Well, he's got that right. Did he tell you her story—why she's upset?"

"After she and her two boys came to Canada from Russia, her younger son dropped out of school, got involved with the Russian mob and was killed by a drug addict. She'd had great hopes for him, and his death toppled her over the edge."

"Killed by a drug addict," Rhona said thoughtfully. "Do you know her surname or where she lives?"

"Her son said she comes to the park every day. I don't know her name, and I know him as Spike."

Rhona made a note. "Why are you here?"

"I upset her when I spoke to her earlier in the day. I wanted to make amends," Hollis said as she patted MacTee, who had sadly watched the sausage lady's departure.

"Who is Willem?" Ian asked.

Oh my God, the Katerina situation had wasted precious minutes. "He's a Russian linguistics professor at the University of Toronto. I asked him to translate something I found in Danson's apartment. He did but he told me to give it to you—that it could be dangerous."

Rhona crossed her arms, narrowed her eyes and frowned. "Not again. Why didn't you?"

Hollis couldn't meet Rhona's gaze. "I thought it would lead Candace and me to Danson or at least give us some clues as to his whereabouts. I planned to turn it over to you if Willem hadn't found out what the note meant in twenty-four hours."

"I can't believe that after your experiences you'd do this again," Rhona said.

"Truly, I intended to, but, as I was talking to Katerina, Willem phoned me from his office. He started off normally. Then I heard him being attacked and he shouted, 'phone 911' and the line went dead. I made the call and headed for the university. When I arrived, a staff person who viewed me suspiciously briefed me on events. She claimed Willem left peacefully with two men. When she told this to the police, I suppose they thought the call had been a prank, because they left." She didn't confess that she'd hung up when she'd been told to stay on the line.

Rhona was already on her radio.

Ian shook his head. "Where is this paper?"

Hollis scrambled in her bag, extricated the translation and handed it to Ian, who read it and passed it to his partner.

Rhona zipped through the note and glared at Hollis. "You thought this wasn't important enough to give to us," she said.

It was not the time or the place for Hollis to allow anger

and outrage to seep into her voice. She might have been wrong, but her intentions had been good. "When we started our search for Danson, there was no police investigation. It was after Candace viewed that horrible body and you informed us about his car that we really believed something terrible had happened to him. I was doing my best to explore every possible angle."

"Initially, maybe that was okay, but you should have given us this," Rhona waved the paper, "the moment you found it." She smoothed and folded the translation in thirds before tucking it in her bag. "By withholding this evidence, you may very well have sealed Danson's fate." Without waiting for Hollis to respond, she continued. "Now you know how serious the matter is, you must give us any other information, and you must stop investigating."

"I'm frightened for Willem." Hollis frowned. "This was my doing. I feel horribly responsible. Do you know who or what the Super Bug mentioned in the translation refers to?"

Ian, who'd been following the conversation while stroking MacTee, intervened. "Don't you realize that even if we know, we can't discuss it with you? Why don't you take this lovely dog for a walk and forget your amateur detective work?"

Hollis promised nothing. Instead she said, "You will keep Candace in the picture? She's frantic to know what's happened to Danson. Myself, I feel horrible about Willem. He was doing a good deed, and he's gone."

Rhona sized Hollis up in a way that told her the detective had noted her failure to promise to stay out of the case. "We will let you know any news that relates to Danson or Willem," Rhona said.

Hollis accepted the remark and headed for her truck, where she flipped on the all-news radio station to get the time. Was Vancouver three or four hours behind? Prairie, Mountain and Pacific—three hours. When she returned from work, Candace had promised to phone Vancouver and demand that Poppy answer their questions.

Fifteen

That woman," Ian sighed as the car hummed to life. "Now we have work to do." Rhona was already on the phone. "Get the surname and phone number of the bouncer at the Starshine nightclub," she instructed. Call finished, she shifted and said, "We're visiting Katerina at home when we know where she lives."

"Katerina?" Ian sounded surprised.

"Yes, I think she might be our killer."

"She's mad I agree, but a killer—that's a stretch."

"Maybe, but we should check it out. First, I'm giving the Eastern European experts this translation. I don't know what Super Bug means, but I'm sure if anyone knows, they will." She punched in more numbers on her cell phone and passed the information along." Seconds after she hung up, it rang again. She identified herself and reached for her pen and notebook. "Got it," she said and snapped the phone shut.

"Okay, we have it. An apartment on Carlton Street, along with her phone number and her son's numbers at home and work. We may need his help. I'll call him."

"If he warns her we're coming, she'll leave," Ian said.

"If Hollis is right, he's worried about his mother and will cooperate. I'll call him."

After identifying herself, Rhona told Spike what they wanted. She listened, nodded and pursed her lips. "I suppose that's true. We'll wait outside."

"What did he say?" Ian asked.

"He wants us to wait until he gets there. He says his mother hasn't let anyone in her apartment for a long time. He doubts his mother will unlock her door but says that if we have a warrant, the manager, who lives in the basement apartment, will open it for us. His mother fears police and having them enter her apartment will unhinge her. He says he needs to be there, because when his mother's upset she only speaks and understands Russian. He'll translate and try to calm her down. It will take him about forty minutes to get here."

"I can't believe you think that woman would have murdered the men," Ian said.

"She has the motive—a druggie killed her son. With her warped view of police, she wouldn't believe they'd do anything about it, so perhaps she took on the task of avenging his death."

"What about getting the search warrant?"

"Definitely." Rhona flipped her phone open. Once she'd established the seriousness of the request and its urgency, she set the machinery in motion to speedily obtain a warrant. They reviewed the case on the drive back to pick up the document.

"Everything seems connected to the Russians, doesn't it?" Ian said.

"Not everything. We know Gregory must have been in the mob or connected to it because he was killed in their distinctive fashion. We don't know if he wheedled his way into Danson's apartment because he wanted to recruit Danson or to spy on him or to stop him. From the translation, I'd guess Gregory was ordered to kill Danson, and that may explain Danson's disappearance. That fits together." She paused.

"What doesn't fit the pattern?" Ian said.

"Why they would go to the trouble of driving the car to Niagara Falls? Why would they want us or the family to think that he'd either committed suicide or run away?"

"Maybe Danson was working for them. His cover had been blown and they were going to set him up somewhere else?" Ian ventured.

"I don't think they work like that. As far as we know, Danson didn't speak Russian, didn't have access to any confidential information and wouldn't have been useful to them. No, I think we're missing something." Rhona shifted to look at Ian and yelped. "Damn hip, it should be better by now. I'll listen to the instructor next time."

*   *   *

After her confrontation with the detective, Hollis was glad to arrive home. She and MacTee climbed the stairs, and she knocked on Candace's door.

"Tee, Tee," she heard Elizabeth shout. When Candace opened the door, Elizabeth scooted out and wrapped her arms around MacTee.

"That was one terrible day," Candace said, leaning on the door frame. "I can't concentrate on anything. My boss asked me a question three times before I registered that she was talking to me. I'll lose my job if I don't get my act together. All I want to do is phone Rhona Simpson to see if they've found anything." She scrunched her lips and shook her head.

"It's terrible when you can't focus," Hollis said.

"I'm not the only one affected. When I picked up Elizabeth at day care, they told me she'd been behaving badly. Apparently she wouldn't settle for her nap, wouldn't play with any one and bit poor little Caroline when she came over and tried to hug her. They asked me what was wrong. I told them we were worried about my brother who was missing." She shook her head again. "No one who doesn't know our family circumstances would understand why that would upset Elizabeth. I'm sure they thought it was a lame excuse. They must have given Elizabeth grief, because she sulked all the way home." She looked past

Hollis at Elizabeth and MacTee. "Good thing you brought MacTee. He distracts her. What happened at your lunch with Willem? Come in and tell me."

"Willem tried to uncover the paper's meaning. Thugs abducted him while I was on the phone with him."

Candace covered her mouth with her hand.

"I called the police, told Rhona and gave her the paper. It's time to face up to the fact that we're dealing with a serious situation. I'm here to say again as forcefully as I can that we must talk to Poppy. Please phone and pin her down and make her commit to a time when we can have her undivided attention."

"Poppy? What's happened that you need to talk to her?"

When MacTee moved, Elizabeth lurched forward and fell. She began to howl.

"Not the best time to talk," Candace said bundling Elizabeth into her arms.

Elizabeth snuffled. "Bad Tee," she said.

"No. He didn't mean to do that," Hollis reassured her. Better give Candace a chance to pull herself together? "Elizabeth, I've made a flock of chickens. They need names. Would you come up and tell me what you think I should call them?"

"Tikens?"

"Paper birds Hollis made," Candace explained. "Like the dog outside her door."

Elizabeth's brow wrinkled.

"Remember the birds, the parrots, that we saw up there a week ago?"

"Tikens." Elizabeth wriggled free and headed for the stairs.

"Call Poppy. Demand that she tell us what she knows about the stamp and who might have placed the notice in the paper," Hollis instructed.

Upstairs, Elizabeth admired the chickens.

"What will we call them?"

"One, two, three, seven?" Elizabeth offered.

"Maybe, but those are numbers. We don't usually call things by number," Hollis said, although she could think of exceptions. Her great-grandfather, the eighth child in his family, had been Octavius.

"Can't know," Elizabeth said.

Hollis had planned to name them after particularly delicious chicken dishes—marsala, korma, cacciatore, Creole, tandoori, tetrazini. Elizabeth no doubt didn't know that the meat and poultry she ate came from formerly living animals. This wasn't the time to enlighten her. "We'll think about it and come up with good names," Hollis said.

Elizabeth had joined MacTee, who stared fixedly alternately at his dinner dish then at Hollis.

"Elizabeth, do you know what MacTee wants?"

The little girl bent down and picked up the bowl. "Dinner, Tee wants dinner," she said.

"You are such a smart girl. Would you like to scoop the kibble into his dish?"

Elizabeth did, and as Hollis set it on the counter, Wagner thundered through the room.

Although she used her phone frequently for outgoing calls, she had only given the number to her mother, Candace and Willem. Where was the damn phone? Her coat and shoulder bag hung beside the door. She scrabbled in her coat pocket and realized the sound was coming from her bag. "Don't hang up, don't hang up," she mumbled groping in the bag then dumping the contents on the floor and lunging for the phone.

"Hello," she said and waited anxiously to hear who was calling.

"It's Willem."

"Where are you? Are you okay?" Suspicion gripped her. "Are you alone?"

"Yes."

What if he was lying? What if the thugs who'd frog-marched him away were standing over him? What if they'd made him tell who had given him the information about the Super Bug? He'd called her on her cell. That was good. At least no one would be able to trace the number.

"Are you there?" Willem said.

"Yes. I'm afraid you aren't alone. Let me ask you questions that you can answer yes or no to."

"I am alone, but do it if it will make you feel better."

What if he was calling from a phone that had a speaker, and anyone else in the room could listen to what she was saying?

"Are you sure you're okay?"

"I'm not great, but I'll live."

"What did they do to you?"

"I'm okay."

"Why are you calling me?" Oh dear, that sounded ungrateful and suspicious. She'd been worrying about him and feeling guilty, but that wasn't what her words conveyed. "I'm sorry that didn't come out right. I'm glad you phoned, because I was terrified that something awful had happened to you."

"We need to talk."

Was this a trap, a way for his abductors to identify her and where she lived? She couldn't ask why they needed to talk in case someone was listening.

Elizabeth was hunkered down, examining the eclectic collection of things that had spilled from Hollis's bag. She reached forward, extricated a hand mirror, peered into it, smiled at herself and replaced it before she grabbed a ball point pen.

No way she was going to let Willem come here. Maybe they could meet somewhere very public. Somewhere she could reach by subway to prevent anyone from following her home. Where? She traversed an imaginary map. Not a coffee shop, not a store. In her mind she left the subway at Bloor Street. No place in the concourse under the stores. She climbed the stairs to Yonge Street and inspiration struck.

"The Toronto Reference Library on Yonge Street."

"What?"

"I'd feel safe meeting you there."

"Okay. We'll meet in the lobby outside the coffee shop by the water feature in an hour," Willem said in a shaky voice and hung up.

MacTee gave a low growl. A pool of drool marked the spot where he'd sat patiently staring up at the bowl while she talked on the phone.

"Sorry," she said and moved his food to the floor, where he inhaled it in seconds.

Elizabeth watched but didn't go near him. Hollis and Candace's warnings not to approach any dog that was eating had sunk in.

"Time to go back to your place. Would you like to bring MacTee?" Hollis said.

"Candace, Willem phoned and asked me to meet him. He said it was urgent. I have to go and find out what happened to him."

"Do you think it's about Danson?" Candace said hopefully.

"I don't know. He didn't give me any clues."

"I called Poppy. She and Alberto compete again tonight. They're doing well, and many dancers ordered costumes. Do you know she didn't even ask about Danson, she said to call her tomorrow when I get home from work. I know you want to find out if she knows any more, but I could tell by her tone that we wouldn't get any useful information from her today."

His mother's lack of interest in her son's welfare continued to amaze Hollis, but she mustn't be judgmental. Poppy didn't know the nasty details and was currently immersed in the preparations for the dance competition. No doubt that explained her indifference. They'd have to wait until she was available, physically and mentally.

"Would you like MacTee, our very own Nana, to entertain Elizabeth? He's eaten and walked."

"Would we? He's better than *Tree House* as a diversion," Candace said.

MacTee duly ensconced, Hollis had zipped up her green down jacket, pocketed her phone and slung her bag over her shoulder when a black thought raised its ugly head. Could Willem's call have been designed to lure her out in the open so his kidnappers could abduct or kill her? But she could outsmart them. If she left by the back of the house, she could slide through an opening in the fence and emerge on the street behind. It might be over the top, paranoid, but she didn't care. Life was becoming more and more surreal.

She trundled back upstairs, opened the fire escape door and cursed. Why hadn't she called a locksmith to fix it? This was not the time to have such a flimsy lock, but she couldn't do anything about it at the moment. She shut it as firmly as she could and made her way down and away from the house, her mind in a whirl.

Why had Willem wanted to meet her? Hollis couldn't really think of any reason, of anything he couldn't have said to her on the phone. She shrugged—she'd find out soon enough.

*   *   *

At Homicide headquarters, Rhona and Ian waited for the warrant.

"We should wear our Kevlar vests," Ian said.

Rhona knew her face expressed her unwillingness. Despite the many policewomen on the force, her department had not provided a model for women. The vests constricted all but the most flat-chested and were widely disliked.

"To interview an elderly woman with psychiatric problems?" she said.

"Yes. She's a loose cannon. We don't know who she's connected to or if she's part of something larger. This is

201

unknown territory. Better to be safe."

This was usually her line. She hauled her vest from her locker and shrugged it on. "At least it isn't a sweltering hot day. They'll keep us warm in that chilly wind. "

Warrant secured, the two detectives parked close to the apartment. Inside the vestibule they examined the panel of buzzers and rang the superintendent's bell. No response.

"Great?" Ian said. "We can't even get in the building. Now what?"

Rhona waved at the heavy glass door. "Wait for Spike. I expect he knows the code to open this one, and he likely possesses a key to his mother's apartment."

"Yes. She'd want him to come in if she fell or had a stroke."

"Maybe, but she strikes me as paranoid, and she might not have given him one."

"True. Even if he doesn't have a key, he may persuade his mother to let us in."

"Who knows—she may open the door when she realizes we have a warrant. If not, when the super arrives, he'll use his key. Some way we will get into that apartment," Rhona said.

In the vestibule they waited until a heavily muscled, bald young man pushed the door open, stepped in and stopped abruptly when he saw them.

"Spike?" Ian said, and the three shook hands.

"Mother have problems," Spike said apologetically.

This probably wasn't the first time he'd had to intervene in his mother's life.

"We know. We met her in the park and realized she did. Nevertheless, we must talk to her," Rhona said and fished the warrant from her bag. "We do have authorization to enter the apartment."

Spike's lips twisted. "I not go in for months. She meet me in park. Not know why." He smiled ruefully. "I know entry code." He pressed a combination of numbers on the key pad. When the door buzzed, he led the way upstairs to the dimly-lit third floor corridor, where he stopped at a plain heavily varnished door. He pushed the buzzer.

"Mama, it's me, Venedikt. Open door." He shrugged and spoke rapid Russian.

No answer from inside. He buzzed again then knocked.

"I come down. Go down." They heard Katerina's voice from behind the door.

"No, Mama. I come in," Spike responded.

"No one come in."

"Mama, I'm son. Let me in," Spike implored.

No answer.

He turned away from the door, met Rhona's eyes and shrugged. "See. I know she not let us in."

Rhona knocked on the door. "Katerina. It's Detective Rhona Simpson. I'm the woman who spoke to you in the park. Let us in. We need to talk."

A shout from inside followed by what had to be fists pounding on the door. "Never." A torrent of speech, accusatory and high-pitched, and a second thundering volley.

Spike stepped back. "No, Mama. No." He too launched a barrage of words, but the tone was soft and conciliatory.

The response was not. Katerina's voice rose to a scream, and her thudding fists beat an even stronger tattoo.

"I'll see if the super is back," Ian whispered and headed for the stairs.

Katerina and Spike continued their exchange but reached an impasse. Both stopped talking, but the door did not open.

Ian returned, trailed by a short, rotund man dressed in navy coveralls with "Bud" embroidered on the pocket.

"Sorry. I was out back doing something about the garbage. Damn raccoons. Wish we could shoot them." He flourished a bunch of keys. "Did you tell her I was doing this? Katerina can be scary," he said.

Ian nodded to Spike. "Tell her," he said.

Spike spoke at length, his tone reasonable, although a

slight tremor betrayed his nervousness.

No response from the apartment's interior.

Bud shrugged, inserted the key, rotated the knob and pushed the door open.

Katerina was not at the door.

Bud craned his neck to see inside, but Ian moved to block his view, thanked him and sent him on his way before they entered.

"Mama," Spike called.

No response.

They trekked along a dark hall to the living room.

Katerina, knitting on her lap, rocked back and forth in an old armchair. She didn't acknowledge their arrival.

Spike dropped to his knees beside his mother. "Mama," he repeated.

Katerina gave no indication that she had heard him.

Rhona remembered Katerina's frenzy in the park. While she examined the living room, she kept an eye on the rocking woman. Nothing untoward in this room. Large, heavy, overstuffed furniture upholstered in maroon plush filled the space. Russian icons and badly painted landscapes hung in no apparent order on faded, flowered wallpaper.

"Mama," Spike said and slipped into slow, carefully enunciated Russian.

Rhona moved to stand in front of Katerina. She showed her the warrant. "We are here to inspect your apartment."

"No." Katerina spat the words. Her body twitched as if electric currents pulsed through her. "My house." She slammed her fist on the arm of the chair. "Mine. Not for you. Mine." Katerina glared around the room without her gaze fixing on anyone.

"Will you answer questions?" Ian said.

Katerina stopped moving as suddenly as she'd started. Her eyes widened as if she was seeing an alien being, an intruder from outer space.

"Did you know the murdered drug addicts?" Ian said.

Katerina subsided into her chair and smiled.

A chill settled over the apartment.

"Did you?" he persisted.

Katerina resumed rocking, but the smile remained fixed on her lips. A secretive, complacent smile. Whatever information she possessed, she wasn't about to share it.

"Why you think she did?" Spike said. He bit his lower lip and repeated the question.

He deserved an answer. If this had been her mother, she'd want to know why the police were here.

"She's in the park every day. Most of the murdered men lived nearby and may have spent time there. The first time we walked through the park, we saw your mother talking to a young man. It seems likely she was acquainted with the dead men."

"Other people come to park. Why you talk to Mama?" Spike frowned and squinched his eyes almost closed. "Pigeon feeders there every day. Did you talk to them?"

"We've spoken to most regulars. See if you can persuade your mother to answer our questions. She may not have understood us. Convince her that we're interested in everyone who uses the park on a regular basis."

A spatter of Russian from Spike.

Katerina ignored him and continued to rock and smile.

"With or without her cooperation, we have a warrant and will search." She raised her voice and enunciated each word. "We are going to check your apartment," she said to Katerina.

Katerina erupted from her chair, and shot forward, knitting needles together, their tips a sharpened arrow aimed directly at Rhona's chest.

Spike and Ian collided in their rush to restrain her.

Rhona fell backwards. Katerina landed on top of her, raising her arms to stab repeatedly.

It took the combined strength of Spike, the bouncer, and, Ian, the fitness fanatic, to pry Katerina away from Rhona, pin Katerina's arms behind her back, snap handcuffs around her wrists and shove her back into the chair.

Rhona scrambled to her feet. "Thank goodness for Kevlar. They're uncomfortable, but when you need them, you don't care."

Katerina mumbled and repeated a singsong phrase.

"What's she saying?" Ian asked Spike.

Spike, eyes wide, contemplated his mother as if he'd never seen her before.

The singsong drone increased in volume.

"What's she saying?" repeated Ian.

"Not enough, not enough, not enough," Spike said. "What does she mean?"

"We may know in a minute," Rhona said.

Poor man. If they were right, he was about to receive a terrible shock.

"It's time to see what she's hiding," Ian said.

Sixteen

Hollis walked north on Yonge Street toward the Toronto Reference library. She approached cautiously. Several times she stopped and peered behind her before she continued. After she'd covered half a block, she stepped into a Tim Hortons coffee shop doorway and allowed the crowd to swirl past her. Then she reversed and returned to the corner of Yonge and Bloor Streets, crossed to the west side of Yonge Street and made her way northward again. This time she swivelled to look behind her and made a mental note of who she saw before she moseyed into the cookbook store and pretended to examine the books displayed at the front. Instead she watched the passersby and paid particular attention to those loitering in front of the library across the street. As far as she could tell, no one behaved suspiciously, and no one had followed her. She crossed Yonge Street at the light in front of the library and entered the red brick building. People swirled in and out. Students, vagrants searching for a warm place to spend time, older men and women researching a variety of subjects—a crowd always filled the lobby. She'd chosen well.

She allowed her gaze to circle the room, searching for Willem.

Half-turned away from her, he stood beside the pool. Bandaids, taped one underneath another, covered most his cheek. The eye that she saw was swollen shut. He stood hunched over like a man protecting his vitals from assault. Unbidden, a memory jumped into her mind. She'd cracked two ribs in a biking accident and for weeks had walked protectively, guarding them against unintentional contact with anything. She'd slept propped up surrounded by insulating pillows but, every time she moved, pain had jarred her awake.

She felt incredibly guilty. Willem, her Cossack defender, was suffering like this because of her, because she hadn't been sensible and gone to the police. How could she ever make amends?

"Willem," she said, approaching him from behind.

He started and involuntarily gasped as he turned to her.

Face to face, she saw that the damage was worse than she'd thought when she'd seen him from a distance. Both eyes were swollen and bruised, and his lower lip was split.

She reached to hug him, remembered how careful she'd been with her broken ribs, and stopped.

He'd held up a restraining arm as she moved forward. "Don't. I hurt everywhere."

"Oh, my god, I'm sorry. This is my fault. Oh, Willem, I'd give anything not to have phoned you, not to have asked you to translate the message."

Willem gingerly placed his hands on her arms. "Hollis."

Reluctantly she fixed on his battered face.

"This is not your fault."

"How can you say that? Of course it's my fault."

He squeezed her arms. "Listen to me. You did not ask me to investigate. You asked for a translation, and I volunteered. Got that—volunteered to see what I could find out about Super Bug."

"Initially, that was true, but when you said I should go to the police, I didn't."

Willem released her. "No. I could have said no. I'm an adult. Grown men have choices. I made a bad one, but it's not your fault."

He withdrew his hands, touched his cheek then again

extended his hands for her to see. "I have both my hands and all my fingers. It could have been worse. They roughed me up a bit, but I have no seriously broken bones,"

"Seriously broken? What does that mean? What bones are broken?" Hollis said.

Willem said nothing.

"They cracked your ribs, didn't they? That happened to me once, and I stood like you're doing." How could he downplay broken bones? "Anything that's broken is serious."

"I'm alive." He pointed to his face. "No permanent damage. This will heal."

Her anger ebbed as rapidly as it had come, but she still felt overwhelming guilt, despite his reassuring words. More than that, she needed to know what the thugs had tried to beat out of him and what he'd told them. Given his condition, it would be crass to pursue the subject, but she had to know if she'd endangered Candace and Elizabeth.

"I gave the translation to the police."

"About time. Does that mean you've stopped your Nancy Drew stuff?"

Hollis ignored the question. "I hate to ask, but I'm going to. What did they want to know? What did you tell them?"

"I'll tell you, but I need coffee and something sweet. My blood sugar level is nonexistent." Willem attempted a smile that must have hurt, since it disappeared almost as soon as his lips curved.

"My treat," Hollis said, reaching into her bag for her change purse. "Find a place to sit down, and I'll bring it to you. What do you want?"

"Thanks, even though it was my suggestion, I accept. A chocolate doughnut and a cappuccino, and bring several envelopes of brown sugar," Willem responded.

Snacks in hand, she joined him on an unoccupied slatted bench facing the indoor pond.

"Well," Hollis said.

Willem eyed his cup as if he feared the pain that might result if the hot liquid touched his split lip. He blew on it and took a careful sip. A light foam mustache decorated his upper lip.

Hollis longed to reach forward and gently wipe it away but restrained herself.

"Something wrong?" Willem asked.

"A mustache," Hollis said.

Willem tidied himself, tentatively broke off a small morsel of doughnut, opened his mouth a crack and slid it in.

Hollis waited.

"They wanted to know where I'd heard about the bug. I stuck to my subway story."

Having been holding her breath, she expelled a puff of air and relaxed the tension in her shoulders.

"Where did they take you after they forced you away from your office?"

"A garage somewhere. Then they hauled me into a car and dumped me in an industrial park near Overlea Boulevard. Once I regained consciousness, it took me more than an hour to get on my feet and clean and patch myself up. For a while there, I didn't think I'd be able to do it. Waves of nausea hit me every time I moved. I could see the sign for the East York Town Centre and limped over. I don't know if you've ever been in that mall, but you see everything and everybody. Even though I was a mess, no one looked at me or phoned the police. I bought bandaids and cleaned up in the washroom. Then I found a payphone and called you to arrange a meeting. I don't trust cell phones. I wanted to pass on what I'd heard in person."

He had to relate all of this in his own way and time.

"In the garage, when they knocked me down and kicked me in the head, I pretended I'd blacked out. They conferred about reviving me. They said they had orders from the boss to find out how much I knew about Super Bug returning. Then they kicked me again in the head and I passed out for real. Next thing I knew I was behind a dumpster in a parking area for a factory that was closed."

Hollis heard "kicked in the head". "Willem, look at me," she ordered.

She examined his pupils. The right was much smaller than the left. "We have to go to the hospital, to St. Mikes, immediately," she said setting her cup on the bench and standing up.

"What?" Willem's face registered his confusion.

"Any kind of head injury can result in a concussion. That can lead to a brain hemorrhage. You need to go to hospital and have them monitor you on an hour-to-hour basis," she said, offering him her arm.

"Are you crazy? We'd spend the entire night waiting to be seen. I've been to the ER before, and I know what I'm talking about." He settled back. "Get this. I am not going anywhere except home to bed. I came here against my better judgment, because I knew you'd be worried." He stopped and glared at her. "Not about me. That would be too much to expect. But about what I'd told them. You didn't say, but other people must be involved in this, whatever this is."

He might as well have slapped her face. Not worried about him? How unfair. Well, maybe not unjust—he'd warned her that she was meddling in something dangerous, and she'd ignored his warning and persuaded him to continue. She couldn't let him go home. What if he had a stroke or bleeding in his brain and ending up lying alone in his apartment?

"Seriously, both your pupils should be the same size. They aren't. Something is happening in your brain." She'd appeal to his common sense. "If you want to continue to be a linguistics professor and, even more, if you want to go to law school, your brain has to be fully operational. You don't want bleeding to wipe out neurons you'll need."

"I am not going to the hospital. The thugs didn't get anything out of me. I don't know why they didn't finish the job, why they dumped me. Maybe they figured I was dying, or they thought I really didn't know anything. If they know

I'm alive, their boss may order them to try again."

Hollis registered what he'd said viscerally. Her stomach contracted, and her breath came in short gasps. "You think they may still intend to kill you," she said in a high-pitched voice she hardly recognized as her own.

"Maybe yes, maybe no. It wouldn't surprise me."

They hadn't killed him, and he needed medical attention. If he wouldn't go to the hospital, she couldn't make him. Even if she called 911 and the police, fire and ambulance services arrived, they had no power to force him to seek medical help. What if she offered to go home with him and wake him every hour? If he lapsed into unconsciousness, she could call an ambulance. But what about MacTee? She couldn't leave him, because Candace couldn't walk him at night when Elizabeth was in bed. They could grab a cab to her place, collect MacTee, pile into her truck and go to Willem's place. It was one option.

He grimaced as he sipped his coffee. Was it from his lip or his ribs or his head? He must have a massive headache. Was that a sign of brain damage? She wished she had more medical knowledge.

"You mustn't be alone," she said.

She'd pick him up like a bulky parcel and take him home with her. What if the thugs had followed him? What if they waited outside or right here in the building? She glanced around to see if anyone seemed out of place in the library. An impossible assessment. The variety of people in the lobby told her nothing except that Toronto was a multicultural, multiracial city where people came to the library for as many reasons as there were patrons. Maybe Willem would refuse. Maybe they'd sit here until the library closed then deal with the situation. She had to try.

"Willem, come home with me and let me monitor your eyes, make you chicken soup, do what caring women have always done. It's the least I can do," she said.

He didn't smile. Didn't say he'd love chicken soup. Instead, he sighed, winced and shook his head. "They were serious. I don't want to risk bringing harm to you."

"Do you think they followed you?"

"No. Once I'd phoned you from the shopping centre, I hailed a cab. There's a stand outside the grocery store. When we arrived at Union Station, I struggled inside, then staggered out and took a second cab up here."

How careful he'd been to cover his tracks. He'd prolonged his pain, his desire to get to his own bed and collapse, in his single-minded determination to meet her, to warn her. Tears welled. With a golf-ball-sized lump in her throat, she'd have a hard time speaking, but she had to persuade him to stay with her.

"You have to." She attempted a smile, a lighthearted remark. "You have to do it for selfish me, so I'll be able to live with myself. If I leave you here to find your way back to your apartment where the mob guys may be waiting to see if you made it back, I won't be able to maintain my façade as a nice, caring person."

Willem didn't smile, but he did nod. "Well, I couldn't be responsible for a drop in your self-esteem, could I?"

While they'd talked, he'd lost colour, become a sickly yellow-grey, a sign of total exhaustion or something more serious. She reached in her bag and pulled out her wallet. "I carry a taxi card. I'll call, then I'll help you outside."

"Okay. Hard for a macho fellow to admit, but I've about reached the end of my endurance."

Inside the cab, Hollis resisted the urge to ask the driver if anyone was following them or to stare out the rear window. Instead, she held Willem's hand and said nothing. At the house, she paid, came around, opened the door and helped him out. He wobbled and took one step before he stopped.

"I can't even take a deep breath," he said shakily.

"Unfortunately, I live on the third floor," Hollis said.

How to get him up there? The front steps—surely they could make it that far. Then she'd help him sit down.

"There's a young man in the basement apartment. Let's get you to the steps. Then I'll get him. We need help."

"Yes, we do," Willem whispered.

Slowly, almost inch by inch, they edged up the short walk. Willem transferred what felt like his entire weight to Hollis, who kept telling herself to hang on, to make one more forward move before she collapsed. At the stoop, Willem crumpled against Hollis, who lowered him to the second step where he sagged back with his eyes closed.

She wished she'd instructed the driver to take them to the nearest hospital emergency. Maybe it wasn't too late.

"Why don't I go in and call an ambulance?" she asked.

Willem didn't open his eyes.

"Should I?" she said.

"I heard you the first time," Willem said in a nearly inaudible voice. "No. We'll make it. I just need to rest for a moment."

She prayed Jack would be home. Inside the vestibule, she buzzed his apartment and held her breath.

"Yes?"

"Jack, it's Hollis, the top-floor tenant. I have a friend who's coming to stay with me, and he's ill. Would you help me get him up to my apartment?"

"Give me a minute, and I'll be out."

When Jack emerged, his smile evaporated when he saw Willem. "What's wrong with him?" he asked.

"He's weak," she said.

"He looks like he's been beaten up. Is that what happened?" Jack said.

Willem opened his eyes. "I've been sick, and I had a bad fall. Thanks for helping," he said in a nearly normal voice.

"Can you use the hand rail to pull yourself, and I'll come behind and push?" Jack said.

"No. I have broken ribs," Willem said.

"Crawling might be the best way," Hollis suggested.

"It might. My knees are okay, and my arms. I don't have

214

any strength though."

"We'll be on either side, and we'll help move and lift your arms and knees if you can't," Jack offered.

Stair by stair, they began the trek.

When they reached the landing between the first and second floor, Willem held up his hand. "I have to rest," he panted, and they eased themselves to the floor.

Candace's door opened a crack, and she peeked out.

"It's me and Willem and Jack," Hollis called.

"What are you doing? Why are you on the floor?" Candace asked stepping into the crowded hall.

"Willem had an…" Hollis paused. "Had" wasn't exactly the right verb. She should say that two men from the Russian mob kicked the shit out of him and left him for dead, but this wasn't the time, particularly with Jack there. "…an accident and he's going to stay with me tonight." She hoped her tone conveyed the sense that the circumstances, however bizarre, were perfectly okay. "His ribs are damaged, so he can't use the railing, and Jack is helping him," she said.

"Willem? You did say Willem?"

"Yes." Silly in the circumstances, but she added, "Willem, this is Candace."

Candace must have figured it wasn't the time to comment on Willem's role in their lives or on his arrival. "It's a good thing Jack was home. Do you need me to help too?" she said.

"We're doing okay. Slow and steady," Hollis said.

"Glad to meet you, Willem, even if the circumstances aren't the best. Hollis, I have mac and cheese left from our dinner. I'll bring a dish up once you're settled," she said and returned to her apartment.

"Your landlady?" Willem asked.

"Yes." Hollis wasn't about to talk about their friendship. They continued to sit on the floor, waiting for Willem to signal his readiness to continue.

"I'm the downstairs tenant," Jack said. "I'm here because

215

Candace's brother, Danson, is a lacrosse player and scout for the Toronto team, and he persuaded his sister to allow me stay here." Why he needed to explain this to Willem was beyond Hollis. Maybe he felt he should make conversation.

"Have you heard any more about Danson? Has anyone figured out where he's gone? The team needs him," Jack said to Hollis.

Damn. Willem might make the connections if Jack didn't shut up.

"You okay, Willem? Can we do the last flight? I'm sure we're keeping Jack from something important," Hollis said.

"No, seriously, something must have happened to him. I mean guys go AWOL if the loan sharks are after them or they want to run away with a woman, but Danson was keen about this year's team. I can't see him doing an end run like this."

"It is strange," Hollis agreed.

"Have you filed a missing persons report?" Jack persisted.

"Jack, we have. Nothing has turned up. Now let's get Willem upstairs."

"Missing person," Willem mumbled.

The jig was up.

Seventeen

"Good thing we wore the vests. She could have done you serious harm," Ian said as Rhona straightened her clothes and collected herself.

"Who knew she was that strong," Rhona's jaw set in a hard line. "Enough pussyfooting around. Time to take the place apart."

Hands cuffed behind her back, Katerina slumped in the chair, talking to herself exclusively in Russian.

"My god. I'm sorry. I never think she attack you. She crazy," Spike said. "I watch her for you." He patted his mother's shoulder and said something that sounded reassuring.

Katerina paid no attention. She'd retreated to another reality.

Hand still on his mother's shoulder, his gaze moved from one detective to the other. "She had really hard time when she came to Canada," he said. "She had profession in Russia. Here she clean houses. Then my brother was killed. He her star, her hope for future. She go crazy."

Despite the attack, Rhona felt sorry for the wreck huddled in the chair. She always wanted to know the back story—how people got to be the way they were.

"Was she right? Would your brother have been a success?"

Spike patted his mother's shoulder again. "Who can know? I not think so. He want quick money." He sighed. "He think crime pays. No, he not her hope for future, but she believe."

"Let's do our search," Ian said.

They left Spike talking gently to Katerina.

The kitchen, messy and stacked with dishes and half-eaten food, told them nothing except that Katerina was a poor housekeeper. The dining half of the living room held a large table, almost obliterated by piles of books and papers, baskets of wool. One corner was devoted to picture framing. At least six deep shadowbox frames were piled precariously one on top of the other. A hammer, staple gun, glue and tape lined up on the edge of a rectangle of oilcloth provided an indication that Katerina was sometimes tidy and methodical.

"Seems like she was in the picture-framing business," Ian said. He allowed his gaze to roam the walls of the combined living room dining room. "She didn't hang them here."

Rhona opened a sideboard crammed with dishes and dusty glasses. Books were piled on the floor.

"What you looking for?" Spike asked from the living room where he'd pulled a chair close to his mother and sat watching the two detectives.

"This and that," Rhona said.

Katerina's head snapped up, and her body tensed as if she was about to spring from her chair. "Secret police take everything." She raised her voice. "No good. I have no money. Nothing to take. Thieves. Secret police are thieves."

"Katerina." Rhona scrunched down until she was on eye level with Katerina. "Katerina, do you have something you'd like to tell us?"

"Tell you?" Katerina repeated and smiled her chilling smile. "You find out. I not have to tell." She smiled again and dropped her head. "You find," she said and reverted to Russian.

"What's she saying?" asked Ian.

Spike cocked his head to one side and leaned close to his mother. He listened for some moments before he lifted his gaze to Rhona. "She not making much sense. She keep saying rhyme that has to do with numbers and colours."

"Can you translate?" Ian said.

Spike listened again. "One for one, red for you, two is more, green for go, three four, three four, purple blue, purple blue, never a gun, never run…" he stopped. "I not understand the rest."

Rhona suspected she knew exactly what the rhyme was about. She hoped she was wrong. "We'll make a quick survey."

Ian opened the bedroom door, stepped in and stopped as if he'd smacked into a wall. "Oh, my god," he said.

Rhona, following behind, repeated, "Oh, my god," and added, "trophy cases. She was making trophy cases. Like a big game hunt."

"She wasn't finished," Ian said.

"That's why there are several finished boxes and the materials to make more on the dining room table."

"They're pretty, in a macabre way."

Rhona regarded the black-framed shadow boxes lined up on the wall. Each held a similar composition.

On a roughly painted red background, knitting needles crossed at right angles, precisely dividing the space into four squares. A cardboard figure with outstretched arms was affixed to this crucifix. Wool wrapped the entire body, except for the head. Each head was black with a white oval mouth opened in a scream and solid white eyes. A scarf of the same wool hung on the right edge of the case.

"That was how she did it. Won their trust. Made them a scarf. Presented it, wound it around their necks and stabbed them with the knitting needles." She shook her head. "It's ingenious." A noise behind her caused her to whirl around.

Spike's hands covered his mouth and his eyes, widened with shock, stared at the grotesque montages. He'd gasped when he'd seen what the boxes held and heard their conversation. His gaze moved from the boxes to them and back to the boxes again.

"She killed drug addicts," Rhona said as she reached for her cell phone and asked for back-up. "We have to take her in," Rhona said.

They turned to Katerina, who had stopped mumbling and begun a keening, high-pitched wailing as her rocking increased.

"What will happen to her?" Spike said. "She need help." He shook his head. "I feel bad. I know she need help and not make her go." He glanced at the knitting that had fallen to the floor when his mother had launched herself at Rhona. Then he swung around and counted the boxes on the wall. "She kill six men? Mother kill six?" His eyes revealed his incredulity, his inability to accept that his mother was a serial killer and, if the boxes on the dining room table told the tale, had intended to kill many more.

"Rats," Katerina said.

Spike focused on his mother. "What rats?" he said.

"Them," she said and pointed to the bedroom. "Rats die. I do it. Not sorry." Having said that, she lifted her head and tried to rise. With her hands pinioned behind her back, she found it impossible. "Help me up," she said to Spike.

He didn't move.

"Go ahead," Rhona said.

On her feet, Katerina spoke again. "We go," she said and moved toward the door.

"What will happen to her?" Spike asked again.

"I can't say for sure. There will be a bail hearing within forty-eight hours, but I'm sure she won't get bail, that she'll be referred for psychiatric assessment. After that, the court will likely send her to mental health court, where they may sentence her to a long-term commitment in the hospital for the criminally insane in Penetanguishene. I don't know for sure, but that is a possibility."

Spike absorbed the information in silence.

Much later, once they'd delivered Katerina to the cells, the two detectives looked at one another.

"Next question is, was she connected to Gregory's murder and Danson's disappearance?" Ian said.

* * *

Hollis thanked Jack after he'd assisted Willem to her bedroom. Although she realized he wanted to stay and quiz her, to learn what had happened to Willem and what she knew about Danson, she shepherded him to the door.

"Thanks again. We couldn't have made it up here without you."

"You'll tell me if you have any news about Danson?" Jack said.

She promised and shut the door.

Willem lay with his eyes closed. How serious were his injuries? If his assailants had left him for dead, they must have done serious damage. Internal, invisible injuries could kill him. His pallor frightened her. She should call an ambulance, hand him to professionals who could assess his injuries and take appropriate action. She sighed. If he deteriorated, she would. For now she'd do her best to care for him.

She untied his polished brown brogues, noticing their quality as she carefully removed them. Willem sighed, but his eyes remained shut. His hands lay palms up at his sides. They were marked with traces of blood, as was his face. She gently pulled the folded quilt from beneath his feet and draped it over him. Then she fetched a bowl of warm water and a wash cloth. Without applying pressure, she sponged his hands and face.

His eyes remained closed, but he spoke. "Give me half an hour to recover from Mount Everest, and we'll talk."

In his condition, he was making jokes! Mount Everest indeed. "We don't need to talk," Hollis said although she desperately wanted to know what he'd found out about the Super Bug. "Sleep. I'll wake you in an hour to check your pupils."

Willem's lips curved, but he winced as the gesture pulled on his split lip.

Hollis left the bedroom door slightly ajar to hear if he

called out. In her combination living room and workroom she stood in the middle of the room and weighed her options. Before she'd finished, Candace, carrying a covered white bowl and a baby monitor knocked and entered the apartment.

Hollis placed her finger on her lips and nodded toward the bedroom.

Candace plugged in the monitor, and lowered the volume. The repeating CD of soothing lullabies that Elizabeth listened to each night invaded the room.

"Heck of a way to meet Willem," Candace said in a low voice with a faint smile.

Hollis didn't think it was a moment for levity. Willem was badly hurt, and she felt horribly guilty

"Sorry, I didn't mean to take it lightly," Candace said.

"I know. I'm being hypersensitive, because if he hadn't offered to help us, he wouldn't be in this state," Hollis said and pressed her lips together to keep from crying.

"Never mind how you feel. This isn't about you," Candace said.

The reproach reached its target. It was time to stop thinking about herself.

"You're right. I'm making him open his eyes hourly to see if there's any change. He has a concussion. If he gets worse, I'll call an ambulance."

"Does what happened to him have any connection to Danson?"

"I don't know. Two guys beat him up because he'd been asking questions about the Super Bug in the wrong places. After it happened, he called me because he'd found out something, but I won't know what it is until he's in better shape."

Willem moaned.

"Come and tell me if you think he should go to the hospital," Hollis said.

Both women stood beside the bed. Willem's eyes remained closed. He shifted and groaned, took a deep breath and again adjusted himself with an accompanying moan.

"His poor face. It will be weeks before those black eyes are okay and it doesn't stop hurting him to eat or smile or move his mouth," Candace whispered.

"It's like weight watchers," Willem whispered.

"Willem, how can you joke when you must hurt like hell?" Hollis said.

Willem opened his eyes. "I'm glad I'm alive."

Once again, knowing he believed the thugs had intended to kill him shocked Hollis. She felt like she'd been kicked in the chest—she found it hard to draw a breath. "I'm glad you are too," she said.

"Were you followed here?" Candace asked. Hollis heard the anxiety, the underlying panic, in her voice.

"Willem did everything he could to make sure he wasn't," she said reassuringly.

"They thought they'd killed me," Willem said. He moved slightly and groaned involuntarily. "Damn near did. You don't follow a dead man."

"If they kicked you until you passed out, you may have internal bleeding. It could kill you, and then they would have succeeded. You don't want that, do you?"

"You don't want to be responsible for a dead man in your bed do you?" Willem answered.

"I'd prefer a live one," Hollis said.

"I'm volunteering," Willem said. He opened his eyes and locked his gaze with Hollis, who felt herself blush.

"Let me see your pupils," she said. "I'll get a flashlight."

When she shone the flashlight in his eyes, the right one was about the same—still a different size.

"Try to rest. I'll do it every hour all night. I was once in the hospital from a fall downstairs and they woke me every hour."

"When was..." Willem said, but Hollis placed a finger near his lips. "Not now. Someday I'll tell you," she said.

Back in the living room, Candace turned off the lights.

"What are you doing?" Hollis asked.

"Scoping out the street," Candace said over her shoulder.

"And?"

"Jack is getting in his car. He must have a practice."

"It's late, isn't it?"

"Maybe he has a date?"

"Never mind Jack. The question is—does the Super Bug have anything to do with Danson?"

Eighteen

Ian and Rhona accepted congratulations. Their chief had arranged a press conference in the amphitheatre. He would do the talking, but he wanted the two detectives there to receive press accolades. He wondered aloud what the headlines would be. All agreed that the *Sun* would have the best one—it always did.

Rhona celebrated their success, but she wanted to get on with the investigation, to pinpoint the connections, if there were any, with Gregory, the murdered Russian, and Danson, his missing landlord. There had to be a link, but she couldn't join the dots. While her fellow detectives speculated on the headlines, she pulled out and reread the translation Hollis had given to her.

Super Bug—she was aware of what that meant in terms of hospitals and medicine, but that meaning didn't fit in this note. Unless it referred to a terrorist attack that would be launched with a super bug. Germ warfare had been a feature of the Cold War, and certainly there had been a scare in the U.S., when poisonous powders passed through the mails. Several people had died. The Russian gang experts should know. She picked up the phone.

* * *

"Go to bed," Hollis said to Candace. "I'm going to set the alarm and wake every hour to make sure he's okay."

"He should be in the hospital."

"I know, but…"

Retching from the bedroom.

Hollis reached Willem first. He was leaning over the side of the bed. A thin trickle of pink liquid slid down his chin and pooled on the floor.

It was blood. Willem might have internal injuries.

"Sorry," Willem whispered.

Hollis grasped his hand. "It's okay. Not your fault, but there can't be any argument. You absolutely must go to St. Mike's."

Willem said nothing.

"You won't be alone. I'll come with you. "

"I'll be okay," Willem whispered.

Hollis gently squeezed his hand. "No, you won't. No one should be by himself at the hospital. You always need someone with you."

Willem drew a ragged breath. "Will you say you're my wife?" His battered lips moved into a facsimile of a smile. "I'm a fast worker."

Although Hollis returned the smile, she didn't feel like smiling.

"If you say you are, they'll tell you what's wrong," Willem added.

"You're right. The next-of-kin stuff. Of course I will," Hollis said. She wanted to smooth the hair back from his forehead, to kiss his bruised face, but contented herself with holding his hand while Candace called 911.

Minutes later the ambulance arrived, and the attendants, sweating and straining, manoeuvered the stretcher down the stairs. Each time it banged the wall Willem winced.

Hollis had collected Willem's wallet before they left the apartment. When she claimed to be his wife, the paramedics allowed her to ride in the ambulance.

At St. Michael's Hospital, Hollis offered Willem's driver's license, and the triage nurse recorded pertinent information. She assured Hollis that they wouldn't have long to wait. Hollis didn't know whether to be happy or sad. This was triage. Rapid entry meant you were seriously injured.

Hollis stood beside Willem's stretcher and held his hand. He opened his eyes briefly and gave her what might pass for a smile. "Hell of a way to get a wife," he said and shut his eyes again.

The wait was mercifully brief. The paramedics spent little time shifting Willem from their stretcher to the hospital's and left to answer the next emergency call. Hollis wasn't allowed to enter the treatment rooms, but the attending nurse promised the doctor would speak to her, and she could be with Willem again when he was out of the examining room.

The Emerg doctor spoke to Hollis before he hurried away. "We're running tests to determine the extent of the internal injuries. He certainly has broken ribs. We don't have beds upstairs, so we'll keep him in Emerg until we diagnosis what we're dealing with. The nurse will tell you when he's back from x-ray."

When they transported Willem to a four-bed room in Emerg, Hollis foraged, found a battered molded plastic chair and perched beside him. Three o'clock in the morning might as well have been noon—the hospital throbbed with activity.

"Go home," Willem whispered. "I'm in good hands. They'll call you. Get some sleep."

Sensible advice, which she hated to take. Leaving him seemed like a betrayal. However, exhaustion wouldn't leave her as sharp as she needed to be. Outside the hospital, she hailed a taxi from the waiting ranks. Half an hour later she fell into bed.

*　　*　　*

Shrill screams pulled her from sleep's deep pit.

MacTee's barking added to the cacophony of noise.

"Noooooo, noooo," a voice shrieked repeatedly.

Hollis stumbled out of bed. The clock said nine. Was it Candace? Elizabeth? What had happened?

MacTee whined and nudged her hand.

"It's okay," she reassured him, although she was quite sure it wasn't. Groggy, she staggered out of bed. Most normal people had dressing gowns, but if you had a dog and no fenced yard, you didn't haul yourself out of bed in the morning, pull on a dressing gown and let the dog out. Instead you rose, dressed, and walked the beast. Her pyjamas would have to do.

As she pushed her feet into her slippers, a barrage of bangs thundered on her door. Whoever it was continued to repeat her keening mantra in a high-pitched voice. Bizarre. She couldn't think of an explanation, but in her foggy state that didn't surprise her.

"Okay, okay, I'm coming," she shouted.

When she flung the door open, she confronted Poppy. "My god, what's happened?" Hollis said.

MacTee raced forward to present a toy monkey.

"No. Not now," Hollis said and pushed him away.

Poppy stopped screaming, sucked in air and released it in ragged gasps.

"What is it? What's wrong?" Hollis said.

"Stolen. It's gone," Poppy said.

"What? What's gone?"

"My safe. I was sure I hid it well enough that no one would find it." Poppy shook her head rapidly and moaned, "Nooooo, noooo, noooo, it can't be gone."

"Did you call the police?"

Poppy stopped howling. Still hyperventilating, she managed to snap, "Of course not."

"That's what police do. Investigate burglaries." Hollis stepped back from the door. "I'll call them."

Poppy grabbed Hollis. "No, you won't."

"Why not?"

Her breathing slower and her words measured, Poppy's gaze locked with Hollis's. "Because no one broke into my apartment. Do you know what that means?"

Hollis waited.

"My keys are special ones. They can't be copied at the hardware store. That means someone who has a key took the safe."

Hollis remembered the missing key on Danson's ring. Candace had wanted to change the front door lock, then they'd decided that there was no point—too much time had passed. Obviously a bad decision.

"Who has a key?" Hollis asked.

Poppy's eyes no longer stared wildly, and her breathing had returned to normal. Sharing her news had calmed her.

It was the perfect time to pin her down and finally get straight answers.

"It could only have been Danson or Candace," Poppy said. "Alberto has a key, but he was with me."

"Danson? Why would Danson, who's disappeared, come back and steal your safe?"

Poppy shrugged. "Who knows?"

"I think you do," Hollis said. "Come and sit down. It's time to talk about Danson, the safe and whatever was in it." Poppy didn't move. Hollis placed her hand on Poppy's arm.

Poppy scrutinized the hand as if it belonged to a prehistoric reptile. She shifted and flipped her arm. When Hollis did not remove the offending hand, Poppy raised her eyes and glared at her.

Hollis tightened her grip. "It's time for truth-telling. Things have been happening that you should know about, because you and that article in the paper are right in the middle of this mess." She thought about Willem's pain, about Candace's overwhelming anxiety, about Danson and the murdered Russian. She frog-marched Poppy inside the apartment.

"Sit down. We're going to get to the bottom of this."

"I don't see what business it is of yours," Poppy said coldly.

"It's my business, because Candace asked me to find Danson, and I agreed to try. I'm doing my best, but I think you're withholding information that would make the job easier."

Poppy perched on the sofa, physically and psychologically uncomfortable.

Hollis yanked a chair from across the room and sat directly in front of Poppy in order to monitor the expressions on her face, to identify the tiny, giveaway signs that Poppy was lying.

Surprisingly, Poppy did as she was told. She groped in the depths of a large patent leather handbag, hauled out and flourished an electronic gadget.

"Whoever took the safe won't be able to open it," she said, a note of triumph in her voice. "I wasn't stupid enough to leave this at home." She smiled a tight little smile that held no warmth or humour. "At least I wasn't stupid enough to pack it in my carry-on. Imagine what airport security would have made of it?"

Hollis, who'd never had occasion to think about, let alone use a safe, hadn't known electronic controls had replaced the combination lock

Poppy crossed her long legs and waved the remote. "If he's after what's in there, he won't risk damaging it."

"What *is* in it? Did Danson or Candace know what you kept in the safe?"

"Danson knew about one thing I have in it."

"And that was?" Hollis asked and hoped she sounded patient. After her night with Willem and her truncated sleep, she felt anything but patient. She wanted to shake Poppy until the information spewed forth.

"Do you really think Danson could have come back for it?" Poppy said. She re-crossed her legs. "Maybe someone." She paused.

Obviously she had a specific someone in mind but didn't plan to name him.

"What if that someone learned what I had in there and forced Danson, maybe at gun point, to unlock the door and let him steal the safe? Maybe that's why Danson left? Maybe he felt guilty…" Her voice dwindled away and her brows lowered. "How would he have known…"

Poppy was driving Hollis crazy.

"Who are you talking about?" she said.

Poppy started. It was as if she'd forgotten where she was. "What?"

"Who are you talking about?" Hollis repeated. "What did Danson know? Who was the mysterious someone?"

Poppy didn't respond.

Hollis took another tack. "Is this connected to the article in the paper? The request that someone who had a particular stamp should connect with the person who'd run the notice in the paper?" Hollis watched Poppy as she asked.

Poppy's gaze shifted. She eyed Hollis speculatively. "It could be," she admitted.

"Why did Danson think the article was meant for you?"

"Because one of the stamps I have is rare and few exist. It could have been meant for me. Danson assumed it was."

"Now what do you think?"

She thrust her lower lip forward and pursed her lips. "Maybe."

"Precisely what are we talking about?"

"An 1851 Queen Victoria 12-penny black," Poppy said as if this would have been obvious to anyone.

Hollis's cell phone rang. She wanted to ignore it and keep Poppy talking. That wasn't an option.

"Hollis, it's Willem."

"How are you? What did the tests show?"

"Thank god, nothing life-threatening. Two broken ribs, major bruising. I'm okay. Stiff and sore but okay."

"What about the concussion and the bleeding?"

"My pupils are now the same size. They couldn't find anything to explain the blood. My spleen was intact, as were the other organs. They don't know what caused it."

Relief. "I'm so glad."

"They want to send me home, but they won't release me unless someone comes to get me." Brief pause. "They told me to call my wife."

Hollis laughed. "Your wife will do that. When?"

"Could you come right away?" Willem sounded apologetic.

After what he'd endured because of her stupidity, she didn't want him to feel apologetic. "Of course. I have to let MacTee out for a minute, and I'm on my way. It should take me twenty minutes."

"You'll have to come in, or they won't let me go. I'm still in Emerg."

She wanted to swear, to throw something—anything to express her frustration. She'd finally pinned Poppy down and dragged information out of her. She hadn't had time to persuade Poppy to tell her what else the safe contained. Given Poppy's reticence and insistence on privacy, she might never have another chance. She'd have to risk it, because she couldn't let Willem wait.

"Poppy, I think you should go to the police."

The woman shook her head.

Hollis hadn't expected her to agree. Poppy had led an interesting life, which no doubt had included a brush or two with the law. Whatever her past, she clearly did not want to involve the police.

"If you won't call them, we have to figure out what happened to the safe. I'm collecting a badly banged-up friend from the hospital." She let Poppy absorb this information before she added. "He was beaten up because of a good deed he did for Danson." She spaced her words to add to their impact.

"For Danson? Who is this person? Why would your friend be involved with Danson? You didn't even know Danson. Well, maybe you met him, but you certainly didn't know him." Poppy resembled an enraged dog, hackles raised, teeth bared.

"After going through his papers and reading what was on his computer, I know him better than almost anyone else," Hollis said, keeping her voice level. "I found something written in Russian in his apartment that," she considered what noun she should use, "a friend translated for me. My friend took it upon himself, as a favour to me, to ask others in the Russian community what it might have meant. This curiosity led to his attack."

"Attack? What was in the letter? What was Danson doing?" Poppy continued on the offensive.

"That's exactly what we have to figure out. I'm picking up my friend. When I return, you and I will talk, and you have to tell me the whole truth. Nothing else will do."

If Poppy took that as a threat, it was okay with Hollis. Even thinking about Willem and the damage he'd survived made her angry. Poppy, self-centred and impervious to others, could have helped and she hadn't. Hollis intended to wring the truth from her.

"I'll be down to see you when I get back," Hollis promised.

At the hospital a tired, battered Willem tried to smile, but his split lip refused to let him. The expression in his eyes told her how happy he was to see her. She knew her own eyes mirrored the feeling.

"Hello, wifey," Willem said.

Hollis crooked her arm through his and led him to her truck. He refused help and boosted himself in but not without a groan escaping his lips.

"Give me directions to your house," Hollis said.

What if the mobsters who had beaten him up had staked out his place?

"I live…" Willem began but didn't get a chance to finish his sentence.

"That could be dangerous, couldn't it? Come home with me. Let me provide TLC. It will be an act of charity, because if I can help you I'll feel less guilty. When you're ready, you can fill me in on what you discovered."

"I accept. Not because I think you have any reason to feel guilty, but because I'd like some TLC," Willem said as he sank back against the seat.

Back at her place, Hollis helped him up the three flights of stairs. MacTee welcomed him with a tennis ball and was rewarded with a pat. Willem insisted he was well enough to remove his shoes at the door, although he gasped when he bent over and had to anchor himself against the doorframe. Hollis scooted to his side.

"Let me do that."

Willem agreed she could do the job and worked his way upward in the doorway almost as if climbing the rigging of a sailing ship.

He leaned on Hollis, and she escorted him to bed. Once he'd painfully folded himself down, she took off his shoes and pulled the quilt over him.

"What would you like? Food, talk or sleep?"

"They gave me toast and juice at the hospital. Sleep would be great. Then we can discuss strategy."

Strategy—what was he thinking? They were out of the chase game, at least he was. Never mind, she'd deal with this later.

"I was talking, maybe interrogating would be a better word, Poppy, Danson's mother, when you called. I'm going down to finish the 'interview'," Hollis said. "I'll fill you in later. Will you be okay?"

"More than okay. A good sleep will be wonderful." Willem replied.

Downstairs, Hollis banged on Poppy's door, which flipped open almost immediately. Inside, Hollis expected vivid colours, dramatic flourishes. The simple, elegantly understated décor surprised her. She'd applied a stereotype— exotic dancer equalled garish colours and cheap furnishings.

Hollis followed Poppy to the living room and, invited to sit down, waited for the dancer to gracefully fold herself into a chair upholstered in a deep green velvet that complemented her hair. Hollis chose a matching chair which faced Poppy's. Two cats lying on the thickly cushioned window seat soaking up the thin early winter sun raised their heads to inspect her but didn't rise. Perhaps they recognized her as a dog person.

Poppy didn't ask how Willem was: Hollis hadn't expected her too.

"Where did you keep the safe?" Hollis asked.

"In my workroom. I have baskets and baskets of fabrics. I slid it under a pile of batting in one of the baskets. When I came back, the apartment didn't look as if it had been searched. Whoever was here put everything back where he found it."

"Did Danson and Candace know where it was?"

"Danson did. Candace wouldn't have been interested. "

"That means we can eliminate Candace, doesn't it?"

"I suppose. Who else could have entered the apartment? I have a Medico key. They can only be duplicated through Medico. My idea is that Candace or Danson accidentally left my door unlocked when they came in to water the plants or feed the cats." She recrossed her legs and leaned forward with a puzzled frown creasing her brow. "The vestibule door is always locked too. I can't imagine how someone got in." She raised her chin and her voice. "The main thing is to locate the safe. It's important."

Hollis thought again about the keys that had been in Danson's car, keys that were duplicates. A vision of her own door to the fire escape flashed through her mind. It would be easy for a thief to enter the house that way. No point in telling Poppy about either possibility. The theft had happened. Now they had to deal with the aftermath

"Why was the stamp important?" Hollis said.

"It's worth thousands and thousands of dollars and part of an extensive valuable collection I kept in the box. I should have stashed it in the bank, but I don't trust banks."

There hadn't been a bank failure in Canada in a very long time, but if that was how Poppy felt, that was how she felt. "What else was in there?"

"Nothing important. The usual documents people keep

in safety deposit boxes—wills, birth certificates—that sort of thing," Poppy said in an offhand way without meeting Hollis's gaze.

Again it sounded like a lie.

"I'd like to know exactly what was in there. Make a list for me. Concentrate on the stamp collection. Since it was hidden, I'm assuming it wasn't yours, that you yourself don't collect stamps and are interested in the collection only because of its value. Is that right?"

Poppy nodded.

"Where did you get it—how long have you had it?"

"A few years."

"Where did you get it?"

Poppy's cell phone shrilled from her purse set on the floor beside her chair. She grabbed for it, said hello, listened and inspected her jewel-encrusted watch. "I'll be there in a few minutes. Keep talking to them. Tell them how well we did in Vancouver. Give them hope that they can do the same."

She clicked it off. "Sorry, I have the keys to the studio. Alberto and the eleven o'clock class are waiting." Her eyes expressed her relief. "I'll be home this evening. Come and talk to me then." As she spoke, she rose, collected her bag and stepped towards the door.

Getting tiny dribs and drabs of information was driving Hollis crazy. Unless she was prepared to throw herself on Poppy and wrestle her to the ground she'd have to wait until she had another opportunity to talk to her. Poppy's refusal to acknowledge her role in Danson's disappearance puzzled and infuriated Hollis, but she couldn't do anything about it.

Knowing the stamp's identity, she'd hit the philatelists and see what they could tell her. She guessed that the collection's owner had given it to Poppy or had died and willed it to her. That explained the purchase of a safe three years earlier. The information and the time frame should help to identify the previous owner. She had a lead, and it might take her to Danson or at least explain what had happened to him. This was wonderful news.

Upstairs, she peeked at Willem who lay on his back, a peaceful smile on his battered face. She wrote a note telling him where she'd gone and directing him to help himself to anything he fancied. She could have added, "including me," but she didn't.

Nineteen

Rhona had asked Spike to come downtown and talk to them. When he arrived, they entered one of the homicide department's interview rooms.

"How is mother?" Spike demanded. He looked every inch the bouncer ready to deal with recalcitrant patrons. Rhona imagined he'd intimidated more than a few unruly men or women.

"I need to see her. She will be scared." He punched his meaty right fist into his left palm.

His fear and worry impressed Rhona. She tried to think how she'd feel if this had happened to someone in her family, but it was impossible. Who thinks of her mother as a serial murderer? She didn't know whether to tell him that when she'd phoned to see how Katerina was doing, the news had not been good. Would it make him more or less anxious? The truth was always better. Katerina was his mother—he deserved to know.

"She's had a psychotic breakdown. She's receiving medical help," Rhona said.

"What that mean?"

"She has retreated, gone back to her own world."

Spike's brow furrowed. "Own world. Russia?"

"No." Rhona thought for a minute. "She's not talking, not responding to anyone, not eating. She's been transferred to the mental hospital and apparently she lies on her bed with her eyes closed, singing to herself in Russian."

Tears filled Spike's eyes. "Poor Mama," he said.

He sat down. Rhona opened a notebook, turned on the tape recorder and noted the time and the subject of their interview.

"I come to help. Why you doing that?" Spike said, pointing to the machine.

"It's a formality," Ian said. "We like to have a record of our conversations."

Spike eyed the machine suspiciously.

"We'd like to know about your mother's friends and associates."

"Short story—none," Spike said. "I try to get her to go to church, to meet others." He shrugged. "She say church stupid. Priests stupid. Not like incense. Not like standing up. Say it hurt her legs. Sometimes I take her to Russian restaurant. In restaurant, she glare at everyone. Then in loud voice she say, 'Who kill my Boris, who in mob do it.' I give up."

"What did happen to Boris?" Ian asked.

"He work for mob. Got killed in drug deal. That why she hate drugs, hate addicts, hate everything." He sighed, "Too bad I not favourite son—I never do drugs, I work, have family." His eyes filled. "Two grandsons, good boys, and she not care. Not want to come visit. All she do is knit. Sad for boys, for her, for me. Sad, sad story."

Rhona felt her own eyes fill with tears. The story of rejected children. She'd never liked the tale of the prodigal son, it had always struck her as unfair. Poor Spike. His family would suffer the publicity, the photos and probably learn to beware of journalists who would hang around harassing them with endless questions.

"I'm sorry. This must be hard for you," she said.

Spike brushed a large beefy hand across his eyes.

"Did your mother have any connection with the Russian mob?"

"You kidding? After what I say, you ask that?" He snorted. "No. She hate the mob."

239

"What about you?"

"After what happen to Boris? No. I know who they are. Not a secret."

"Did Danson Lafleur have anything to do with them?"

Spike straightened. His brows drew together and he peered at her. "Danson. Why we talk about Danson?"

"Because he's missing, and we think it might be because of the mob," Ian said.

Rhona wondered if Ian should have revealed this much. They only had Spike's word that he had nothing to do with the mob."

"I dunno."

"Did you ever talk to him about Russian gangsters?" Rhona asked.

Rhona watched Spike and saw what people meant when they said a light went on. Spike's eyes sparked, and he grinned.

"I did. Other lady ask me, and I tell her about conversation we had."

"Tell us," Rhona encouraged.

"Late night I eat souvlaki and see guy I think big wheel, but sent back to Russia. Same guy but different. I tell Danson how he is different. Danson very interested."

Given Danson's obsession with returning criminals that information would set him off on a hunt. If the description came close to the man in the morgue, the mysterious Gregory, they'd know who he was. If it was Gregory, and Gregory was in the Russian mob, why had Danson rented a room to him?

"What did he look like?"

"Now hair brown, was black, eyes brown were blue, wore glasses, was thin and before was fat. But have same face." Spike made a triangle with his hands. "Can't change that."

"Tall or short?"

Spike didn't say anything. He must be running a memory video. "Maybe six foot, but he have little feet."

Size eight shoes. That had been the clue for Candace—the man's shoes had been too small to have belonged to her brother. Gregory's feet were small—they had a pair of his shoes.

They continued to ask questions about the mob, and Spike shared what information he had but added nothing that the departmental specialists weren't aware of. His primary concern was his mother and what would happen to her.

"You do know that when the press gets hold of the story, they'll find you and your family?" Ian asked.

"My family." Spike's voice reflected the anxiety on his face.

"Yes. You should go home and warn them. They may try to ask your sons about their grandmother. How old are they?"

"Two and four."

"They'll be okay, but the press will try to talk to whoever takes care of them, to your friends and neighbours. It won't be nice," Ian warned.

Spike stood up.

Ian and Rhona also rose, and Rhona extended her hand. "Thank you for your help. Good luck."

After he'd left the two detectives exchanged sympathetic glances.

"Not his fault. He tried to help, but there will be those righteous ones who'll say he should have tried harder, should have realized how deranged she was," Rhona said.

"Could anything have been done?" Ian responded. He answered his own question. "We couldn't arrest her for obsessive knitting, could we? She had to commit a crime before we could intervene. Damn mental health act. You can't protect people from themselves, can you?"

Rhona nodded. There was no satisfactory answer.

"Gregory is the key. He rented a room in Danson's apartment. Now, he's dead, and it was a mob killing. It's possible he was Super Bug. Now we still need to know who killed Gregory and why. We also have to find out what happened to Danson," Ian said.

*   *   *

As always, a Google search would provide information. Hollis typed in "rare stamp dealers Toronto," and read the listings. The firm she chose to start with provided a Google link and map which she printed. Straight up Yonge Street to North York should be a breeze. Poppy had confirmed the rare stamp's identity and that it had been mentioned in the *Globe* article.

Before she left, she propped a kitchen chair under the fire escape door. Unlikely that the burglar would return or that Willem's assailants would discover his whereabouts, but at least the crash when the chair hit the floor would awaken him. It might even stimulate MacTee to bark.

"You take good care of Willem. Bark if anyone tries to come in," she told MacTee as she closed the door behind her.

*   *   *

"Two down, one to go," Rhona said at two o'clock on Friday afternoon.

"Does it strike you as odd that we haven't heard from Hollis recently?" Ian said, raising his eyes from his paperwork.

"Hollis is a devious woman."

"Why do you think she doesn't share information?"

"I don't know, but she's nearly got herself killed because of her insistence on following up on her ideas instead of turning information over to us."

"Do you think she's still tracking Danson?" Ian said placing ticks in appropriate boxes on the form in front of him.

"Are you kidding? She's as tenacious as one of those gila monsters in Arizona."

"Gila monsters?" Ian laid his pen down.

"They're lizards. Big ugly things. Sometimes, if a golfer searches for a lost ball and disturbs one, it clamps on to his hand."

242

"His?"

"Women don't reach under bushes when they've been told snakes, lizards or poisonous insects may be hiding there. Anyway, it's impossible to dislodge the lizards. The victim is taken to the hospital with the thing hanging from his hand. I'm not sure how they remove it once he arrives."

"Wouldn't you think golfers would be more cautious if they knew gila monsters were there?" Ian laughed.

"You would, but some aren't. Anyway, Hollis reminds me of a gila monster."

"I don't think she'd like the comparison," Ian said with a smile.

Rhona picked up the phone. "I'm going to be proactive," she said. The phone rang until the call answer came on. "Hollis, it's Rhona Simpson. Call me when you get in," she said, leaving both her office and her cell numbers.

*   *   *

In her battered truck, Hollis again vowed to clean up the accumulated dreck and smiled, knowing her tendency to procrastinate would determine that it would remain a mess. As she drove north, she watched the numbers. The one she wanted was well into Richmond Hill in the area referred to as 905. In the amalgamated GTA, the greater Toronto area, central Toronto phone numbers began with 416 and suburban ones, with 905. The rivalry between the needs of the two communities continued to be a source of irritation for city dwellers and suburbanites.

Once she'd located the number, she saw that it was a suite, which meant it was upstairs in a low-rise building. She hated entering businesses like this. Her latent claustrophobia kicked in, and anxiety about escape tightened the muscles in her stomach and dried the saliva in her mouth. The same panic engulfed her in big box stores when she couldn't see the exit and feared mountains of cartons would topple and crush her.

This claustrophobia had plagued her for years. She'd worked hard to deal with it, to learn various coping mechanisms to divert or suppress the panic. Now she forced herself to enter, climb to the third floor and push open the appropriate door. Inside, she surveyed the glass cases housing displays of stamps. A poster advertising Ottawa's postal museum caught her attention. She hadn't realized such an institution existed.

The young man behind the counter clearly was not one of the owners pictured in the website advertisement. She asked to speak to one of the brothers who ran the business. Earlier, she'd decided she wouldn't lie, wouldn't say she was a private sleuth, but would try to give that impression. It was almost noon, and she had her fingers crossed that the man she wanted to talk to had not gone out for lunch.

The dark-haired, swarthy man who emerged from the back of the store matched the photo on the web, although he'd aged since the picture was taken. She introduced herself and launched into her speech.

"I'm investigating the whereabouts of a collection that features a Canadian 1851 Queen Victoria 12-penny black. Several weeks ago on Saturday, October 14, there was a request in the personals column of the *Globe* that anyone knowing where they could find this stamp should phone. A young man who answered that advertisement disappeared almost immediately afterward."

The man's eyebrows rose. Clearly unexplained disappearances were not what he usually heard about.

"Do you know and can you share the names of those who possess this stamp?"

"We normally protect collector's privacy," the man said smoothly and firmly, but his eyes betrayed interest in her unusual story.

She'd known this would be difficult but hoped the dealer might give her a lead.

"Thieves who specialize in this area are aware of the stamps' value," the man continued.

A small spark of hope. Perhaps she had come to the right place.

The man rested his arms on the counter top and peered at her. "It's odd that you ask," he said. "One of our regular buyers noticed the item in the paper and drew it to our attention. We decided it wasn't coincidental that the previous week a young man had come in and asked us the same question."

Could Danson have been the young man? "Did he tell you his name? Can you describe him? Was he tall and athletic-looking? Were you the one who spoke to him?"

The man held up his hand like a police officer stopping traffic. "One question at a time. Yes, I was the person who spoke to him. He didn't identify himself. Even when I asked, he refused to say who he was. This made me think he was up to no good. Of course, I told him nothing. As for his description. He was about my height. I'm five-foot-six. Maybe thirty and very ordinary-looking."

A new player. Was this the man responsible for Danson dropping out of sight?

"You didn't answer his question."

"That's what I told you," the man said, a note of annoyance creeping into his voice. "To tell you the truth, he made me nervous. He had that hyped-up, jittery body language that I associate with drug addicts. I did wonder if he might be going to rob us, and I stood very close to the bell on the floor."

"Bell on the floor?"

"I can step on it without alerting anyone standing in front of me, but it rings in the back and in the security company's office, and they notify the police. That's one reason we like being on the third floor at the back. A thief has to get out of the building. If we're lucky, there's time for the police to arrive."

He paused. Hollis could see that he was wondering why he'd given her this information.

245

"Anyway, I didn't tell him anything. I sent him packing."

Hollis fished in her bag and handed him her out-of-date business card.

"I don't live in Ottawa or teach at the community college any more, but the cell phone number is the same. The young man we're searching for, Danson Lafleur, is the brother of my friend and landlady, Candace Lafleur. We're pretty sure there's a connection to the stamp and a collector who possesses or did possess it. We need that information to find out what happened to her brother." She offered this information and waited for his answer.

"Have you reported his disappearance to the police?"

"Of course, but, as you can imagine, young men leave for many reasons. Although they have the report, they're not yet pursuing it with interest."

This definitely wasn't true, and she felt bad about breaking her resolution not to lie. If she went one step further and suggested that Danson had been murdered, she didn't think he'd tell her anything.

"We haven't had one of these stamps come up for auction for several years. We can locate most of them. I don't see that it would help you if I gave you the names."

"Probably not. Have you heard that one of the owners died recently, and did you expect the collection would come in for appraisal or be put up for auction?"

Hollis held her breath while she waited for his response.

He studied her with the intensity he must use to authenticate stamps. She almost expected him to take out a magnifying glass. As he peered at her, she realized how red her face must be, and exhaled slowly.

"Actually, you'll probably locate this information sooner or later. Three years ago a passionate collector stopped coming in. We called him a couple of times, but he said he had given up his hobby. There was nothing more to do—it was his decision."

"Would you give me his name?"

"Normally, I wouldn't, I'd respect the collector's privacy. However, I read his obituary in the paper more than a month ago. Ever since, we've been expecting whoever inherited his stamps to come in or, if he didn't choose us, we thought we'd see that the collection was up for auction. It hasn't happened."

Three years before, Poppy had purchased a safe. That must have been when she'd received the stamp collection. It explained her extreme distress when it had been stolen.

"I would appreciate knowing his name," she said.

"Charles Smith, Charles Garfield Smith," the man said.

"Thank you." Hollis extended her hand. "You've helped me enormously."

"Let me know if you find your missing man. A stamp collection is a wonderful thing, but not a reason for foul play if that's what happened to the young man."

Hollis promised. Outside the building on the way to reclaim her truck, she mulled over what she'd learned. Why would Charles Smith have given Poppy the stamps years before his death? Why wouldn't he have kept buying and selling until he died? Why hadn't he merely designated her as the recipient in his will? Why had she been sure of the identify of the person who'd stolen the safe and been frightened by the knowledge? Questions, questions—time to hound Poppy until she revealed the answers.

It was early Friday afternoon. Wills were probated, and the public could read them. His will would answer some of her questions.

Government offices often closed at four and never opened on the weekend. If she wanted to know the terms of Charles Smith's will, she had to get downtown fast. Because of an earlier involvement with wills, she knew exactly where to go and what to say.

November afternoon traffic sputtered and jerked. The urge to speed, to pass the dawdlers who ambled through lights leaving her to await the next green enraged her. Calm down, she ordered herself. Take it easy. You're closing in on important information.

The will had been probated and was available for a fee, which she paid. She took it to the area set aside for research and collapsed on the seat with the bulky official document.

A quick skim.

Charles Smith had left his house and the cash in his bank accounts to his son Jacob. No surprise here.

He'd left one million in trust for a child, whom he hadn't named but whose identity was known to the sole executor, a lawyer with the firm of Ritter, Johnston and Thompson. He stipulated that if the child died, the money would be divided between his son and the Sick Children's Hospital Foundation.

This was decidedly weird. Hollis hadn't thought it was possible to leave money to someone without identifying them. Why would he do this?

One possible answer frightened her. He could have believed the child would be in danger if he or she was identified.

As she zipped through the legalese, she realized that no mention was made of a stamp collection.

The will was relatively short. Its implications frightened her.

Jacob Smith must have known his father collected stamps. The dealer had valued the collection at well over a million dollars. How enraged the young man must have been when he learned not only that he wouldn't inherit it but that the bulk of his father's estate had been left to a child probably unknown to him.

Time to find Jacob Smith. He had to be the key to the puzzle.

Twenty

Hollis's first step was to find out where Charles Smith had lived. Since his son had inherited his house, he might always have lived with his father, or he might have moved in after his father had died. If she went unannounced, she'd have a better chance of surprising him into sharing whatever information he had. Perhaps he could tell her where Danson had gone or at least reveal if Danson had called or come to see him.

Back in her apartment, she found Willem sitting on the bed cautiously spooning peach yogurt into his mouth. MacTee had parked himself close to Willem and fixed his gaze on the spoon.

"I think I'm going to be on a semi-liquid diet for quite a while," Willem said, giving her a lopsided grin.

"You're better, aren't you?" Hollis said.

"I am. I got up to answer the phone, but I took so long, I didn't make it. What did you find out?"

Hollis pulled a chair close to the bed and told him about the safe, the stamps and the connection to Danson before she asked, "Now tell me what you overheard the thugs say."

"That the Super Bug was back and had a really big project. Their bosses and the Bug were worried someone would recognize him before he did what he'd come for. One of them grumbled that he thought the Bug must have switched sides or be working as a double agent, or he wouldn't have been able to get back in the country easily."

"Unfortunately, it's easy for criminals to return. Finding those who've done that is Candace's brother's obsession." Sadness swept through her when she thought of Danson and his one-man crusade to rid the country of overseas criminals. "I think the Super Bug is dead."

"Why do you say that?"

"Because I think he was Gregory, the man who rented a room in Danson's apartment. I suspect he wanted to see how much info Danson had about him and other Russians like him who had been deported and returned."

"Pretty ballsy. If Danson and the authorities knew what he looked like before he was deported, wouldn't he be taking a risk, even if he'd had plastic surgery or dramatically altered himself?"

"Danson wouldn't have seen him the first time. He's only been in the tracking business since his girlfriend, Angie, was killed three years ago," Hollis said.

"I still don't understand why you think Super Bug is dead."

"It's a long story, but the essence of it is that when Candace reported her brother's disappearance, the police asked her for something with his DNA."

"Surely that isn't routine procedure," Willem said.

"No, it isn't. They had an unidentified body in the morgue they thought might be Danson."

"I don't get it. Why didn't they ask her to come and see if it was Danson?"

"Because the face was smashed beyond recognition, and it had no fingers."

Willem shifted and winced. "A mob execution. Maybe my source was right when he suggested his loyalty was in question."

"Because the DNA matched the dead man's, they thought he was Danson." She shook her head. "He wasn't. It belonged to a man who called himself Gregory. Now we think he was Super Bug, but we haven't found out what happened to Danson."

"Do you think he was killed too?"

"Not until a body turns up," Hollis said. "Danson could have been tracking Gregory, or he could have been following another trail altogether. An item relating to his mother, Poppy, was published in the personal column in the paper. Right now, I think that's the more likely path."

Before she went address searching, Willem required her attention. "Would you like more to eat—soup, a milkshake, ice cream, a smoothie?"

Willem attempted another lopsided grin. "Sounds great, but," he ran his hand over his chin, "I'm a man who likes to shave. I feel dirty if I don't. If you have a razor, I'll do that and maybe have a shower."

After the talk of mutilated bodies, thinking of Willem's body in the shower with rivulets of water coursing over it was a welcome relief.

"Sure. I have hot water, soft towels and a new razor." She grinned. "I could do candles and soft music too."

Their eyes met and held. "Another time," Willem said.

He meant it. Hollis's heart did a flip flop.

"Would you like help getting your clothes off?" she said and felt a telltale flush warm her face.

"What red-blooded man would refuse an offer like that? Seriously though, I can't manage my socks and if you unbutton my shirt, I can do the rest."

She did as she was asked and carefully refrained from stroking his bruised body although, to herself, she acknowledged the strength of the urge. Instead, she did the job quickly and held out a hand to help him up. He leaned heavily on her and took small cautious steps to the bathroom. He hung on to the door frame and staggered to the sink, where he anchored himself to the vanity with one hand and set about his task with the other.

"You're sure you can manage? Why don't I turn the shower on and get what you need?" Hollis said.

Willem, shaking slightly, looked as if he wished he

hadn't embarked on this program. "I'll shave first. Then, if I'm okay, you can come in and start the water."

Message received. He didn't want her watching him shave. She closed the bathroom door and waited outside for a few minutes.

"I don't think I'll have the shower," Willem said from behind the closed door. "Could you help me back to bed?"

When he'd lowered himself carefully to the bed, she did up his shirt buttons before she lifted his feet and helped him lie down.

"That was frightening. I'm really weak," Willem said.

"To be expected. I'm going to make you an easy-to-swallow power drink to start you back on the road to health."

"I'm in your hands," Willem said and attempted a roguish grin. "I wish."

"Me too. All in good time," Hollis said and hurried to whip up a comforting mixture of banana, yogurt, apple and carrot juice. Once he'd drunk it and taken his pain pills, she encouraged him to sleep again. Five minutes later, he was.

She checked to see who had phoned and picked up a message to call Rhona.

What to do? If Rhona had news about Danson she would have called Candace and Candace would have told Hollis. More likely Rhona had called her because she wanted to know what Hollis was doing. If she contacted Rhona, the detective would ask questions that would be hard to answer truthfully. Hollis shook her head. She had Rhona's card in her wallet. Maybe later she'd return the call, but right this minute it was phone book time.

*   *   *

Hollis opened the Smith pages. Why couldn't the man have had a unique name? Smith—that was a joke. She couldn't face the idea of calling all the Charles and C Smiths in the book. There had to be an easier path. Who would know where he lived? Of course? The stamp dealer. Should she phone and ask? His reluctance to give her information flashed through her mind. It would be too easy for him to say no and hang up. Face to face, she would do her best to explain why it was important and why he wouldn't be violating ethical reservations if he did.

She grabbed her bag, left another note for Willem and raced to her truck. As she headed back up Yonge Street, she formulated her speech.

Inside the store, she did a rapid reassessment. The man behind the counter was not the one to whom she'd spoken earlier. No welcoming smile and his, "how can I help you," did not promise easy access to the information she needed.

"I came earlier today and spoke to another gentleman. Would he be available?"

"I'm here alone this afternoon."

She repeated her story. He gave her little encouragement, but finally she screwed up her nerve and said, "Could you give me Charles Smith's address?"

The man, whose long face had remained expressionless during their exchange, paused and examined her. His eyebrows rose and his lips reformed into what could be described as a sardonic smile. "So that you or your accomplices can break in and see if the collection is in the empty house? I wasn't born yesterday. The answer is no. My brother shouldn't have told you as much as he did, and I'm certainly not going to share any more information."

"Thanks anyway," Hollis said and slunk from the store. Damn. She'd have to make those calls after all.

Back at the apartment, Willem sat on the sofa contemplating the gold painting.

"That has potential," he said.

She'd almost forgotten her trouble with the painting. Other issues had taken precedence in the last week.

"I'm having problems with it," she said.

"Is it one of a series? I'd guess it's autobiographical, maybe about exploring."

Hollis thought about it. She hadn't cottoned on to the fact that it might relate to her own life, although almost all art was self-referential. She'd thought about it as a painting where things were half-hidden, half-revealed. Her life was like that. Almost at the halfway mark, and she hadn't found the answers she was looking for. Very perceptive of Willem to home in on the ambivalence and ambiguity in her life.

"It is. I thought I was exploring colour as well as burying and retrieving information, but you're right. Thank you."

"Any time. I may have a new career as an art critic. So where have you been? Did you find out anything?"

"The identity of the stamp collection's owner."

Willem raised an eye brow. "That's enigmatic."

"You're the one who intends to be a lawyer. I'll share the contents of a will that I read and you can tell me what you think it means. First I have to see where Charles Garfield Smith lived." She examined Willem. "You had a shower?"

"I did. Now I wish I had clean clothes. I hated putting these back on." He brushed a hand over his filthy pants.

Would her clothes fit? She stood six feet tall in her stocking feet and owned a number of men's shirts she used when she painted or made her papier mâché animals.

"Maybe I can do something about that," she said, heading towards her closet. She pulled out a clean but paint-stained blue shirt.

"You can wear this on top and wrap a towel around your waist. I'll throw your stuff in the washer in the basement."

"I accept," Willem said and slowly levered himself to his feet, took the proffered shirt and shuffled to the bathroom. When he emerged, it almost covered his chest, and he'd draped a white towel like a sarong around his waist. He clutched his bundled clothing.

"Very fetching," Hollis said, taking the clothes and heading for the door.

When she returned, Willem had returned to bed.

"Anything I can get you?" she asked.

"Every time I do anything, I'm exhausted. My body tells me to take it easy, to take another nap, and I'm listening," he said.

"If you do want something to eat or drink give a shout," Hollis said. "I'm going through the phone book searching for Charles Garfield Smith's address."

She left the bedroom door ajar and crossed the room to collect a highlighter. MacTee, who'd been lying by the front door, rose when she walked through the room. He stared at her and went back to the door. A glance at the clock and she realized he hadn't been out since just after she'd spoken to Poppy that morning. The search for Charles Smith would have to wait. She reached for her hoodie and, with MacTee at her heels, set off for a walk.

Indian summer, if that's what they'd been having, was over. Grey clouds stacked in horizontal layers, a chill wind and a dark afternoon that had become a sombre evening reminded her that November's dark days had arrived. Time to haul out the winter clothes and prepare for the cold.

Deep in thought, she didn't notice Jack pull up to the curb beside her as she neared the house. The slam of his van's door didn't break into her reverie, but his inquiry did.

"How's the patient?" Jack asked and touched her arm.

She jumped then felt embarrassed at her skittishness.

"Sorry, I was thinking about something. Wasn't expecting to talk to anyone."

"How's your friend doing?"

"Much better. Thanks for your help. Were you coming from practice or work?"

"What?"

"I thought you might be returning from work or a lacrosse practice."

"Work," Jack said and peered at the house. "Did the dancer get back?"

His voice betrayed his conviction that a woman Poppy's age really couldn't be a legitimate dancer. Since Hollis too had been startled when she'd learned Poppy's occupation, Jack's attitude didn't surprise her.

"She did. Came in on the red-eye from Vancouver this morning."

By this time they'd reached the door and separated.

"MacTee, sometimes walking you helps me clear my mind. Same thing for meditation. Walking didn't help, and I haven't got time for meditation. I'm going to have to wing it with a muddled mind," Hollis said to the dog when they were back upstairs.

In the apartment, Willem slept with his mouth open, snoring gently.

She pushed the chickens to one side and plunked the massive phone book on her work table.

Smith, Charles.

Should she phone each one and ask for Charles? The Charles she wanted was dead. If a family member answered the phone, her call would be a hurtful reminder of their loss. Other Charles Smiths might also be dead, and that reasoning would apply. For her particular Charles Smith, the only family member who might answer the phone would be Jacob. She was guessing, but she didn't think he'd been overcome with sorrow when his father died. Anyway, it had to be done because he was the one she wanted.

Trying to locate Charles Smith would be even more tedious than sending the e-mails.

An hour later, she'd made no headway and developed an admiration for telemarketers. There had to be another way. One more thing to try. She moved to her computer, typed in the phone number that had been in the *Globe* advertisement and went on a reverse search. She hadn't known how to do this when she'd called the number before.

It worked. She had the address. Now it was time to see if anyone was home.

Twenty-One

Six o'clock on a Friday night in November. She'd wait until seven, when anyone living in the house would have had time to return from work and then she'd scout the place. Meanwhile, she and MacTee would update Candace on her activities.

Candace, clutching a bag of groceries in one hand and guiding Elizabeth up the stairs with the other, reached the top step as Hollis and the dog descended. Hollis thrust out her arms for the groceries, leaving Candace free to fumble in her shoulder bag for her key.

"Tee, Tee," Elizabeth shouted and swarmed forward to grab the dog's neck.

MacTee surreptitiously licked her. This was his alternate form of greeting when he didn't have a toy to present. Elizabeth shrieked. "Kiss, Tee kiss me."

Candace herded them inside, flicking on lights as they moved to the kitchen. She unpacked hamburger buns, meat and a pre-washed salad bag along with a Spanish onion and a tomato. She waved at the collection, "Want to stay for a hamburger and a salad?"

"Love to, but not tonight. I'm feeding Willem before I embark on a special mission."

"Willem's back. That's great. What happened at the hospital? What mysterious mission are you on?"

Hollis brought her up to date on Willem's condition, on his information about Super Bug, her own stamp collection investigation and about Charles Smith's house. "It's time

257

Poppy came clean about her stamp collection and told us why Charles Smith gave it to her. Why hasn't she told you about it? And most of all, why did Danson go off to see someone about the stamp?"

"She has the key to all this, and she isn't talking. It's as if she's protecting someone and ignoring the fact that by doing that she may have put her own son in grave danger," Candace said. She unwrapped the hamburger, tossed it in a bowl and added seasonings. Forming patties as she talked, she said, "What do you think you'll find tonight?"

"Probably nothing. Don't get your hopes up. The house may be unoccupied. It may even have been sold. I'm keeping my fingers crossed that, Jacob, Charles' son lives there."

Candace, ready to slice tomatoes, stopped with the knife suspended above the cutting board. "Hollis, have you considered that if this was the man Danson talked to before he disappeared, you may be in danger if you confront him?"

Hollis had weighed this possibility. Having read the will with its strange wording, she understood that Jacob might be dangerous. She could think of no other reason for hiding the child's identity. It partially explained why Poppy had been uncommunicative. However, she believed she might uncover a vital clue leading her to Danson and was willing to gamble that she wouldn't come to any harm. She ripped a sheet from the memo pad beside the phone, extracted a slip of paper from her pocket and copied the address.

"If I don't return by nine thirty or ten, phone Rhona Simpson, she's the detective I know, and bring her up to speed." She smiled. "It's great to have a detective on call in case anything bad happens."

"She'll be mightily pissed off that you haven't shared this information; that you've trotted off on a wild goose chase on your own."

"Maybe, but let's face facts. The Toronto police have not found Danson. Moreover, because they suspect him of killing Gregory, they may have marshalled their forces to locate him. I'm worried that if they think he may be hidden or hiding at Jacob's, they'll marshal the heavy artillery. If Jacob has kidnapped Danson, he's a bold guy, and if he suspects the police are closing in on him, I'm afraid that if he hasn't already killed Danson, this might compel him do it. I want to find Danson, not collar this guy. You're right. If Jacob does turn out to be bad news, Rhona won't be pleased that I didn't tell her about him."

Elizabeth stopped further conversation by falling. She'd been leaning on MacTee, and he'd walked away letting her crash to the floor. Her mouth opened on impact, and she howled.

Candace wiped her hands on her apron before scooping Elizabeth into her arms. "Sweetie, dogs aren't like chairs or tables. You can't lean on them, because they move. MacTee didn't mean to hurt you. He's sorry. Give him a pat and tell him you love him."

Elizabeth stopped crying. "Tee, see Tee," she said. After Candace set her down, the toddler wrapped her arms around the dog.

Upstairs in her own kitchen, Hollis found the table set and tomato basil soup simmering on the stove.

"Thought it was time I did something," Willem said with his half-smile. "Since liquids are my option, I rummaged around and found soup."

Hollis added bread and grated cheese to the meal.

"Soak the bread in the soup until it's soft enough to eat. If you cut the cheese in tiny bits you'll manage it too, and it'll provide the protein you need."

They sat down and ate companionably.

"Time for me to go home," Willem said. However, his tone of voice made it a question not a statement.

Hollis had risen to spoon ice cream into two bowls. She spoke over her shoulder. "Not as far as I'm concerned. However, if you think you should go back and get on with your life, I'll understand." What she didn't say was that she would be quite happy if he stayed for an indefinite period.

"It isn't that. I must be a nuisance. I'm not used to being dependent."

"You aren't." She brought the dishes to the table. "I worry about the thugs who beat you up. If they had instructions to kill you, somebody is not going to be pleased to discover they blew it. I don't want them coming back to finish the job."

Willem's warm hand covered hers. "I don't either. The mob must have realized that if the unidentified body is Super Bug's, the police would identify it eventually. The danger may be past. Once the mob bigwigs know the police have identified him, they won't be interested in me." He squeezed her hand.

Hollis wanted him to hang on to it forever.

"Can't hold hands and eat ice cream," Willem said with a second half-smile and released her hand.

"I'm going out tonight to follow a lead that may take me to Danson."

"Why don't you let the police do it?"

"Because I'm afraid they might go the assault route with sirens, guns, loud hailers—the whole nine yards."

"My god, why would you think that? If the police would react that way, there's no way you go," Willem said.

"I don't think it'll be that dangerous. I've already left the address with Candace. If you don't hear from me by ten, you both have my permission to phone Detective Rhona Simpson and tell her what's happening and where I've gone."

"I wish you wouldn't go, but in the short time I've known you, I've become perfectly aware that you'll do whatever you have to do to locate this guy. All I can do is wish you luck," Willem said.

"I'm taking MacTee. There's no better way to inconspicuously assess a neighbourhood than to have a dog. When we walk dogs at night, we take a flashlight to see what they've done."

Willem wrinkled his nose.

"Sorry, more information than you needed. Anyway, I've often thought burglars should employ dogs when they case a house or a neighbourhood. A well-dressed thief accompanying a dog would attract no attention whatsoever."

"Maybe that's what they do. Who knows how they zero in on a target."

Hollis wrote the address and left it beside the phone. She removed MacTee's leash from the hook beside the door. When she did this, he shot into his anticipatory dance. He leaped in the air with four paws off the floor and rebounded when they hit the floor.

"Too bad he doesn't like going out," Willem said.

Hollis had googled the address. It was uncanny how you could examine a house right down to the location of the garbage cans. This too must help thieves. It saved them wandering around wondering where the doors and windows might be.

Although she'd reassured Willem and Candace that this was a routine reconnoitre, the tightness in her shoulders and dryness in her throat told her she'd lied. If visiting this house was the last thing Danson had done before he disappeared, she must be careful. At least she could be found if anything happened to her. Being found and being safe were not the same thing. Bodies were found—she didn't want to be one of those.

Her beat-up truck could draw unwanted attention if she parked it near the house in the upscale neighbourhood. Instead she left it in a strip mall several blocks away on Avenue Road. There were two take-out restaurants in the mall, and since it was Friday evening, the stores were open. Her truck would be unremarked. After she locked it, she wondered if leaving it here was a bright move. What if she had to run for her life?

Run for her life—it sounded like a B movie. "I'm in high drama mode," she said to the dog who paid no attention. She hadn't said biscuit, dinner, walk or bed—those were the words he listened for. Instead of paying attention to her, he sniffed his way from bush to bush surveying the record of the dogs who had preceded him. Friday must have been garbage collection day—empty recycling bins littered the street and gave MacTee more tantalizing smells to investigate.

Forty-seven Cormetto street lurked well-back from the road. In this affluent north Toronto neighbourhood the houses had been built on large lots. A street light revealed it to be a two-storey brick centre hall plan with an attached single car garage. It resembled many other houses she'd passed on her walk down the street.

No lights burned in the house.

She checked out nearby houses. Lights shone toward the rear of the nearest house on the right. A porch light glowed above the front door of the house on the left, next to 47's garage. Flyers strewn on the porch suggested the owners had been away for some time.

Although no one appeared to be home, the darkened windows might mean that the occupant had drawn the curtains tightly. Caution was required. She released MacTee's leash and encouraged him to accompany her up the drive. Instead he wandered off on a tangent, and she let him go, knowing he'd be fine and not wanting to call him until she'd finished her surveillance.

What if Danson was imprisoned inside? If he was and she rang the doorbell, she'd alert his captor. What would she say if someone answered the door? If it was spring, she could say she was canvassing for the Cancer Society. Snowsuits—she'd claim to be collecting for needy children. But she wasn't going to ring the bell. Instead, she'd circle the house to see if any lights shone from the windows. If the house was totally dark, it would be time to discover if Danson was inside.

Toronto's glowing night sky reflecting from low-lying clouds didn't provide much illumination. What if she stepped on something or bumped into a metal garbage can? What if there was a dog? She gave herself a mental shake. Enough of the "what ifs".

It was stupid to bumble along in the dark. Time to risk someone seeing her flashlight's beam and calling the police. She flicked it on and slipped along the side of the garage to survey the back of the house.

No lights, no noise. It seemed unoccupied, but that didn't mean Danson wasn't inside.

Something moved in the deep shadow near the back door. She jumped, directed her light and confronted a masked face. One of the millions of raccoons that inhabited Toronto. Their adaptation to city life had swelled their numbers to the point where statisticians claimed they outnumbered humans. Not what she wanted to see. She retraced her steps and stopped well away from the beast.

There was a pause while she peered through the darkness and listened for the dog. She couldn't see or hear MacTee but willed him to stay away from raccoon territory. MacTee hated the masked marauders and responded by barking and chasing—the last thing she needed.

Standing in front of the house, she hesitated. How could she let Danson know a friend, a rescuer, was outside? As the cold seeped through her thin-soled shoes, she remembered one of Candace's conversations with the police. She'd told them about the nail polish on the key and about another signal she and Danson shared.

What had she said? The sensation that information was almost but not quite within her grasp drove Hollis crazy. She tried word associations. Little boy, danger, door. Closer. It had something to do with the door, with Danson coming home when Candace was alone. What was it?

*   *   *

Five o'clock. With Gregory identified as the Super Bug and

the multiple drug addict murders solved, the two detectives anticipated a long-awaited, free weekend.

"Planning anything special?" Ian asked. A breakthrough, she thought. He'd asked a personal question. To date their relationship had been businesslike, and he'd revealed little about himself and shown no interest in her life, although she'd shared bits and pieces.

"I love biking on Toronto Island, but in November when the weather man calls for traces of snow, it's not an option. Doing absolutely nothing, vegging out sounds good. Saturday paper, a little shopping, maybe a movie. What about you?"

Ian nodded. "Probably much the same."

Definitely not a breakthrough in their relationship. Their desks clear, they collected their coats.

"Should we call Hollis again?" Ian said.

"I have my cell phone."

"You'll be off-duty."

"True, but I can connect her to help if she needs it. I'm uneasy about Hollis. These connections to the Russian mob are bad. If she had a clue about them, she'd back off, but that isn't her style. If Danson's disappearance is mob-related, she's in over her head and in danger if she muddles around and upsets them. They don't take kindly to nosy people."

*   *   *

Shifting from one frozen foot to the other, Hollis glimpsed MacTee's shadowy form sniffing closer and closer to the dark house. She had to act before he picked up the raccoon's scent. What had Candace said? She searched frantically through her jumbled thoughts seeking a replay of the conversation. It had been when the police had discussed keys—that much she remembered.

Then it came to her.

When either Candace or Danson approached the house,

264

they whistled a specific tune to tell who was at the door. It had been a children's song.

She ran through a roster. First, nursery rhymes, but it hadn't been one of those and understandably so. What if Danson had been bringing a friend home and he'd had to whistle baby stuff? It had been something to do with animals. A sense of panic. Animals. Horses, cows, dogs, cats—none of the above. More than one animal. No, Candace had said they'd been living in Quebec and chose an appropriate song. Something in French. French songs? "Au Claire de la Lune"? "Alouette". That was it—the song about plucking feathers from a lark.

Nothing happened when she pursed her lips and blew. The cold had stolen her whistling power. She wet her lips, inhaled and started again. This time a thin, almost inaudible, sound quavered forth. Whistling wasn't going to do it. She'd have to sing and sing loudly.

Her mind flashed back to grade school when the music teacher had gently suggested that she mouth the words to a song the class was performing in the Christmas concert. Ever since, self-consciousness about her voice had kept her from singing in public.

But there was no public here. She wasn't making her stage debut. There appeared to be no one home in the Smith house or the house next door. If there was a chance that Danson was inside she needed to risk all, fill her lungs and bellow.

When she finished several verses accompanied by appropriate references to *tête*, *bec* and *ses yeux* she stood still and listened. First, she heard the hum of distant traffic, the wind swishing in nearby trees, then it came—the faintest whistled rendition of "Alouette".

Absolute shock.

While she'd hoped Danson was inside, in her heart she'd believed this was an exercise in futility, because his protracted silence meant he wasn't here or he was dead. It took seconds for her mind to process reality.

He was alive.

"Danson, where are you?" she shouted before she could stop herself. Singing was one thing, but what if calling out alerted Jacob that she was there?

"In the garage," he replied in a faint voice.

How could this be when she stood in front of the garage door? He couldn't be gagged, or she wouldn't have heard him. He must be ill.

"Are you okay?"

"No. But I'm alive," he said in a voice so quiet, she strained to hear.

She rushed to try the door. Grasping the handles, she strained, then said, "I can't budge this. If I break a window, I can get in the house and let you out."

"No." His voice was stronger.

"What?"

"No." His voice grew stronger. "There's no time to spare. Jacob broke into the safe an hour ago. He told me because he wanted me to know he'd found the vital information he needed. Since I would not longer be useful to him, he was leaving me here to die. Have you got a phone?"

Sadistic bastard.

Hollis reached into her purse, clutched her phone and pulled it out.

"Phone 911. Don't stay on the line. Go home. Now. As fast as you can. Make sure Elizabeth is okay. Guard her with your life then call the police."

"Elizabeth? What does Elizabeth have to do with anything?"

"Jacob found her birth certificate. She's inheriting from Jacob's father. If she dies, Jacob gets more. He said he'd get rid of her. Throw her from an overpass was what he said."

"I'm gone," Hollis said as she called to MacTee and headed down the street, wishing she hadn't parked in the strip mall. They broke into a run. At Avenue Road, with MacTee right at her heels, Hollis zigzagged across the street, narrowly avoiding honking cars and screeching brakes. In the parking lot, she opened the passenger door, boosted MacTee in, ran around and flung herself in the driver's side.

Time for the cavalry.

It took seconds to punch in Rhona's number. When the detective answered on the second ring, Hollis, backing out of her parking space, gave her the address where Danson was imprisoned and told her the danger Elizabeth might be in before she hung up. She didn't have time to answer questions.

Careening down Avenue Road then down Yonge Street she made herself slow down. Being in a crash wouldn't help anyone.

As she drove, she sorted through the implications of what Danson had said. Poppy had the stamp collection. Likely Poppy and Charles Smith had been lovers. Okay, that was fine. Given what she knew about Jacob, his father must have believed the stamps would never get to Poppy, unless he gave them to her himself. Why had he done this three years before? Unless he'd known he had some dreadful disease.

She braked hard to avoid a car that had turned left from the right lane. MacTee catapulted to the floor. Stupid drivers.

Where did Elizabeth fit in the picture? If he'd left money to Elizabeth, why wouldn't he have left something for Candace? This didn't make sense. Before she could worry the problem further, she reached the house.

Friday night. Not a parking space to be had. She felt like abandoning the truck on the street, flashers on to alert motorists, but she couldn't risk others' lives. Instead, she backed up and jerked into Candace's driveway, pulled up behind Jack's van, which was parked in front of the garage, and threw herself out of the truck. With MacTee at her heels, she raced around the house, unlocked the door and pelted inside, colliding with Candace, who was coming up from the basement holding a mop and a pail.

Scrambling to her feet, she sprinted for the stairs without stopping to help Candace.

"What's wrong?" Candace shouted after her.

The door to the apartment was open.

Hollis tore inside. Had Jacob already abducted Elizabeth? Too awful a thought.

"Elizabeth. Where are you, Elizabeth?" she called.

"She should be in her crib. Jack said he'd watch her while I checked out the flood in the basement," Candace said coming in behind her. They ran to the baby's room.

"My god, she's gone," Candace cried.

For Hollis, everything suddenly fell into place. Jack was Jacob. He'd been living in the house since he'd appropriated the identity of a lacrosse player when he read Danson's e-mails and took Danson's keys. Before Hollis could digest all of this information, she heard Willem's shouts and Elizabeth's screams.

"Upstairs—the fire escape," Hollis said, already moving toward the door and the stairs. Surely Jack wouldn't throw Elizabeth from the fire escape? He'd realize the game was up and back off. But he didn't know she'd blocked his van, didn't know she'd found Danson, didn't know she knew who he was. Why hadn't she cottoned on sooner? When she'd asked him questions about his job or the lacrosse team, he'd always taken time to reply. Now she realized he'd needed to reorient himself to his acquired personality. When she noticed that his van had Ontario, not Quebec plates, she should have followed up.

Upstairs, Hollis and Candace confronted a bizarre scene.

Twenty-Two

Rhona was on the way to the Metro store on Eglinton Avenue when she received Hollis's call. She pulled over, phoned in and had the dispatcher send cars and officers to rescue Danson and to block Elizabeth's abduction.

Shopping could wait. She screamed into a U-turn and headed south to Belsize Drive. It wouldn't be long until the street swarmed with police cars. Just as she'd feared, Hollis hadn't shared the information which had brought things to this crisis.

* * *

Jack stood with his back to the open fire escape doorway. His arms wrapped under Elizabeth's arms as he anchored her to his chest. Willem clutched Elizabeth's legs. It looked as if they might pull her in half.

Elizabeth continued to scream.

"Let her go," Willem shouted.

How was he able to hang on like that with his broken ribs? He must be suffering excruciating pain. In two strides, Hollis flew across the room and head-butted Jack's stomach.

"Fuck," Jack gasped. He released Elizabeth.

His sudden action caused Willem to fall backward with Elizabeth on top of him. Hollis lay on the floor, where she'd dropped after attacking Jack.

Candace swooped in, enfolded the toddler in her arms

and crooned comforting sounds to the frightened little girl.

Hollis scrambled to her feet and heard a scream and a thud.

Either the rusted railing had given way, or Jack had jumped. The rusted iron had always made Hollis nervous, made her edge downward with her hand on the substantial brick wall rather than the railing.

Hollis moved first. She stepped onto the fire escape landing. The railing was gone. Reluctantly she peered down. And saw nothing. November's blackness encased whatever horror lay below.

Not for long.

Sirens wailed ever closer. Footfalls echoed as someone ran into the backyard.

Powerful flashlights flicked over Hollis's truck, the van and rested on Jack lying spread-eagled on the paved driveway.

As Hollis watched anxiously, a police officer bent over him, straightened up and spoke to other officers crowding into the yard.

The door bell chimed.

Back in her kitchen, Hollis knew she must look as shell-shocked as the others did. Candace continued to rock Elizabeth, who'd stopped crying and squirmed to get down.

Hollis's cell phone rang. She fished in her pocket and pulled it out.

"Hollis, Rhona here."

"Did you get Danson?" Hollis asked.

Candace jolted as if the word Danson had been a bolt of electricity directed at her body. "Danson," she echoed.

"They're there now. What's happening where you are?" Rhona replied.

"We stopped him. Elizabeth is fine."

"I'm on my way. *You* have some explaining to do," Rhona said.

Hollis didn't like her tone. This would not be a pleasant encounter, but it was true, she *had* withheld information. It was sheer good luck that had saved Elizabeth. She should have gone to Rhona, and she would have if she'd had any clue that Elizabeth was threatened.

"Danson's alive," Candace exclaimed joyfully. "He's alive. That's wonderful." She flipped to Willem who stood next to her and flung her arms around him. "Alive, Danson's alive," she sang and squeezed Willem, who gave an involuntary gasp.

Candace released him. "I'm sorry."

"It's okay." His white face indicated he was anything but okay. "Where's Danson?" he said to Hollis.

"I don't know. Maybe the hospital. Rhona is on her way. She'll tell us," Hollis said.

"Where was he?" Willem persisted.

"Jack, who isn't Jack—he's Jacob Smith—imprisoned him in his father's garage. He's been there since he disappeared. Right before I got there, Jack cracked open the safe he stole from Poppy and told Danson he was leaving him to die in the garage."

"Thank god we never gave up, that we kept searching." Candace stepped forward and threw her arms around Hollis. "Without you, Danson would have died. Hollis, how will we ever thank you?"

Hollis returned the hug. "Candace, a lot of it was luck. When Rhona gets here, she's going to be damn angry."

The bells peeled again. Before the sound died away, thunderous banging reverberated up the stairwell.

Hollis disengaged herself. "I'd better let them in before they break the door down," she said and headed downstairs. When she opened it, a bluecoated covey of bodies surged past her.

"We have the child—she's okay," Hollis said, and the men stopped.

The lead officer went upstairs to confirm what she'd said. She followed.

After the site had been secured, the officers wanted to interview Hollis, Willem and Candace. Hollis, who'd been working through the details in her own mind, welcomed the chance to sort it all out.

"We'll do it downstairs in my apartment," Candace said in the tone of voice that suggested there was no alternative.

Willem took a minute to gulp painkillers. The tussle with Jack had taken its toll.

Candace's living room proved small for the group. The officers, Candace, Elizabeth, Willem, Hollis and MacTee positioned themselves, and Hollis began.

"Candace's brother, Danson Lafleur, has not been seen or heard from since Saturday, October..."

Poppy's arrival interrupted her speech.

"Danson's okay," Candace shouted to Poppy.

"What are these police doing here?" Poppy demanded.

At this point Rhona arrived.

The situation reminded Hollis of English comedies, where people entered and exited and created chaos.

One of the officers stepped forward as if to take charge. Candace held up her hand in the universal signal to wait.

"It's a complicated story. Hollis will tell us," she said.

Hollis began again. She didn't give every detail, didn't talk about Gregory or the Russian connection. After she'd sketched in the background, she pointed to Poppy.

"This is Poppy Lafleur. She is Candace and Danson's mother. If I'm right in my assumptions, she's also Elizabeth's mother." Candace gasped but said nothing.

Elizabeth, hearing her name, smiled. "Poppy, Poppy, Poppy," she said.

Poppy nodded. "You're right. I was too old, too selfish to bring up another child. Candace and I agreed that it would be better if Elizabeth thought I was her grandmother."

That was one thing successfully figured out. Now for the rest of the story.

"Elizabeth's father was Charles Garfield Smith," Hollis said.

Again Poppy nodded.

"He gave Poppy his valuable stamp collection when she told him she was pregnant. Once Elizabeth was born, he made elaborate provisions for Elizabeth in his will but didn't name her, because he recognized that his son, Jacob, aka Jack, might be a psychopath who would kill her."

"Charles was a good man. I miss him. He often talked about his son. He did everything he could but said it was hopeless, that as a little boy Jacob tortured animals and related to no one. He'd raised Jacob alone, and he felt guilty about him." Poppy sighed. "I should have realized Jacob would stop at nothing."

"You knew the message in the paper came from him?" Hollis said and heard her voice rise.

"I suspected it had."

Candace jerked to her feet and pointed an accusing finger at her mother. "Poppy, if you thought that, why didn't you tell us after Danson disappeared?"

Poppy lowered her gaze and examined her shoes. "I should have, but I hoped I was wrong. I wanted to protect you and Elizabeth. She's a baby who can't look after herself. Danson is a man."

Maternal feelings were distributed unevenly if this woman had ignored her son's danger and continued to deny her involvement. She was what she was. The important thing was that Danson had survived. Hollis directed her next question to Rhona.

"How is Danson?"

"The paramedics toted him off to the hospital. I'll find out where they've taken him and see what his condition is," Rhona said.

After several calls she addressed the room "He's at Sunnybrook. He's suffering from hypothermia and starvation. Because he was in good shape before his ordeal, they say he should recover fully."

Before she'd finished, Candace moved toward the door, still holding Elizabeth. "I'm not leaving her with anyone," she said. "We're going to the hospital. Hollis, you should come too." She avoided looking at her mother.

"Give Danson my love and tell him I'm sorry," Poppy said.

Candace glared at Poppy. "Poppy, I can't tell you how angry I am. How stupid you were. How you endangered us by your refusal to face reality. I don't think I can ever forgive you." The evenness of her voice underlined her fury.

Poppy said nothing.

"I'll give Danson your message," Candace said. "He's such a caring man, I'm sure he'll forgive you and want to see you soon." She shook her head. "How you could hide your head in the sand the way you did is beyond me."

"We'll go in my truck. I don't think you can get your car out of the garage," Hollis said. She didn't add the obvious—that Jacob's body lay on the asphalt, and his van blocked the garage door. "You'll need Elizabeth's car seat."

"We'll get the officers outside to do that," Rhona volunteered and got on her phone.

"I'll pick you up at the front door," Hollis said. It was important that Elizabeth not see what had happened to Jacob.

After fastening the car seat in the truck, they headed for the hospital. Elizabeth did not fall asleep during the drive. No doubt the adrenalin generated when Jacob and Willem had fought to possess her was keeping her awake.

Candace entered the hospital room and stopped dead when she saw Danson. "My God, what did he do to you?" she said as she clasped Elizabeth tight to her chest.

Thin to the point of emaciation, Danson lay with an intravenous tube dripping in his arm. He lifted his free hand, gave a tiny wave and a broad grin. "I'm going to be fine. Great to see you. I have to thank you for not giving up on me, or I'd still be locked in that garage."

Candace scooted to his bedside, and lowered Elizabeth to give Danson a kiss. She backed off, set Elizabeth down and pulled Hollis forward.

"Hollis did it. What exactly is wrong with you?" Candace asked in a trembling voice.

"The bastard starved me. He gave me water because he wanted to see how long I'd last. Said he had to keep me alive in case he needed me."

"You're much bigger and stronger than Jacob. How did he imprison you?" Hollis asked.

Danson sighed. "How? By luring me to his house with the promise that if I had or knew of the whereabouts of a Canadian 12-penny black 1851 stamp, he could give me a terrific deal. Poppy told me not to do it, but I didn't listen."

"Why did you go? The stamp belonged to Poppy," Candace said.

"I wanted her to do it, to phone, check out the article and go and see what the guy was offering." He shook his head. "Thank God she didn't. She told me it was a come-on, that those little items that promised the person would learn something to his advantage were always bad news. I didn't listen. I was sure I could get her a good deal, a better offer than she'd receive from stamp dealers or at auction. She'd been saying she might sell her collection, and I wanted her to get as much money as possible."

"You talked to him, and I assume he invited you to his house. Then what happened?"

"He was friendly. Asked if the stamp belonged to me. I was smart enough to say I represented a family member, but I didn't say who. Anyway, he offered coffee and I accepted. The next thing I knew, I had a monstrous headache and was lying on the cement floor in the garage. Jacob was shouting at me through a little grate in the wall."

"Grate?"

"I guess it used to be a milk box when the house was built."

"Milk box?"

Danson sighed. "Tradespeople used to deliver milk, bread, groceries. The milkman would open the outside door, collect the order and leave whatever the family had ordered. The home's residents opened the box from inside and collected the order. This particular box had had iron bars installed on both sides." He made a rueful face. "Well-anchored iron bars."

"What did Jacob say?"

"Once he saw that I was awake and struggling to stand up, he giggled and said he'd heard in prison that the date rape drug worked like a charm and was easy to get, but he'd never believed it worked so quickly and effectively. Then he said that he had my keys and my wallet, knew all about me and intended to get the stamps. I guess that was Saturday. The next time he opened the box, it was Sunday evening. He said he'd been to my apartment, read everything in my computer and files. He was mad that the stamps weren't there but smug about a plan he'd concocted."

That explained the heavy-footed tramping back and forth that the downstairs tenant at Danson's apartment building had heard on the Sunday.

Candace, gently rocking Elizabeth who'd gone to sleep, reached forward and squeezed Danson's hand. "Why didn't you shout and bang on the garage door? Surely someone would have heard you," she said.

"The house is set way back on the lot," Hollis explained.

"And the next-door neighbours spend the winter in Florida," Danson said. "Believe me, I did make as much noise as possible when I realized that I was trapped. Jacob told me to forget it, that no one would hear me, and I needed to save my energy."

"It's been cold. How did you keep warm?" Candace said.

"Jacob left one of those upright water coolers, a sleeping bag, a plastic pail and a roll of toilet paper. There was nothing else, absolutely nothing else that I could use to pry the door open or make more noise. Every day he'd open the little window and give me an update on his progress in tracking down the stamp. No food. In fact, he'd say hello and ask if I was getting hungry."

"That's fiendishly cruel," Candace said.

"That wasn't the only cruel thing he did. I heard word for word every call he made to Candace. It tore me apart, because I knew how upset she must be, and he was twisting the knife each time he phoned her. He's a grade A sadist, and I felt so guilty that I'd been stupid enough to walk into his trap."

A nurse hurried into the room, looked at Danson who had closed his eyes at this point, and whispered that they should leave.

"He shouldn't exhaust himself. He needs to get his strength back," the nurse said.

Hollis touched Candace's arm. "We'll have to wait for the rest of the story later."

Candace nodded, kissed Danson and followed Hollis from the room.

"There's one more thing I still need to find out. I want to know why Super Bug was killed," Hollis said.

*   *   *

Rhona couldn't wait for morning. She phoned

"It's over," she said.

"What's over?" Ian answered.

"The case. Danson's back." She filled in the details.

"It's a good thing Hollis pursued it, isn't it?" Ian said when Rhona had finished her tale.

"I hate to admit it, but you're right."

*   *   *

Hollis, Candace and Elizabeth returned from the hospital close to ten. They were barely inside the front door when Poppy emerged from her apartment.

"How is he?" she asked.

"Terribly thin, undernourished and weak," Candace said. "His mind is fine, and he's anxious to leave and get on with his life. They'll let him out in a day or two after his shrunken stomach is accepting food again. I guess when you've been starved, there's a science to feeding you to prevent your body from going into shock."

"Did he tell you what happened?"

"He did. I'm still angry, but I'll share the details after Elizabeth is in bed," Candace said.

"If Willem's up to it, he'll want to hear too. I'll go and see how he is," Hollis said.

Upstairs, MacTee presented her with a ragged Teddy Bear he'd had since he was a puppy. She patted him and tiptoed to the bedroom where she pushed the door open. Willem lay on his back snoring gently. No need to wake him—he'd hear the story when he awoke.

After she came back from visiting Candace he was awake and sitting in the kitchen. She made him a smoothie, repeated what they'd learned and helped him back to bed. In the morning, while she walked MacTee, he prepared breakfast and later told her he planned to go home as he no longer had a reason to fear the mob and had to prepare for a seminar.

But now, it was time to go to the hospital with Poppy, Candace and Elizabeth to see how Danson was doing and hear the last details of his imprisonment. When they arrived, they found Rhona and Ian in Danson's room.

Danson looked better than he had the night before. Presumably the nutrient drip was performing its magic.

It was time for Hollis to apologize for her lapses. "Sorry I didn't get back to you with what I learned," she said.

"It is a prosecutable offense," Rhona said. "But we think he," she pointed a finger at Danson, "might not have been found until it was too late if you hadn't persevered." She shook her head. "Not to say that we approve of what you did, but the outcome was happy."

"From what Danson has told us, Jacob intended to kill Elizabeth," Hollis said.

"He did," Danson said. "He told me there was no way he was sharing his inheritance with some brat his father had conceived." Danson shifted, and his blue hospital shirt slipped sideways to reveal his sharply defined and protruding collarbone. "Jacob figured his father wouldn't have given Poppy a letter saying he'd given her the stamps. He gambled that if that was the case she wouldn't go to the police if he stole the stamps, because she had no proof that they were hers. Once he had the stamps, he'd track down and kill Elizabeth, then he'd be free and clear to enjoy everything."

"Where did Gregory fit into the picture?" Hollis said to Rhona.

Rhona and Ian exchanged a glance.

"Given the part you've played in solving these cases, we think you deserve to know," Rhona said. "He was a Russian double-agent who thought Danson not only was on his track and would blow his cover but conceivably had figured out the espionage network they'd established. Before he could take action and remove Danson, Jacob did it for him. However, the mob had figured out Gregory was doubling, and they took him out. End of story. In a way it was good Danson disappeared when he did because Gregory clearly had been instructed to kill him," she explained.

"Thank you for telling me. Now all the pieces fit together," Hollis said.

"Jacob thought he could cut away everything that stood in his way, but he didn't factor you into his calculations, did he?" Ian said. "Didn't greed and a sense of entitlement take him down?" he added.

Hollis smiled. "I agreed to help. That's what friends do." She looked at Danson. "Speaking of which, your friend Molly is worried about you. I promised we'd tell her when we found you, but I think she'd be happier if the news came from you."

Danson returned her smile and nodded.

Friends. This was the second time she'd stepped in to help a friend. Was there something about her that attracted those in trouble? Silly question. It had been purely coincidental that she'd happened to be there when bad situations had arisen.

Now it was time to resume her normal life—exercising herself and MacTee, creating her whimsical animals and painting. Willem's insightful comments about the half-finished gold painting flashed into her mind. She felt the familiar tingling in her fingertips that meant the creative block was gone, that she was ready to paint. One problem solved.

But what about Willem? Was there a future for their relationship?

Back in her apartment, he was up and shaved. "I waited until you came home. I didn't want to leave until I'd thanked you for taking care of me." He paused and held out his hands. Hollis took them. He smiled his careful half-grin. "I plan to return the favour with interest."

Nothing could have pleased Hollis more.

As a member of the Ladies' Killing Circle, Joan Boswell has published stories in each of their seven books: *The Ladies' Killing Circle, Cottage Country Killers, Menopause Is Murder, Fit to Die, Bone Dance, Boomers Go Bad* and *Going Out With a Bang*. She has also co-edited the last four books. In 2000, she won the Toronto *Sunday Star* short story contest. She has published three Hollis Grant mysteries with RendezVous Crime, *Cut Off His Tale, Cut to the Quick* and *Cut to the Chase.* Joan lives in Toronto with two Flatcoated Retrievers.

More info on her activities is online at:
joanboswell.ca

I would like to thank my critiquing group, The Ladies' Killing Circle, Vicki Cameron, Barbara Fradkin, Mary Jane Maffini, Sue Pike and Linda Wiken. Also, love and appreciation to my family for their support.